Praise for
FALLING OFF
A CLIFF

"In *Falling Off a Cliff*, Rose Senehi plunges us into a world rich with a unique sense of time and place. This haunting tale is more than setting, more than a glimpse into the ways of a disappearing Appalachian culture, but rather a story of two strong women, a generation apart, whose sole ambition is to bring healing to their community despite the challenging terrain and suspicious attitudes. But for one of them, healing must also come from within as she searches for her lost past shrouded by a dark, impenetrable secret. The satisfying mixture of history and mystery yields a novel that will be remembered well beyond the turn of the last page."

—*Mark de Castrique, Author, Fatal Scores,*
A Sam Blackman Mystery

"Rose Senehi knows and loves her mountains and their people—their peaks and valleys, both physical and personal—and in *Falling Off A Cliff* she shares them with an unerring eye and a fine sense of detail. But this is not just another mountain book. It is the riveting story of two women on journeys at the core of their lives—Lula Mae, striving toward her future, and Holly, in search of the mysteries of her past. It is a superb piece of fiction from a gifted storyteller."

—*Robert Inman, Author, Home Fires Burning.*

"It's always a pleasure to immerse oneself in a world that an author creates with a good story. Holly Baldwin's search for the truth by following her heart in Senehi's *Falling Off a Cliff* encourages me to jump off my own cliff and dive for the truth in my search for my foreparents. It's everyone's center.

—*Emöke B'Rácz, Poet and Founder, Malaprop's Book & Café,*
and Downtown Books and News, Asheville, NC

"With *Falling Off a Cliff* Rose Senehi continues her exploration of a special area with a very special history. Holly Baldwin's search for her origins offers the story of a culture well nigh forgotten and of a way of life now abandoned. Yet, at its heart, this novel is a love story we all happily recognize."

—*Fred Chappell, NC Poet Laureate Emeritus, Author, Ancestors*
and Others and Look Back All the Green Valley

"Senehi weaves a romantic tale of history, mystery, love, loss, and redemption as she tells the heart-breaking challenges faced by public health nurses in an isolated and suspicion-laden mountain vastness."

—*Vickie Lane, Author of And the Crows Took Their Eyes and of*
The Elizabeth Goodweather Appalachian Mysteries

ALSO BY ROSE SENEHI

CATCHING FIRE

CAROLINA BELLE

DANCING ON ROCKS

RENDER UNTO THE VALLEY

THE WIND IN THE WOODS

IN THE SHADOWS OF CHIMNEY ROCK

PELICAN WATCH

WINDFALL

SHADOWS IN THE GRASS

FALLING
OFF
A CLIFF

Rose Senehi

To Barbara,

Rose Senehi

KM

Published by

K.I.M. PUBLISHING, LLC

Post Office Box 132
Chimney Rock, NC 28720-0132

Cover Photographs: Lee Barker

Published in the United States of America.

PUBLISHER'S NOTE

PUBLISHER'S CATALOGING-IN-PUBLICATION DATA

Names: Senehi, Rose, author.
Title: Falling off a cliff: the story of a mountain nurse / Rose Senehi.
Description: First paperback edition. | Chimney Rock, NC : K.I.M.
Publishing, LLC, 2021.
Identifiers: ISBN 978-1-7360168-0-0—(paperback)
Subjects: LCSH: Domestic fiction. | BISAC: FICTION / Southern. |
FICTION / Small Town & Rural. | FICTION / Cultural Heritage.
Classification: LCC PS3603.S475 2021 (print) | dcc 813/.6—DC23.

Library of Congress Control Number: 2021931040

First Printing: January. 2021

For Holly Barker

CHARACTERS

1923

Lula Mae McWade: Born in 1916, we meet her at the age of seven
Granny McDowell: An oldtime herb doctor who mentors Lula
Essie Gordon: A self-ordained granny doctor
Helen Baldwin: A well-to-do spinster who moves to the mountains
Hattie McWade: Lula's mother
Billie Boy, Luke, Big James, Nancy, Ned, and Jake: Lula's siblings
Zeb McGee: Works for Lula's brother and operates a still
Gus Gibson: Owns a sawmill at the bottom of the mountain
Carrie Sutter: Gus Gibson's neighbor
Father Phillips: Circuit-riding Episcopal priest
Molly & Robert McGraw: A mountain barrel maker and his wife

1960

Holly Baldwin: A newly minted public health nurse we meet in 1960
Jeff Garrison: A young, promising apple grower
Granny Garrison: Old mountain woman who is Jeff's grandmother
Myrtle (Myrt) Ryan: A widow who takes Holly in as a boarder
Ella Rockwell: The village postmaster
Doris Hensen: Holly's childhood housekeeper
Jenney Howard: Public Health Nurse and Holly's supervisor
Lucy: Public Health Nurse who Holly is replacing
Patsy Burrows: Child with scoliosis. And her mother and father
Annie Barnwell: Old mountain woman

The Lost Colony

Henderson County, NC

(Estimated Size: 1 by 3 Miles)

Located on a plateau/mesa atop the Southern Blue Ridge escarpment, what is now referred to as The Lost Colony of Henderson County was established shortly after the Revolutionary War. Surrounded by mountains, this isolated, self-sufficient settlement thrived throughout the 1800s, until the changes brought about by the Industrial Revolution finally seeped into its coves and ridges and ended the era.

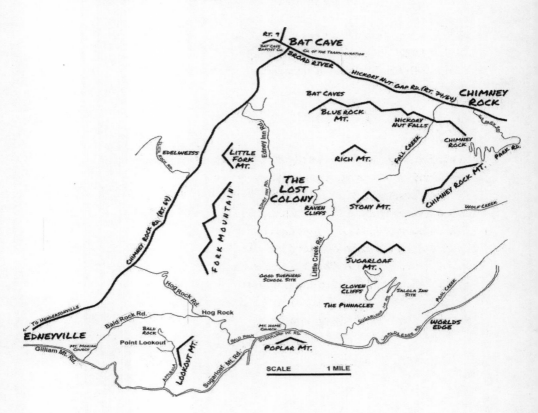

CHAPTER ONE
1923

"Thar 'nough?" The little girl tilted the small wooden crock so the old woman could peek inside.

Granny McDowell took a pinch of the powder and rubbed it between her thumb and forefinger. "Jist right." She poured the ground holly tree root into a pottery jar. "Take a bit a this and make up a batch a tea fer yer pa, and he'll sleep a whole sight better."

The woman wiped the chestnut mortar clean with her floor length apron and placed it on a shelf along with the wooden pestle. "I do believe ye be a yarb doctor jist like me." She nodded toward the open door. "Lula Mae, that patch a meadow out thar is our medicine chest, an it be time to be diggin a mess a blood-root. An come week next, I be needin ye ta fetch the roots a the lady slipper. Women folk be needin it fer their nerves."

The old woman gathered a basket and digging tool and pressed them into the seven year old's hand before leading her to the door of the dirt-floored log cabin.

"Jist look fer purdy white flowers like I done showd ye. Be back by the time the sun starts fallin behind Lil Fork Mountain cuz your ma will be lookin fer ye bout then."

Lula hurried across the narrow porch in her bare feet, ran down the split log steps, and set out into the woods. Seeing that the sun had started its journey west, she determined to fill the basket well before dusk so she could get home in time to get her chores done. Her father was doing poorly after being kicked by their mule, and now the heavy work fell on her mother and six siblings who already had plenty to do.

But she wasn't about to rush the digging of bloodroots. She had to take care like Granny had showed her. She was already one to always take care—especially when her labors were to help sick folk in need of comfort.

Sorry as the state of things were at home, Lula felt she was doing her share collecting herbs for the granny doctor and helping her on visits to the small cluster of families still living atop Chimney Rock Mountain under the shadow of the Sugarloaf Mountain dome. As payment, the old woman would stop by their cabin and share some of her treasures upon returning from a trip down the mountain where she traded herbs and potions for salt, pepper, tea, and coffee. Times Granny had ginseng to trade in the valley, she'd bring back gun powder and lead for her father.

On those occasions, Lula's father would pat her on the head. That small gesture from a man who rarely showed what was in his heart made her feel proud.

Lula's path wound around a bald-faced section of the mountain onto a meadow. She hurried past one of the many deserted log cabins dotting the plateau, afraid a bear or coyote might have taken up residence inside. Martha Garrison, who lived in a nearby cabin with her eight children, once told her that when she was young, a panther had fallen through their roof and raised havoc before they were able to chase it out. Lula was glad all such critters had been run off the mountain or hunted down.

Spying a drift of snow-white blossoms hugging the earth ahead, she approached the thick cluster, sank to her knees, and pulled the digging fork from the basket. She needed to get busy, but couldn't resist taking a moment to absorb the sheer beauty of the flower smiling up at her.

Moments like this, when she could look upon something so perfect, brought glorious pleasure. Even more glorious than when a circuit-riding preacher carried the gospel to their little colony and everyone sang until their hearts were filled with the joy of the spirit, or when a teacher visited for a spell and thrilled everyone with a bit of learning. She understood the plainness of her existence, the need to make do, the endless day-in and day-out struggle to produce food and fuel to cook and heat.

She gently coaxed the fork into the moist, loamy ground surrounding the plant and lifted it out. Bit by bit, she brushed aside the soil to reveal its bright red stem and root, all the while careful not to scratch it so the valuable red-orange sap wouldn't ooze out. She held it in the air and thrilled at the wonder of the dozen perfectly shaped pearly-white petals and vivid yellow cluster in its center.

After months in the darkness of their cabin with little color other than from the pure white of the snow that blew in through the cracks in the logs and the yellow and orange flames licking the hearth, the perfection of this small gift from the earth roused her senses. A surge of gratitude for being alive and part of the natural world rose from within her. She was sure the earth's richly colored spring awakening was the reward God gave folks for enduring the hardships and gloom of winter. Though she felt guilty for pulling this treasure from the ground that gave it life, she knew its sacrifice would serve a higher purpose.

Granny would dry the roots, and Lula would grind them into a powder that could be used to relieve folks who were ailing from throat and breathing maladies. A lot of it went into the stinky little bags she filled with pungent herbs for folks to hang around their necks. Lula was proud that, when called upon, she could make herself useful. She knew what color cloth the granny doctor wrapped the bloodroot powder in and had no trouble quickly retrieving it from the old woman's bag, for she had watched her dye it with sap of the root.

Up until a few months ago, her entire world consisted of the colony's patch of dirt on the side of the mountain. She hadn't even imagined there was any other place beside just where they were until one of her father's kin, gone ten years since leaving to serve in the Great War, came back up the mountain. As the family gathered around the open hearth at night, he told of things he'd seen that were more magical than the tales her mother's old aunt would spin. And that's what she thought they were—stories and places he had dreamt up. Still, she was mesmerized.

The first time she had actually laid eyes on anything beyond her familiar surroundings was when her brother, Billy Boy, took her with him to the far edge of the colony where the creek fell off the face of the earth. He had held her hand tight as they ventured to the edge and watched the rushing water plummet hundreds of feet to the silvery thread of a river that snaked through the gorge below. Then they hiked east along the ridge a good way, until he stopped and pointed to a huge rock jutting out from the mountain below.

"Looks like a chimney," said Lula.

"That's why they be callin it the Chimney Rock," said Billy Boy.

They had headed back to the falls and sat resting on a fallen tree, enjoying the cool breeze sweeping down the gorge. He told her that years ago their land had been cleared and tilled by oxen pulling plows smithed in the colony's own forge. He told her about the grist mill that had sat on the very creek they had run along, and how it would grind their corn into meal and grits between stones the owner had chiseled out himself. Then he told her about the flood of 1893 that sent the mill crashing down four hundred feet to the bottom of the gorge, never to be replaced.

"But the Flood of 1916 was the worse one I knowed bout. That's the summer Uncle Ezra got took off to war," he had said. "Hit poured rain ever day fer weeks til we finally lost our corn, an the hay field got itself under water. It done poured a whole heap one day, as iffin the bottom ad fallen out a the sky. That night, with all the waters overflowin, we heard one terrible roar an ran out, afeared a what we'd see. We could hear Fork Mountain apeelin straight away, and trees, rocks, mud, water rushin down inta the valley. And in the middle a it, you got borned. That night there were so many horrible sounds ye could hardly hear a body talk ifin they were right next ta ye. Come morn, Pa brought me ta this very spot an we saw the road down there washed clear away an the river piled high with what looked more like kindlin than broken trees."

Lula loved when Billy Boy would tell her stories about the community's past, but the thing that had fascinated her the most that day was the handful of buildings along the road that ran with the river. From up on the mountain, they appeared as small as the tiny log cabins her father would sometimes carve. She had asked, "Billy Boy, who lives in the one with so many windows?"

"It's a inn," he answered.

"What's a inn?"

"I don't rightly know, but Aaron's father done pointed it out, an that's what he said it tis."

Lula smiled to herself remembering all the times with Billy Boy, but she had to get back to work collecting the bloodroot. She dug them up and carefully placed them into her basket for most of the afternoon. The basket now full, she started back. Granny's cabin came into view, and she spotted her coming from out of the woods.

Granny greeted her breathlessly. "Good. Ye back. Jist been visitin with yer momma. Asked bout ye comin with me tomorrow." She took the basket from Lula and entered the cabin. "We be visitin folks on Sugarloaf an Stony Mountain."

That night, Lula lay on her straw-filled tick mattress filled with anticipation for her first trip beyond her small world to the places she'd only heard mentioned as the family gathered evenings around the hearth.

She had seen with wonder the comfort herbs had brought the ailing and felt a deep contentment knowing she was a part of it. Then she thought of Granny McDowell. She and Granny were alike. When she saw how the tinctures Granny gave to someone took away their hurt, her heart would grow in her chest and feel like it would burst. She laughed. Billy Boy was a hard enough worker and kind of heart, but he didn't have what she and Granny had. She couldn't imagine him wrapping a poultice around a foul smelling wound. He never even took heed of himself when he was hurt bad. No, it was a special something, and she and Granny had it.

CHAPTER TWO
1960

Holly Baldwin pictured the dangling onyx stones dancing from her aunt's ears to the ragtime rhythm of the Charleston. Though the image made her smile, tears welled in her eyes. She reached into the jewelry box for an amethyst brooch, held it up to the light, and marveled at how the exotic purple and pink facets mirrored the North Carolina skies just after sunset. She wondered if it had been dug out of the hillsides of Hiddenite or maybe Spruce Pine. She always wanted to know the origin of things, a bothersome habit that had plagued her for most of her life as she wondered where she came from.

She tried to pick up a necklace, but its chain got snagged on something. She coaxed a darkish strand out from underneath. Nothing but a string of long, black seeds randomly threaded so they stuck out every which way. She laughed at the thought of her aunt wearing anything so crude around her aristocratic neck and tossed it into the wastebasket. She fingered another brooch while the old itch to know crept up on her.

"That ratty old string of seeds wouldn't have ended up in these treasures unless it meant something to Aunt Helen," she mused. "Could it be seeds from her past. Something she couldn't let go. If so, why didn't she share it with me?"

Her thoughts were interrupted by a car pulling up outside.

She quickly retrieved the seed necklace from the wastebasket and placed it back into the box, snapped it shut, and put it into the trunk. As she began stripping the bed, she waited for the familiar footsteps on the stairs.

"Downstairs sure looks strange without furniture," Doris Henson remarked as she entered the room. She'd served as the family's housekeeper for as long as Holly could remember. Doris placed a box on the dresser. "I brought something for you to eat on your trip. Knowing you, you're not going to stop for anything til you get there." She ran a hand lovingly across the dresser's marble top. "I've dusted this bedroom set a million times. Are you sure you want to give it to me?"

"I'm sure," Holly replied.

"Are you sure you're sure? Your aunt always said it was Eastlake and worth a lot of money."

"I put everything I want to keep into storage," Holly answered. "Just be sure to get it before Monday. I told the new owners I'd be out by then."

Doris glanced around the room shaking her head. "I don't know how you can give up this place or that job at the hospital you jabbered about nearly your whole life. How can you just pack up and go?"

Holly finished folding the bed sheets, hoping Doris wouldn't make leaving the only home she'd ever known harder than it already was.

"I hope to God you're not chasing another one of those crazy hunches of yours," Doris said.

Not getting a response, she tugged on Holly's sleeve. "Please, tell me you're not, so I can stop worrying about you."

Holly didn't answer, but picked up a blanket and carefully folded it.

"Sometimes I wonder about you, child," said Doris. "I remember the big fuss you caused when your aunt sent you to camp, and you told everyone you were an orphan from Sir Walter Raleigh's Lost Colony."

Holly gave her a weary glance. "I was eight for heaven's sake. Dreaming up some exotic past is normal for kids."

"You're right, but they know they're pretending. You, on the other hand, let your imagination run off like a pack of wild horses just because you heard some ole fogey visiting your aunt mention a lost colony. Good Lord, that place vanished three-hundred years before you were even born."

"Well, I haven't done anything like that since I was ten."

"No!" she scoffed. "You've just ratcheted it up a notch. Now that your aunt has passed, you're not going to be satisfied until you go digging around in places you have no business digging around in."

Holly rummaged through the trunk for space for the blanket. "When I think of it, that storytelling business was kind of sad. I was just a little kid trying to erase the stain of being an orphan." She finally squeezed the blanket in. "A lot of it was Joey Sullivan's fault."

"Those Sullivans were a wild bunch," agreed Doris.

"Wild is an understatement. They were cruel. One day, when I was in the first grade, I was coming home from school and they blocked my way. Joey was the biggest one. He had to be eleven or twelve. I'd heard enough about those kids to be scared, so I dropped my lunch pail and took off through someone's back yard. But they came after me. Joey caught me and pinned me to the ground with his knee on my chest. I'll never forget that sweaty red face and him demanding I say my mother never wanted me. Then they all started chanting it. When I wouldn't say it, Joey forced mud into my mouth."

Holly stood motionless, remembering the words that were like razors slashing her insides. "You think you're high and mighty," the hideous beast spit out, "but everybody knows you're a throwaway. You may be living in that fancy house with that mean old lady who made my brother do the ninth grade again, but you're nothin but an orphan nobody wanted. Not even your mother. Now, say your mother didn't want you. Say it!"

Holly was quiet for a long moment, then she stared hard at Doris. "I never did say it. I spit the mud in his face and he started punching me, but I never said it."

"Oh, I'm sure you didn't."

"Mary Murphy's mom finally came out with a broom and ran them off."

Holly checked the closet for anything she might have missed. "I guess that's when I started making up stories. At any rate, that part of my grim little past is history."

She turned and smiled at the woman who had always been like a second mother to her. Noticing the concern on her face, Holly forced a lighter tone. "Do me a favor and check all the drawers to make sure I haven't left any gold or diamonds behind."

Doris started going through the dresser, wistfully reminiscing while Holly stood at the open window gazing at the rolling countryside surrounding Pittsboro, North Carolina. The beautiful vista was beginning to wake from the winter. She felt a pang of regret as she stared down at her aunt's prized rose bush twining around the garden trellis. How she hated to leave it behind. She could still picture her aunt pruning it with care and love. The memory of the bush's beautiful pink roses and intoxicating scent along with Doris's fond ramblings brought back another warm early spring afternoon. She had gleefully come home from school, and upon opening the door, found Doris anxiously waiting.

"She wants to see you," Doris had gravely announced, then gently patted the ten-year-old on the head and whispered, "I don't know what you did this time, young lady, but I'm sure it's a lulu. She's been on the phone with the school all afternoon."

Doris nudged her toward the parlor. "When she's done with you, come in the kitchen. I've got fresh-baked cookies."

Holly entered the parlor with a pretty good idea of what her aunt wanted to talk to her about. The woman was sitting at her desk surrounded by the antebellum furnishings she had inherited from the estate of her father, who at the turn of the century was a prosperous merchant and customs collector in Columbia, South Carolina. Although she had spent most of her adult life in North Carolina, she still exuded the unmistakable aura of beguiling charm and equanimity that could only belong to someone born to wealth and manners in the deep South.

Her aunt motioned for Holly to near, then caressed her and lovingly pushed the stray blonde locks from her face.

"What am I going to do with my darling treasure?" she said as she cupped Holly's face in her heavily veined, but still elegant, hands. "Tell me, child, when are these unsettling reports from the school going to end?"

Holly twisted her lips in a stubborn pout and looked away.

"Just what secret did you make that new girl swear to keep?" her aunt asked.

Holly sullenly traced the edge of the Empire mahogany desk with a finger.

"Is it true you told her your mother was the daughter of the Russian czar and she gave you to a peasant before the whole family was executed?"

"It's possible, you know! You've told me a thousand times you don't know who I am."

Helen Baldwin caressed Holly again. "I have to admit, it was better than the tale you told the milkman. Really, Holly, how could you expect Mr. Boswell to believe you were found floating in a basket as the Titanic sank. For land sake, girl, you'd be in your twenties by now!"

She stuffed the tail of Holly's blouse back into her skirt. "I love you Holly, and it comforts me to know you love me." Helen hugged her tenderly. "I can't blame you for wondering, my precious. I only wish I could give you some piece of mind, but I can't. Sometimes we have to accept things as they are." Her face took on an expression that came as close to stern as she could manage. "Now, as far as those stories of yours go, enough is enough. Promise me you won't ever do this again."

Holly bit her lip, took a deep breath and said, "I promise."

Helen gave Holly a quick peck on the cheek. "Now go get some of those cookies Doris made for you."

Holly raced toward the kitchen with her aunt calling out, "I know you're never going to stop spinning these fantasies in your head, child... but *for heaven's sake* do keep them to yourself."

The sudden shutting of a drawer woke Holly from her

thoughts. She smiled to see Doris wiping away a tear.

"I'm going to miss you, Holly. God knows how much I miss your aunt."

"Are you gonna be all right?" Holly asked.

"Staying with my sister is working out better than I expected, and with what your aunt left me, I should be fine." Doris looked lovingly around the room. "Thanks again for the bedroom set. It means a great deal to me."

"You're the only one in the world who I'd want to have it," said Holly. "It's going to link you, me, Aunt Helen, and this place together forever."

"Darn you, Holly Baldwin. You always say things that just about break my heart."

With the earnestness of someone making a desperate last ditch effort, Doris pleaded, "Holly, please don't go. Stay here with people who love you." She clasped Holly's arms and looked into her eyes, searching for an answer. "I know you wouldn't be leaving all this behind unless you're planning on chasing down that crazy notion about your Aunt Helen living in the mountains. Tell me you haven't taken a job in that godforsaken wilderness because some cousin at her funeral mentioned your aunt used to live there. It doesn't make sense. Can you really see her in a log cabin? She traveled all over the world. You were a foundling and could have come from anywhere."

Holly pulled away and slapped the trunk shut. "Aunt Helen lost almost everything when the banks closed in '29 and I was born five years later. She could've been teaching in that area about then." Holly raised an eyebrow and looked dead on at Doris. "It's not a notion, it's a clue."

Two hours later, Holly was driving her aunt's '56 Ford Fairlane west on Route 29 headed for Hendersonville, North Carolina. Doris might be the nearest thing she had to a grandmother, but the kindly woman never understood the longing that ate at her. Every time she saw a little girl being cuddled by her mother, she'd wonder what it was like; or when she'd see a woman in a store, on the street, in a restaurant, she'd wonder if her mother would've looked like her.

But, beyond the thirst that nothing would satisfy, lay the grim blanket of abandonment that fell over her every time she heard a kitten mewing for its mother or a bird, fallen from its nest, desperately chirping for its parents.

As she drove along, she smiled to herself, recalling the words that were about to change the course of her life.

"Are you sure Aunt Helen lived in the mountains?" she had insisted the cousin from Columbia tell her.

"Yes. Before the Depression."

"Where in the mountains?"

"Somewhere near a town called Bat Cave."

"Are you sure?"

"Good gracious, woman, how could anyone forget a name like that?"

It had taken a couple months to land a job and sell the house after spotting an ad in the medical bulletin asking for registered nurses to work in public health in the mountains near Bat Cave, but she was finally on her way.

The farther from Pittsboro she got, the more Doris's words unsettled her. She tried to force the unthinkable out of her thoughts. What if this search led to a dead end? She'd have no choice but to let go of her dream of finding her mother and discovering the reason she had given her away.

Coming out of Shelby, the Fairlane drove around a curve, and the sudden appearance of the Blue Ridge Mountains struck her in awe. Instantly, the exhilarating magnificence on the horizon chased away all her misgivings. Now *was* the time. The answer *was* beckoning. She laughed out loud. The appearance of the distant cousin from out of the blue at her aunt's funeral was a priceless parting gift from the woman who had taken such loving care of her all her life. Finally, after years of agonizing not knowing, she'd been handed a key that could unlock the mystery that haunted her all her life.

CHAPTER THREE

The next morning, Holly sat studying a map in the Hendersonville rooming house she'd found when she came for her interview. She planned to spend the next four days acquainting herself with the area before reporting for work, but first, she had to find a permanent place to live. She jumped up, grabbed her purse, and hurried out to her car.

The highway from the heart of Hendersonville to Bat Cave quickly turned into a narrow two-lane road chiseled out of the mountainside. It wound up and down steep curves and soon swallowed the Fairlane into a dark, forbidding cocoon still drenched in the bleakness of winter.

The sensation of moving like a wary animal through a primeval forest gripped her. Everything was of the earth—monstrous trees, dark mysterious undergrowth, giant jagged boulders. Gnarly rhododendrons hovered above the huge moss-covered rocks and decaying blowdowns crisscrossed the floor of the forest. This interwoven mass hugged the mountains on both sides of the road and beyond.

Every once in a while, she'd catch a glimpse of the creek running alongside the road. It slithered over and around rocks and boulders in the darkness, until a penetrating blade of sunlight made the water glitter with life. Now she understood why her new supervisor, Jennie Howard, hesitated when she had told her she wanted to live and work in the Bat Cave area.

When she came to the stop sign on the other side of a bridge and turned right, she drew a sigh of relief. The sky opened to a brilliant blue framed by steep mountains that towered on either side of the road. She was deep inside a gorge. A few buildings and houses crowded close to the road as if trying to get away from the river.

This must be the village of Bat Cave, she thought. Jennie had suggested she stop by the post office and ask if they might know of anyone looking for a boarder. If that didn't work, she was to try at the churches in town or the fire department, or if she could find one, a Laundromat.

The vast difference between being a nurse in a formal clinical setting like a hospital and being one that operated within the public health arena was brought home to Holly when Jennie emphasized the importance of getting acquainted with all the postal workers. She said they would be one of her best sources for finding patients who lived on nameless dirt roads. She also advised her to locate all the firehouses, churches, and grocery stores in her district so she would know where the nearest safe place was.

At her interview, the health department's executive director had stressed that serving as a public health nurse in the North Carolina mountains would be challenging, but these stratagems so pointedly offered by Jennie were making her wonder. Peering up at the forbidding mountains, Holly gulped. What had she gotten herself into?

Holly hadn't even started her job yet, but she already understood the importance of reaching out. Spotting a small building with a post office sign, she pulled in. Now was as good a time as any to start practicing the concept.

She entered the narrow lobby, barren except for a wall covered with postal boxes and a table cluttered with forms. She found a customer window at the far end, but no one was there. She tapped the bell on the counter and glanced at the bulletin board on the facing wall next to her.

A Polaroid of a bulldog with a bold "REWARD" above it caught her eye. The way the animal's bottom teeth jutted out from its lower jaw made it look a bit daunting. Scrawled below was, "Answers to the name, Cutie Pie."

An older woman suddenly appeared at the window.

"That irksome dog's been found," she said as she strained to reach over the counter and snap off the notice. "Cutie Pie goes missing every other week. Sometimes he wanders in here." She picked up a jar and shook it. "Keep treats on hand for him and any other critters that show up."

"You work here all the time?" asked Holly.

"Yep. I'm the postmaster, clerk, janitor. I'm it! My name is Ella Rockwell. Now, what can I do for ya?"

Holly quickly introduced herself and explained that she would be working in the district as a public health nurse, then she took Jennie's advice and chatted a while.

"Why do they call this town Bat Cave?" she asked.

"Cuz there's a bat cave in it. Supposed to be the largest granite fissure cave in the whole of North America. Don't know why bats come all the way from Indiana to roost in em, but that's what they call em."

After engaging in a little small talk about the area, Holly finally got around to mentioning she was looking for a place near there to live.

"You can ask over at the Episcopal Church or the clinic up the road, or you can try Myrtle Ryan. She lives on that road off 64 before the bridge. Her husband died a few months back, and she mentioned to me she was wantin to take in a boarder."

"How can I contact her?"

"You wait right there, Missy. I'll phone her."

Ella went out of sight, but every once in a while, Holly caught a few words.

"She's from away... looks like a right proper young lady."

The woman returned. "Go back over the bridge, turn left onto River Road, and it's the first place. Go on, now. She's waitin on ya."

Five minutes later, Holly pulled up to an imposing two-story gabled house flanked on both ends by stone chimneys. A spry wisp of a woman waited at the open door and enthusiastically welcomed her inside. She led her to a large, dark parlor—all the while rattling off every bit of information Holly had related about herself to the postmaster.

"I don't use the bedrooms upstairs anymore. The steps were too much for me and my William. You'll have plenty of privacy and your own bathroom up there." She was quick to notice Holly studying the enormous stone fireplace. "Back in the 1800s, that one and the one in the kitchen used to heat this whole house. My husband's father put in ductwork and installed a coal furnace, but when his parents passed and he and his first wife inherited the house, they changed to oil, so you'll have no cause to worry about being cold. Why don't you run up and take a look while I brew some tea."

The staircase was surprisingly wide, as was the hallway upstairs. Holly inspected the four bedrooms and decided the one across from the bathroom would suit her best since it seemed to have the newest mattress. The rooms were too big to appear cozy. Frayed and worn oriental carpets and massive Victorian furnishings spoke of bygone wealth. The elaborate hand-screened wallpaper edged with stains from long-ago roof leaks added to a melancholy aura of abandonment.

She drifted over to a large arched window and looked out at the overgrown garden with its birdbaths and arbors crisscrossed with dried-up vines. A surviving rose bush meekly displayed a few new leaves. She had to shake off the feeling of loss for what at one time had to have been a colorful, butterfly-filled haven.

Descending the staircase, Holly saw the woman busy in the kitchen.

"Come here, darling," she said, pointing to a washer and dryer. "If you decide to board with me, you're welcome to use these and, of course, the phone." She went to the refrigerator and swung the door open. "And you can have the use of this, as well as cooking privileges."

Holly was stunned at what little there was in the refrigerator. A couple opened cans, a jar of jelly, a few apples, and a shelf of condiments. No wonder the woman was so thin. This happens to a lot of widows after losing the spouse they'd been cooking for most of their lives, Holly thought. If she took the room, it was something she'd have to fix.

"Here. Sit yourself down and have some tea," the woman said as she pulled out a chair. "Well?" she asked, making no effort to mask her anxiousness.

"There's no question the room will work for me, Mrs. Ryan. I only hope I can afford it. I'm starting my job on Monday and only make sixty-five dollars a week. And, I'm afraid I can't guarantee I'll be here for more than six months, since I'll be on probation til then."

"First off, everyone calls me Myrt, and never fear about that probation business. I can tell you'll be fine." She pursed her lips and thought for a moment. "Would fifty dollars a month be too much?"

Holly instantly agreed, and with that out of the way, the two settled in on enjoying the tea and each other's company. Myrt proudly brought out pictures of her husband and lovingly introduced her to Oliver, a big orange cat that had been sitting on the windowsill enthralled with the goings-on at the bird feeder.

"My husband came from money, but I was raised on a farm not a half-mile from here," said Myrt.

"Then you know about the people who lived around here?"

"I should. I'm related to most of them."

"Did you know any Baldwins?"

"That's not a common name in these parts, I need to think on it," said Myrt. She picked up the cat and put it out on the porch. "You lookin for family?"

"Yes. I'm an orphan, and I have reason to believe I might've been born around here."

"*Sooo*...that's why you're lookin to stay in Bat Cave. I have to admit, couldn't help thinking it odd that anyone from away would want to board here. So did Ella over at the post office."

Holly couldn't help thinking that the way news traveled around Bat Cave, by now everyone must be thinking so, too.

"It's gonna be tough finding things out," said Myrt. "So many people have moved away, there's less and less old families left. When were you born, dear?"

"1934."

"That puts your momma growing up somewheres in the early 20s. Those were hard times and made for a lot of orphans in these mountains. A fever would go through, and it wasn't uncommon to wipe out whole families. There was no hospital, and doctors were scarce. Back then, folks mostly had to count on granny nurses or herb doctors. When both parents died, folks would take up what kids they could afford to keep. Sometimes the children were lucky enough to go to a relative, but a lot of times they were put out to work. My uncle always said he married my aunt Addie when she was sixteen to give her a home when her parents died."

Listening to this frail, yet feisty woman, Holly was drawn to her. Myrt had been a spinster teacher until, at forty-five, she married a childless widower she knew from church. Now, alone in the world, Holly felt her need, and knew, if she took the room, she would do whatever she could to help relieve it.

While Myrt prattled on about her life, Holly was suddenly filled with an unfamiliar sensation. What was it? she asked herself. Yes, that was it. Like she'd just shed a tight, suffocating costume. All her life she had been careful to keep her orphan state a secret for as long as she possibly could. It wasn't fair to be seen through that lens. Surprisingly, she had just unmasked herself and walked through a threshold she had always doggedly shunned, a door that all the made-up stories protected her from going through. Everything from her old life was now gone—her aunt, her home—and the idea of rebirth in a strange, foreign place excited her. Her path was clear. She was an orphan and she was going to find out why.

HOLLY STUDIED HER reflection in the Victorian dressing table's tall mirror. Her new blue and white stripe uniform seemed so different from the whites she had worn at Greensboro's Wesley Long Hospital. More official, like she was part of a force. With the dress code requiring she wear a girdle, bra, and hose, she looked down at her narrow ankles rising from the clunky black oxfords and grimaced.

She gave herself a final inspection, then patted her badge with pride. Her eyes overflowed with tears as the familiar heavy cloak of loss and disappointment draped over her again. How she wished her parents had seen how she had turned out. But coming from a home without a man, and being raised by a spinster, her heart reached out more to the distant, unseen woman who nursed her at her bosom.

Holly wiped her eyes and shook off the dejection, then raced down the stairs and hollered goodbye to Myrt as she ran out the door. After spending the past three days getting settled, she was looking forward to her first day at the health department as she drove down Route 64 towards Hendersonville. Surprisingly, it only took her thirty-five minutes to arrive at the department's offices on Spartanburg Highway east of the city's downtown. She parked in the lot behind the one-story building that housed the county's Health Department, clinic, and public health division.

She went in the east end of the building and was greeted in the hall by Jennie.

"You're gonna spend most of the day with me," said Jennie, "but first I want to introduce you to the other three nurses on our team and get our morning meeting out of the way."

With everyone assembled in a small meeting room, Jennie looked around. "Where's Louise?"

"She took a call before we got up to come," someone said.

"Okay, then why don't you start," said Jennie. "Have you gotten to talk to that woman up on Sugarloaf yet?"

"I went up again on Friday and knocked at the door a good while, but no one answered. Out of the corner of my eye I saw a curtain move in a window, and considering the long drive I'd just had and all the trips I already made to talk to her about her daughter's curvature, I went up to the screen and peeked in. A little girl looked back at me and said, 'We's hidin from ya.'"

Everyone was laughing as the door opened and the missing nurse came in looking as if she had been crying. The meeting continued with issues of head lice, parents refusing to sign for inoculations and exams, and cases of scabies—all seemingly ongoing problems.

The meeting gave Holly a good idea of what her job entailed, and she felt she was trained to handle it. She could see that most of their clients came from either their free clinic or school visits, and that the county was divided into four sections with a public health nurse assigned to each.

Finally, Jennie asked for a report from the nurse who had come in late.

"Louise, how are you doing with that first grader?"

"The case is closed."

"Closed? Why?" asked Jennie.

"The little girl is dead." Louise closed her eyes and dropped her head in her hand. "She bled to death."

Jennie hurried over and put her arm around the distraught young woman and gave her shoulder a squeeze.

"If only I had followed my gut and brought in Social Services," moaned the nurse. "All my instincts told me she was being molested."

"You did everything you could," said Jennie. "How many home visits did you make to get her mother to sign for an examination, or even shots? Two? Three? God knows you did everything you could."

The woman's face twisted in grief. "All the signs were there. The school never had any problems with that child until her mother took up with the new boyfriend." She sobbed into Jennie's shoulder. "Social Services said the monster wouldn't even let her mother take the child to the emergency room after he did that to her."

Jennie took off her glasses and rubbed her eyes. "All right, ladies. Meeting adjourned."

Everyone left the room, leaving Jennie and Louise alone.

Lucy, the nurse who Holly was replacing, approached her.

"Let's go get a cup of coffee. Jennie's going to be tied up for a while," she said as she steered her down the hall toward the break room. "I know that was a rough introduction for you this morning, but that nurse didn't do anything wrong. It's a tightrope balance in these mountains. If we call Social Services, whether or not they can prove something's going on, we know we'll never get into that house again."

Holly shook her head. "Why don't these women do something?"

"They look the other way because they can't afford to have their men go to jail. They're the ones who work. With no education, no other means of support, it's a burden these women feel they have to bear."

"Unbelievable!"

"In this field, you need to learn to pay attention to your instincts. If a child comes in for an examination and you find they're red and raw between their legs, you ask them if anyone touches them there. When they say yes, my daddy, my brother, my uncle, that opens a whole can of worms. You can't keep it a secret. It's your professional responsibility to report it. The sad fact is, once you do, you're not welcome anymore, and if they can't prove a case against the offender, he goes right on hurting the child with no one to stop him.

"That's why we can't react the minute we get a suspicion. We have to be detectives, all the while gaining the trust of the women. You're always trying to get to that mother's heart with your heart. You have to let her know that you care about her and her children.

"There are always going to be bad days, but you'll find the gratification you get from helping these people more than makes up for it."

They finished their coffee and walked back to their office where everyone was preparing to leave on their assignments.

Holly spent most of the day with Jennie, getting oriented to their system, especially the all important State, County, and Federal laws and regulations. Things like their rigid dress code, standard procedures, and department paperwork were thoroughly reviewed. Holly's favorite moment came when Jennie handed her the official department satchel with which to carry the tools of her trade on her rounds: blood pressure cuff, thermometer, stethoscope, scissors, bandages, a package of sterile instruments for dressing changes. The small contraption for weighing babies amused her.

Holly drove home that afternoon trying to absorb all the information that had been thrown at her. Through all of it, she'd felt the friendly, yet, professional camaraderie among all the public health nurses as well as the office staff. Even though they often felt like the Dutch boy with his finger in the dike, they were all aware they were on a noble mission. Not one that they would ever see completed, but one where they were doing everything they could in whatever small way they could to make people's lives better.

CHAPTER FOUR
1923

Frozen in time, the isolated colony that was settled shortly after the Revolutionary War was nestled on a broad, rolling plateau high atop Chimney Rock Mountain in North Carolina's stretch of the Blue Ridge Mountains. Now, nearly one hundred and fifty years later and spanning at least seven generations, the people who remained were still as staunchly independent as those gritty pioneers who made their way into the mountains by foot, mule, and cart all those years back. Since the turn of the century, however, the community had been gradually disintegrating.

It all started when the men who had gone down the mountain in the late 1800s to trade brought back word of the amazing change and surging growth in the valley to their south. At the same time, the mountain with the famous stone chimney on the north side of the colony was being developed as a tourist attraction, offering work to the men of the colony and access to the growing village of Chimney Rock. The lure of opportunity captured those who thirsted for a better way of life, and slowly but surely, families began drifting off the mountain.

The most crippling blow to the colony came when most of the men who had been pressed into service during the First World War never returned. Left behind were those who simply couldn't leave, or who found it impossible to break from the independent way of life they were content with.

Those who chose to stay, continued to raise cattle and sheep and let their hogs run wild to fatten on acorns, chestnuts, and chinquapins. They still sheared their sheep, and the womenfolk spun it into thread which they wove into cloth and dyed with brews from herbs, roots, and tree barks found on the mountainside. Like they always had, they raised everything they ate and made as many of the things they needed as they could. What they couldn't, they trekked nearly a day down one of the two steep, narrow footpaths to the Edneyville valley or the town of Chimney Rock to trade the things they had on hand for the things they needed.

LULA HARDLY BELIEVED that she and Granny would make it down the mountain with all their fixins. Lula's feet were practically worn to the bone from all the walking on rocks, roots, and rough land. The rag her momma had tied around her sore toe had come off so many times, she finally let it go.

In spite of all she had to carry and the heat and humidity of the summer, she was excited. That past spring, Granny had taken her all over Sugarloaf and beyond, but this was the first time she'd be going all the way to the bottom of the mountain and into the valley.

"I be gettin ya when the sun starts risin oer Chimney Rock Mountain, an we be stayin the night, maybe two," Granny had told her the day before. "It be takin til mid day, but all dem furriners will be at the inn an wantin my potions an asphidity bags."

They came around a patch of rhododendron and welcomed the sight of a rippling stream. Granny told her to sit a spell, then took out a tin cup and some cornbread. She dipped the cup in the stream and offered it to Lula along with a chunk of bread.

"Here, lass. We almost there now. Rest up a bit, an we be on our way."

The sound of a barking dog caught the old woman's ear.

"Mary Laughter's place be jist beyond. She be wantin us to stop."

It wasn't long before they came to a clearing with a small log cabin. As hot as it was outside, smoke still rose from the chimney. A woman stood at the door holding a baby with two little ones clinging to her skirts. The hound barked and strained on its rope, making the goats skitter across the small yard fenced with split logs. A young boy ran out of the cabin to quiet the dog as the two approached.

After a short gab, Granny found some potions in her bags for the woman, while Lula made friends with the shy little toddlers. The woman gave Granny a sack of chestnuts in trade, and Lula added them to her already bulky load before they continued on their way.

Hours later, the path finally flattened out and spilled into a field sprinkled with black-eyed Susans and ox-eye daisies. The rasping of cicadas filled the air. They walked a short distance in the grassy field until reaching a dirt road, wider than any Lula had ever seen. As they trudged on with the sun beating down on them, Lula wondered if they were ever going to get anywhere. A wide, frisky river ran alongside the road that led them into a cool, shady glen. Enjoying the respite from the searing heat, they continued around a curve, until Lula stopped dead in her tracks and let all her bundles slip from her hands.

A huge, white two-story building rose on the horizon two hundred feet ahead. Lula's eyes slowly scanned across the scene in front of her. Elegantly dressed people rocked leisurely in chairs on the wide veranda and covered porch above it, while children in pinafores and high-laced shoes frolicked on the lawn. A horse and fringed surrey stood waiting for someone's luggage to be unloaded. It was almost too much for Lula to take in.

"What's that thar?" she asked.

Granny McDowell snatched up Lula's bundles and shoved them back into the child's arms. "That thar is the Edney Inn, an where I aim ta do a mess a tradin."

Quickly, the old woman ushered her across the lawn to the back of the building and up the stairs to the kitchen. The air was stifling. A heavy-set woman stood over the stove, dark damp circles beneath her arms. Sweat ran in rivulets from her temples.

Spoon in hand, she gave Granny a broad smile.

"I sure hope you brought plenty of them asphidity bags with ya," she said as she picked up her apron and wiped her brow. "Our boarders been askin for em."

A woman rushed in with an armful of kindling. She bumped into a table in the crowded room and sent the wood flying. Lula jumped to the flustered woman's aid and helped pick up the wood and stack it next to the huge cast iron stove. Lula looked up to see Granny McDowell over in a dark corner pulling aside a burlap curtain and motioning for her to come. Lula quickly gathered her bundles and followed her into a small room lit only by a tiny window. Several straw mattresses covered in ticking lay on the floor.

"Here's where we put our heads down at night," said Granny. "Ye rest here while I do me some catchin up."

The old woman disappeared, and Lula quickly ran to the curtain and peeked out. The large, sweaty woman who Lula took to be the cook had set some cups on the table. She had pulled her hair back in a bun and rolled up her long sleeves. She offered Granny a chair, then took a huge pot off the stove and poured them both coffee before sitting down. Lula knew she shouldn't, but couldn't resist the temptation to listen in. She carefully slipped from behind the curtain and, quiet as a mouse, sidled up against a pie safe, out of sight.

"That's a right nice little gal you got there," said the cook. "Keen on bein helpful."

"That she are," said Granny. "Her pa's doin poorly, an there be a need ta take on someone strong. Calls fer her ta be put out ta work. Her ma be trustin me to find a good place. She's her favorite an it pains her ta let her go, but the others are needed more fer workin the farm. Fifty-cents a month plus room an board tis all they be askin fer her labors."

The cook shook her head. "I'm from a long ways back in the hills myself and sure do know about hard times, but times are hard here in the valley, too, and we've already taken on all the help we can rightly use. Strong, hard working men and women at that." She took up her apron and wiped the back of her neck.

"It's all I can do to feed them and all our boarders, and every day the surrey is bringin more folks from the Hendersonville train station. I reckon there ain't no place to escape the heat and skeeters in Florida and Georgia."

THE SOUND OF busy feet and clinking of dishes woke Lula from her nap. Roused by a promising aroma and finding herself alone in the room, she pulled aside the curtain and marveled at all the people rushing around the kitchen preparing the evening meal. She ventured out and gaped at the table piled with bowls of steaming food. No sooner had the cook filled them, when they were whisked away by a waiting maid. The bounty stunned Lula—platters with mounds of fluffy mashed potatoes, as many bowls of vegetables as she had fingers on one hand, and stacks of 'roastin ears' ready for buttering.

When the last of the piles of fried chicken and trays of sliced home-cured ham and stewed beef were finally taken away, the cook shed her apron and flounced her rotund body through the crowded kitchen. The swaying of her long skirt revealed her bare feet as she made her way onto the porch and clanged the bell. In moments, so many people rushed into the building that the noise was nearly deafening. All those feet pounding on the wood floor sounded like a cattle stampede.

With the maids scurrying in and out of the kitchen, Lula was able to sneak unnoticed into a huge parlor where she could look out onto the dining room. Thirty or so guests were seated on both sides of a long table with maids rushing back and forth, pouring coffee and milk and bringing in baskets of biscuits hot out of the oven. Mothers frantically rounded up their children and struggled to get them quickly settled at the smaller tables scattered about. Afraid Granny might have returned and be looking for her, Lula tore herself away from the boisterous scene and snuck back in the kitchen.

"Well thar she is," said the cook. She pulled out a chair for Lula. "You set right there. Miss Bertha is gonna put up your supper."

Lula gobbled down every bit she was served and licked the

rich yellow cream that had been poured on top the blackberry cobbler clean off her plate.

Dishes started coming back in the kitchen, and it soon became noisy and crowded with all the washing and putting away. Later, Lula sat in a corner petting a cat, wondering where Granny McDowell had gone, when she heard the unfamiliar but delightful notes of a piano. She jumped up and started to follow the sound into the ballroom when the cook grabbed her.

"Where you think yer goin?"

Lula looked up at her.

The woman's eyes fixed on the straggly blond hair, ragged dress, and dirty bare feet.

"I'm sorry, darlin, but I can't let you go in there."

Bertha looked into the pleading blue eyes, but all she saw was the bedraggled little girl she had been when she lived in the back-woods. She didn't have the heart to hurt the helpful little angel's feelings. Her pitiful condition wasn't her fault. The woman thought for a moment, suddenly smiled, and led Lula out onto a small back porch. She hefted a box off a crate, revealing a window above. Hearing a fiddle start up, she quickly swung Lula up onto the crate. "Peek through that thar window, secret like, and no one's gonna know the difference."

Lula put her elbows on the sill and nestled her chin on her hands as she watched the finely dressed people assemble on the glistening waxed floor for a square dance. The women and girls were pretty in all their finery, but what struck Lula most was the great delight with which they danced. She couldn't remember ever seeing her mother look so gleeful or smile with so many white teeth.

She suddenly missed the comfort of sitting with her family in front of the warm hearth. When would she see them again? With her pa unable to go into the fields, she couldn't fault her momma for putting her out to work. She had heard such things were done in hard times. Lula knew nothing about money, but still sensed fifty-cents was a great deal of it. Tears welled in her eyes, and a yearning filled her heart for her momma and papa and brothers and sister.

The next morning, it was still dark when the commotion started up in the kitchen again. Lula rose off her straw mat and tiptoed around the one Granny was snoring on. She went out into the kitchen and quickly made herself useful by picking up a broom and sweeping up all the ashes around the stove. With all the goings-on, she knew the fire had to be kept up, so she found something to wrap around the handle of the firebox door and opened it, then she stoked the wood and stuffed in more. With no one telling her to do anything different, she spent most of the early morning tending to the fire, pleased that the cook had readily accepted that the chore was hers. Lula felt it was the least she could do after all the vittles the woman had given her the night before.

One of the kitchen maids asked her for help, and she followed her out to the spring house. The cool dark room had an ice-cold spring flowing through a long stone channel. The maid picked a bucket from it and handed it to her with a warning.

"Don't drop this. It's fresh .churned butter." Then the girl grabbed a basket of eggs with one hand, and a large jug of fresh, cold milk with the other and trudged back to the kitchen with Lula at her heels.

Lula put the butter on the kitchen table and got a breathtaking look at all the preparations for breakfast—hot biscuits, sorghum, hominy grits, cured ham slices, and an endless variety of home-made jellies and preserves. How she wished Billy Boy could see it all.

By now, Granny was up and preparing to go out trading again. "Ye stay here an make yerself useful. I be back by noon time," she told Lula.

None of the help were allowed to sit down to eat until the breakfast was over and all the plates were cleared, except the maids who had to rush upstairs and clean the rooms while the guests were eating.

Seeing the trail of women lugging buckets of water and baskets of clean linen up the back stairway to the second floor, Lula figured they could use some help and ran after them. A women, carrying two buckets of water down the long hallway lined with rooms on both sides, signaled for Lula to open a door for her. Once inside, the maid made quick work of cleaning the wash- stand bowl, filling the empty pitchers with water, and putting up clean towels while Lula gathered up the used ones.

The woman handed Lula a bucket and told her to empty the convenience.

"What's a venience," asked Lula.

The woman rolled her eyes, then opened a door below the stand, pulled out a china pitcher, and emptied it into a slop bucket.

"Ugh," moaned Lula.

"You don't expect these highfalutin folks to go to the out- house in the middle of the night, do ya?"

Lula could hardly imagine anyone being so plum catered to. She'd hardly gotten over her first trip to the fancy outhouse. There were seats for three people and a Sears Roebuck catalogue she at first thought was for looking at. When she asked the maid who had taken her out there where the dried corncobs were, the girl tore off a page and handed it to her. Then she pointed to a wooden box of lime in the corner with instructions for her to scoop some up with the short-handled fire shovel and cover up her 'business' when she was finished. The whole process took some getting used to, but at least the maid had taught her to read two words: men and women.

Later, after the kitchen help ate and finished the breakfast chores, Bertha settled down at the table and relaxed over a cup of coffee. Lula finished sweeping the floor, and one of the maids who looked to be no older than Lula's big sister asked her to come help with getting in vegetables for the midday meal.

Out in back, they passed the barns for keeping the inn's cattle, horses, and hogs, set far enough back so the smell wouldn't reach the sensitive nostrils of the inn's boarders. Lula asked the girl what the boxes fastened to the outside of the barns were for and was told it was where their hens lay their eggs. These strange folk even catered to the chickens, thought Lula.

They reached the fields where bushel baskets of squash, beans, carrots, and potatoes waited at the ends of rows ready to be brought to the kitchen. Two women in long skirts and sun-bonnets were gathering vegetables in the field while several men hoed. Seeing a young fellow emptying a picker's full basket, Lula thought Billy Boy could do that and wondered if they'd give her momma a whole dollar for his labor.

Lunch at the inn was as hectic as dinner the night before, and by the time the whole noisy process of cleaning up was over, Granny McDowell had returned.

"We be settin off to see the doctor woman on Chimney Rock Road," she told the cook. "Hopin the postman be takin us in his buggy when he gits here."

Bertha gave Granny some coins for potions and poultices, then made ham and biscuit sandwiches for them to take. Her trading finished, Granny took Lula in the back room and rearranged the bundles for her to carry—much less than what they had started with. Then the old women pulled up her apron and put the coins Bertha had given her into a leather bag hanging from her waist.

They said their goodbyes and went out to the front of the inn where a crowd waited for the mail. The way some of the children were staring made Lula wish she and Granny could hurry up and get along to where they were going on foot. Lula was relieved when the sound of creaking wagon wheels drew everyone's eyes to the bend in the road.

By the time the horse and buggy appeared, the bevy of boarders had swelled. The buggy pulled up to the row of metal mailboxes standing on the edge of the lawn, and an elderly man got off. He was dressed in what Lula thought was too many clothes for the heat they were suffering. A jacket hardly seemed necessary.

After tying the horse to a hitching post, he announced, "All right, folks, I gotta put the mail in the boxes first, then I'll be sellin stamps and post cards, and takin your parcels."

Many of the letters were whisked from his hand before he could even stuff them into a box. The men retired to the porch as soon as they got their newspapers, but the women couldn't get their letters opened fast enough. The cry, "When's daddy coming?" rippled through the throng as the mothers quickly read their mail.

By the time the postman finished selling stamps and collecting the outgoing mail, Granny had gotten him to agree to take her and Lula as far as the doctor woman's place. With Granny settled on the seat and Lula on the ledge at the rear, the postman climbed up on the buggy. He snapped the reins and clucked, and the horse began a slow, determined trot down the road with Lula dangling her bare feet off the back.

The road ran through a valley surrounded on all sides by mountains. Lula stood up and gripped the back of the section for holding parcels and mail. "Where's we come from?" she hollered to Granny.

The old woman pointed east. "Up thar."

Eyeing the far off monolith, Lula thought it was no wonder it took them most of a day to make their way down.

The road came to a narrow wooden bridge, and once crossed, ended at what the postman called the Chimney Rock Road. Lula wondered if it led to the chimney that stuck out from the mountain that Billy Boy had shown her. The buggy turned left and started up the steep, rutted dirt road that was little more than a logging trail, bumping and jerking over big rocks jutting out of the earth. It had grown cooler now that they were surrounded by the shade of giant oaks, ash, and locust, adding to the joy Lula felt. It was the first ride Lula ever had other than when her father let her get astride their mule as they set off for their fields.

Suddenly the driver yelled, "Whoa, Nellie," and the buggy came to a halt at a big metal mailbox. "Here's where Essie Gordon, the doctor woman, has set up her drugstore," said the driver. "Nearest one for twelve miles." He got off and started to help Granny down. "I have a package for that genteel lady she lives with up there. She's callin her house Edelweiss after some place she's been to in Switzerland. Would like to go up and take a gander at that grand piano everyone's talkin about. Hear it came from Columbia by freight, and she had it brought up by oxen. But I'm runnin behind and would be most grateful if you folks would kindly take the package up to her."

Granny said she'd be honored, and everyone busied themselves loading up their bundles. The package for the lady he called Helen Baldwin was so small, it was hardly trouble at all. They said goodbye to the postman and began an arduous trek up a narrow, winding path. It seemed barely wide enough for two people to walk side-by-side, but Lula spotted several scars in the dirt from buggy wheels and horse hoofs, so it had to be wider than it looked. She eyed the drop-off on one side anxiously. She certainly didn't want to ride in a buggy on this road.

When they finally reached the small log structure that was little more than a hut, they were surprised to find two women who had arrived ahead of them. They carried jugs of honey, eggs, and berries to trade, and, as was the custom for mountain women, wore long skirts with aprons and long-sleeved tops and sunbonnets, all plainly made of homespun cloth.

A little dog ran out from the hut barking, followed by a striking woman who quickly greeted everyone in a most friendly manner. Lula couldn't take her eyes off of her. She was smoking a corncob pipe and dressed like a man, with a rimmed hat, tie, and long pants. She tended to the two women, and after they left, invited Granny and Lula to spread out the herbs and poultices on a table inside.

"I done sold my asphidity bags," Granny told the doctor woman, "but thars plenty a yarbs."

The woman took a puff from her pipe and slowly blew it out. "Do you have any bloodroot?"

Lula quickly produced three small bundles and showed them to her in her open palms.

The woman pointed to another table with her pipe. "Put them over there," then asked, "How about lady slipper?"

Lula snatched a small bundle and showed it to her, and again the woman pointed to the table. By the time they had gone through all the catnip, ramp, and wild ginger, almost all Granny's offerings were on the other table along with the items the other two women had left.

The doctor woman turned to Lula, "You run along outside and play with the dog while we finish our business."

Lula dutifully went outside as bid, but succumbed to her shameful vice and leaned against the door close enough to hear.

"Well? Will ya take er on?" asked Granny.

Lula held her breath as she waited for the woman to answer.

"Here's the half dollar. Tell her mother I'll put her to work for a month, and if she's as good as you say, I'll add a quarter."

CHAPTER FIVE

"I be goin down the road apiece to Bat Cave," Granny told Lula as she left her with the doctor woman. "Ye stay here now an I tell yer ma bout where ye is."

Lula stood alone outside the rustic, windowless little drugstore and watched Granny with her lone bundle make her way down the road until she disappeared out of sight. Lula wiped the tears from her hot, gritty face, then knelt down and buried her face in the little dog's fur until two brown oxfords appeared in front of her. She looked up.

"I'll be busy here for a while," the doctor woman said. "Go up to the house and present yourself to Miss Helen." With that, she turned and went back into the hut.

"What yer dog's name?" Lula called out.

"Jack," came the reply.

Lula started up the road. Ahead, the huge intimidating log cabin with a stone chimney running up its side gave her pause. She turned. "Come, Jack."

The dog wagged its tail and kept fidgeting as if it wanted to go but couldn't tear itself away from its master.

Lula took a deep breath and trudged up the hill alone, and as she neared, for the second time in as many days, she heard the now familiar sound of a piano. Reaching the house, she timidly stepped onto the porch and peeked through the open door. A tall, elegant looking woman in a lacey, high-necked white dress sat playing an enormous mahogany piano. Although her hair was starting to gray, the woman seemed full of youth. She stopped playing and looked up at Lula.

"Come here, little one," she said in the sweetest sounding voice Lula had ever heard. "You must be the girl Granny McDowell has told us about. Please come and tell me your name."

Lula went up to her, her head bowed, and whispered, "Lula... Lula Mae."

"Well, Lula Mae, you can call me Helen and Mrs. Gordon, Essie. Where are your things, darling?"

Lula knew it wasn't proper, but still couldn't find the courage to look her straight in the eye.

"Got none."

"Well, we'll soon see to that, but right now, I think you could use something to eat and a bath."

Helen rose and led Lula by the hand to the kitchen and sat her down with a plate of sweet biscuits, then filled a large kettle with water from a faucet that ran continuously into the sink. Lula didn't raise her head once as she ate the delicious morsels and drank the tall glass of cold buttermilk the woman had fetched from a spring house outdoors, but she knew she was being stared at. She could feel it.

Helen put on an apron and went out from the kitchen to a small adjoining room. Lula, wanting to be respectful, left one biscuit on the plate and followed her.

Lula pointed to a long tin tub set on a wooden frame. Water flowed from a pipe leading from the outdoors and was filling it up. "What's that?"

"That's our bathtub. The sun shines on a big tub of water outdoors and warms it. I had a carpenter set it up, along with another one outside behind the cookstove. That way we have some water in the winter that's not frozen. When the kettle whistles, I'll pour it in and make you a nice bath."

After Lula got in the tub and endured having her hair washed and elbows and feet scrubbed, she didn't want to come out. She had seen Granny give lavender to folks to put in their soap, but had never before had the luxury of soaking herself in the wonderful fragrance.

Helen went from the room for a while, then came breezing back in. "I found you some clothes a church in Raleigh sent us. The next time we get a shipment from them, we'll see if we can fix you up with some shoes, but I'm afraid it will take forever to get those feet of yours looking proper."

She helped Lula from the tub and dried her off, then she reached for the pile of clothes.

"Here put these on. They should fit," she said, handing her a pair of cotton underpants.

"What do I do with em?"

"You wear them under your dress."

"What fer?"

Helen looked away and blinked back a tear. Quickly composed, she helped Lula get them on.

Lula kept running her hands over the lightweight dress Helen had put on her. With its colorful little forget-me-nots, it was wonderfully different from the plain wool she was used to and gave her a thrill. Then Helen led her outdoors and showed her how to open a lever to refill the water tub.

Pointing to a pipe that led from two tubs on the side of the house up to the mountain, she said, "Our water comes from a spring up there. Every time we take a bath, we have to come out here and fill the tub again. It's something I saw when I stayed at a chalet in Switzerland."

"How do ye get the water outta the tub?"

"It goes out a hole in the floor like in the kitchen. There's a trench under the house that it runs along."

Lula's mind spun with all the newfangled fixings. She'd never seen anything like it.

Next she was shown the two-seater outhouse hidden behind a lattice wall. Helen walked with her to their garden, and the two of them pulled up some carrots and beets. As they entered the house through the kitchen door, a young woman came rushing in.

"How's your sister doing, Katie?" Helen asked.

"Right fine. Sorry it took me so long, but I couldn't leave til I had a square meal set on the stove for her family." A proud grin appeared. "My, her new baby sure looks fine." She snatched an apron off the hook. "I'll be gettin right to the supper."

"Take your time, dear. You needn't rush," said Helen.

The three of them worked in the kitchen for a while, and by the time the food was ready to be put on the table, Katie had left for home, and Lula was starting to feel comfortable in her new situation.

Expecting to be eating in the kitchen like she had at the Edney Inn, Lula was surprised when Helen seated her at the table. Lula thought it odd when Helen asked Essie to say grace. Only her father had that honor at home. Lula had her eye on the steaming biscuits and picked one up as the basket was passed. Helen reached over and put a chunk of butter on her plate with a smile. All the fuss Helen was paying her made Lula blush. She smiled back and began spreading the butter on the biscuit.

"Good Lord, child! You have to use your knife to spread the butter, not your fingers," snapped Essie.

Lula bowed her head and somberly wiped her hands on her napkin.

Helen reached over and took up Lula's knife and buttered the biscuit. "Like this, dear."

Lula felt her cheeks get warm, and she started fidgeting in her chair.

"Go on. Eat your dinner," coaxed Helen.

Lula looked up at the sweet smile, then timidly reached over, picked up a juicy slice of ham from the platter and, holding it with both hands, started to take a bite. Suddenly Essie grabbed her wrist and shook it until the ham flopped down on the plate.

"Gracious, girl! Didn't anyone ever teach you how to use a knife and fork?"

Lula gritted her teeth and crunched up her face, now a bright shade of red. She grabbed her knife and stabbed the half-carved ham on the platter, and did the same with her fork, then folded her arms in a pout.

Helen rushed from her chair and crouched down next to her.

With one arm around her, she brushed the locks from her face.

"Essie didn't mean anything by that, darling. You're doing fine."

"No, she's not," slurred Essie before taking another drink of the clear liquid in her glass. "How can I take her round with manners like that."

Helen rose, wrenched the fork and knife from the ham, and proceeded to cut up the slice on the plate. She gently put the fork in Lula's hand and said, "Go on, darling. Eat your supper." Then she took the bottle Essie had been pouring from and put in on the sideboard, saying, "You've had enough... and so have we."

Lula dutifully ate without looking up. No one spoke. All that was heard was the clinking of forks on the plates and the caw of a crow flying over the house.

Finished eating, Lula pleaded meekly, "Hit'll be good ifin I can go up the stair steps ta be a beddin, lest ye be wantin me ta help in the kitchen."

"Of course, you can go up to bed," said Helen. "You must be tired from such a busy day."

Helen rose and took Lula by the hand and led her up the stairs to a small room. Lula stood stoically while Helen undressed her and helped her with a nightgown, neither of them saying a word. Helen tucked her in bed, and when she bent to kiss her on the forehead, Lula turned over on her side and let the tears run down her burning cheeks. All that was left for Helen to do was pat her on the head and leave before she herself burst into tears.

As Lula lay in the bed, it was still light enough to see the leaves on the limb outside the window ruffle in the gentle breeze. She listened to the rapid-fire staccato from a mockingbird and wondered if it had ever called out on her beloved plateau. The beautiful room with gaily printed wallpaper instead of drab, bare wood, the silky sheets and comforter that smelled like a sweet summer breeze, and the scent of lavender coming from her locks gave her no pleasure. She'd as soon trade all of it to be home at the hearth on her momma's lap listening to the rhythm of her pa rocking in front of the fire as he puffed on his pipe with their faithful hound curled up at his feet. Remembering the harsh words the doctor woman spoke brought tears to her eyes, and she fell asleep yearning for the home where she was loved and honored.

"WELL YOU CERTAINLY were a shining example of charity this evening," said Helen as she gathered the left over bowls of food.

"I took on the child like you insisted," said Essie, "but I don't see how she's going to fit in. Take the way she speaks."

"Essie, you're going to have to face the fact that you're getting to an age where you'll be needing help. And as far as the way the child speaks, you need to keep in mind that the isolated community way up on the mountain where she came from has been so far removed from general society there's been no admixture over generations. Good Lord, up until a few years back, they'd been living with no contact with anyone from the outside world since the late 1780s.

"I've read enough Shakespeare and Chaucer to recognize some of their old English words and expressions like fetch and poke. And the way they say church house, biscuit bread, and ham meat is classic old English vernacular as well."

Helen rose and started clearing the dishes. "I'll admit these mountain people speak in a language that is rather original, picturesque, and often incorrect, but much of it has survived from the English spoken at the time of Chaucer. So you can't consider their way of talking as lowly, and at the same time expect the great literature of a few centuries back to be respected."

Helen took the dishes to the kitchen, returned with the coffee pot, and poured Essie a cup. "Here, drink this and try to sober up," she said shaking her head. "This drinking of yours is becoming a serious vice. Look at the way you welcomed that sweet child into this house. It was deplorable. Essie, you simply have to stop accepting that dreadful concoction they call shine as payment for your services. It made your behavior tonight unacceptable. I know you're not that unkind.

"That little darling did everything she could to help out in the kitchen today. When I thanked her, and she said she was grateful for the bread and board and the fifty cents you were giving her mother, it just about broke my heart." Helen stared off into space and tsked. "Imagine being a child and put into a strange house to work, away from your family and the people you love."

"Don't worry, I'll make it up to her tomorrow," said Essie.

HELEN WENT INTO Lula's room the following morning and was surprised to find the bed made, with the dress she'd been wearing the night before lying neatly on top. Wondering if Lula was afoot in her nightgown, Helen hurried down the stairs and was met at the bottom by Essie who was coming from her downstairs bedroom. Katie appeared from the kitchen with a pot of coffee.

"Have you seen Lula?" Helen asked.

"No."

Helen looked accusingly at Essie.

"Don't fret. She has to be somewhere around here," said Essie. "Let's look."

Not finding Lula anywhere in the house, they checked the garden and all around the outside. Helen riffled through the can they used for burning, and as she suspected, the pitiful dress the child had been wearing when she came was gone.

"Now you've done it with your drinking," Helen said with unusual terseness. "All that child wanted was to help her family."

Jack came barking from behind the trellis. The two women looked at each other and rushed to the outhouse. The door was ajar, with Lula on her hands and knees scrubbing the floor. She looked up.

"What are you doing, child?" Helen asked in disbelief.

"Earnin my keep. My ma sorely needs the fifty cents." She turned and went back to scrubbing.

Helen started to bend down when Essie pulled her back, then gently took the scrub brush from Lula and lifted her up.

"You don't have to do the scrubbing, Lula," said Essie.

"Katie and the others will see to it." She spread open Lula's hands. "I need you to use these to help me with my nursing. Granny McDowell told me that's your gift."

Lula was sent upstairs to change, while Helen and the housekeeper worked in the kitchen. By the time they sat down at the breakfast table, the mood had softened a bit, but few words were spoken. Helen was about to pass Lula the jelly jar, when she stopped and listened. Suddenly Jack ran out of the house barking. Hearing the sound of hoofs pounding the earth, everyone rushed to the door and out onto the porch.

The horse came to a halt just short of the porch. A man shouted from the rearing animal, "Mrs. Gordon, you gotta come to the inn right quick. We got a little boy who can hardly breathe."

He slid off the snorting horse and offered the reins to Essie. "Here, take my horse! I'll walk back."

Essie ran into the house and came out toting a carpetbag. She handed it to the man, put her foot into the stirrup, and swung a leg over, then gave Lula a quick glance and shouted, "Get up behind me, girl!"

The man quickly hoisted Lula onto the horse.

Helen handed her the bag with the instructions, "Hold tight to this and Essie."

Moments later, the horse was galloping down the Chimney Rock Road with Lula's arms wrapped tightly around Essie's waist, the bag between them. Essie rode the horse hard to the Edney Inn Road, then straight up to the inn's kitchen steps. She slid off, tied the horse to a hitching post, and ran in with Lula running after her toting the bag.

"Where's the boy?" she shouted to Bertha who stood wringing her hands.

"Upstairs."

"Put on as many kettles as you've got, and send them up aboiling!"

Essie took the back staircase two steps at a time with Lula trailing. Mrs. Edney, who was pacing outside a room, lit up the minute she saw Essie.

"Thank God, you're here," she exclaimed.

Essie rushed into the room to see the boy's mother kneeling at his bedside. She took a quick look and could see he had turned blue.

"Everyone leave," she commanded, then pulled the mother from the child's side. She bent over the boy and put her mouth over his and breathed. She kept at it for the time it took for the first kettle of boiling water to arrive. Then she pulled off a sheet and made a tent over the child to capture the steam. After a few minutes, she whipped off the sheet and started forcing breath into the boy's mouth again. She repeated the process every time a new kettle arrived.

Lula watched in awe as, over the next two hours, the boy's color slowly returned.

Essie, nearing exhaustion, told Lula to get out an asphidity bag and put it around the boy's neck. Next, she turned to the mother. "The steam and then the cool air have helped to open up his lungs." She took up a clean towel and wiped her brow. "Why don't you go tend to your family. I'll sit with the boy. He needs quiet now." Then she asked Lula to fetch her a cup of coffee.

Lula rushed out of the room, raced in her bare feet down the staircase, and burst into the kitchen where preparations for lunch were underway.

"Well, look at you," said Bertha. "It seems you found yourself a right nice situation."

Bertha's kind attention made Lula so uncomfortable she couldn't look up at her as she said, "The doctor woman be wantin coffee."

"Everyone's sayin the boy's gonna be all right," said Bertha as she took the coffee kettle from the stove and poured a cup. "You take that on up with you, and I'll be sending up a nice lunch right quick."

Lula went back up the stairs, careful not to spill a drop. Lula spent the afternoon and into the evening running water and towels while Essie administered them to the boy, taking his temperature often. By nightfall, Essie was confident enough to leave the boy in his mother's care with instructions for her to come in the room next door if his condition changed.

Weary, Essie lifted Lula, asleep in a chair, and carried her to the room where they'd be spending the night. After putting her on a cot and tenderly tucking her in, she took a bottle of colorless corn whiskey out of her bag, poured herself a tall glass, and sat rocking in a chair in the dark.

CHAPTER SIX
1960

"When you work as a nurse in a hospital, your patients have come to your house," Lucy, the nurse who Holly was replacing, had told her as she drove up and down Sugarloaf Mountain the day before, visiting patients. "In the hospital you make the rules and give the orders. But when you're a public health nurse, you're a guest in your patient's house, so you have to do whatever it takes to be invited in and make yourself welcome; and remember, in the back of every parent's mind, is the knowledge that you work for the same government that can take away their kids. That's why we seldom go with anyone from Social Services. It's important you're seen as a nurse, not someone from a county enforcement agency."

The next day, Holly rolled those words around in her head as she drove to make a visit. How strange, she thought, having to earn her patients' trust when she was only there to help. She wished she had a name that was common to those mountains. It would help them accept her. But Myrt had told her "Baldwin" wasn't one she'd heard in those parts before, a statement that made her wonder if her aunt had lived there after all.

She pulled up to a small trailer with a huge antenna on its roof. Lucy had introduced her the day before to a girl who lived there with a new baby. Good, no car. The file had indicated that the girl didn't want anyone to come to the door if a car was in the driveway because that meant her husband was home. The day before, Lucy had emphasized to the sixteen-year-old that she needed to feed the baby. Later, Lucy mentioned she suspected the girl was retarded because she couldn't read or tell time, and the baby was definitely undernourished. He now weighed a pound less than at birth.

"That baby isn't thriving," Lucy told her. "You better check on him every day."

Holly got out of her car and looked around at the abandoned cars littering the lawn. She grabbed the rotting wood handrail and made her way up the rickety set of stairs to the porch. She adjusted her name tag, making sure it was straight, then knocked on the door.

"Come in," someone called from inside.

Holly opened the door, and like the day before, the girl was fixated on a tiny black and white TV, oblivious to the baby screaming in its cradle. Since the girl wasn't breast feeding, Lucy had told her to leave the empty baby bottles out, so they'd know how many had been given. Holly was stunned to discover only three on the counter, even though most babies drink two or three ounces about eight times a day.

She found the baby formula, quickly made up a bottle, and handed it to the girl with the baby. Holly could see the crib the baby had been lying in was in order with a stack of fluffy diapers sitting next to it. When Holly questioned her about the diapers, the girl answered without taking her eyes from the TV.

"My mother lives nearby. She comes a couple times a day with clean ones and takes away the dirty ones," said the girl.

Holly quickly added up the situation. The only time the baby was being fed and changed was when the mother dropped in.

Seeing that the baby had sucked the bottle dry, Holly took out her scale and weighed him. The poor little thing had lost another two ounces since yesterday. Alarmed, Holly knew she had to act fast. She thought for a moment. The girl's whole life revolved around the TV. Maybe she could make that work for the baby. Holly took out her note pad, pushed aside the clutter on the couch, and sat down next to her.

"Tell me about all the shows you watch," Holly pressed.

As the girl rattled off the lineup, Holly was surprised how articulate she was about the shows and their casts.

"Every morning I can hardly wait for all those boring news and weather people to get off so I can watch *Captain Kangaroo.* Then comes *I Love Lucy,* then *December Bride,* and *Love of Life.* I get somethin to eat when *Search for Tomorrow* comes on, then *The Guiding Light.* But my favorite of all is *As the World Turns.*" She looked pleadingly at Holly. "Do you think Oakdale is a real place?"

"I wouldn't know," said Holly. "Now tell me what you watch at night?"

Holly jotted it all down, then made up eight bottles of formula and hurriedly drew simple sketches depicting the shows during which she wanted the girl to feed the baby. She attached them to the bottles and carefully went through them with her.

"When you wake up, you give the baby a bottle, then when *Captain Kangaroo* comes on you give it the one with the man with the roly-poly face and bangs." She showed her the bottle with a drawing of a heart. "This one you give when *I Love Lucy* comes on." By the time Holly reached *The Guiding Light* depicted as a sunrise, and *As the World Turns* as a globe, she was confident the girl understood and would do as instructed. It was clear she loved the baby and wanted to do right by it; however, it was equally clear that she had no clue that, when her baby cried, it needed to be fed.

Holly finished with the girl, telling her to save the empty bottles, and that she'd be back in the morning. Settled in her car, Holly reviewed the file on a new case she'd been assigned that morning. A baby who weighed less than four pounds at birth and was now at home needed a follow-up. She studied the hand-drawn map attached to the file. It showed Sugarloaf Mountain Road with instructions to turn right onto the second dirt road past the Mountain Home Church. An arrow pointed to a place a distance from the turnoff with the notation: "Cross the stream on foot and walk from there."

She passed the road and had to double back. How could any-one call this dirt path a road, she grumbled, after finally locating it. Coming from high on the mountain, the road was mostly downhill. Every once in a while, it leveled out to a rolling pla-teau with hundreds of small trees in rows that she took to be an orchard. The road rapidly led to a dense forest and became steeper. She came around a curve and could see another curve ahead with a drop-off on one side.

It was barely wide enough for one car, and she became con-cerned about what she would do if someone came toward her from around the mountain. Feeling an urge to go back, she looked over her shoulder and decided it was too risky to back up around the narrow curve. She had no choice but to keep going. Slowly, the car edged around the mountain, and as she hit a straight-away and was starting to feel less stressed, she heard a thumping. She stopped the car and got out. The back tire was flat.

She checked her watch. Already one o'clock. Miles from a phone and on a dangerous, deserted road, she had better get busy and change it. However, she couldn't visit a patient in a soiled uniform. Not a soul or a house around, she quickly took off her uniform, turned it inside out, and put it back on. Next, she un-snapped her stockings from her girdle and rolled them down to her ankles.

It took a while, but she finally got the car jacked up and the hubcap off, but the lug nuts wouldn't budge. She was pawing through the toolbox in the trunk for some oil when a pick-up came speeding around the curve behind her and skidded to a stop, slinging gravel around her feet.

A man in a clean white t-shirt and faded jeans jumped out and strolled over wearing a smug grin.

"Lucky for you I came along," he said with a wink.

Holly gave him a long, critical look. She averted her eyes from his biceps and snapped, "I was doing fine before you nearly rammed into me."

He broke into a wide grin and shook his head. "You sure are one feisty little thing." He offered his hand. "Jeff Garrison."

She gave it a brief shake. "Holly Baldwin."

He picked up the lug wrench and went about getting the spare out of the trunk, changing the tire without another word. She watched his muscles ripple under his shirt with every exertion. After thinking her situation over, Holly poked him on the shoulder. He looked up, questioningly.

"I need to do something at the front of the car, and I have to ask you not to look."

He studied her face for a moment, then went back to the tire, shaking his head. "Sure."

Holly grabbed a rag from the trunk and brushed off her hands and knees, then raced to the front of the car. She quickly took off her uniform, crouching down, so if he was rude enough to look, he wouldn't see much. She rolled up her hose, attached them to the snaps dangling from her girdle, then stood up and smoothed out her slip and uniform. Seeing he was putting the jack back into the trunk, she reached into the front seat for her purse and went up to him. "How much do I owe you?" she asked.

"I can see you're not from these parts. Around here, ma'am, we help folks free of charge."

"That's very kind of you, but I've held you up, and I feel obliged to compensate you."

His eyes lingered on her for a moment with a trace of a grin. "Let's just put it on the cuff."

"Well... thank you. I appreciate it."

"Is that some kind of uniform you're wearing?" he asked as he slammed her trunk shut.

"Yes. I'm a public health nurse and this is my territory."

Feeling she had made a statement with that announcement, she opened her door and got back into the car. No sooner had she put the key into the ignition, than he was resting his forearm on the open window and leaning in close enough for her to notice the smell of his soap. She looked into the steely blue eyes and chalked up his arrogance to his being fully aware of the effect his appearance had on most women.

She stared down at his arm, then up at him as if she wanted it taken off her car. He evidently got the message and backed away, then crossed his arms over his broad chest and smiled. As she continued up the road, she found it hard to erase the image of him standing there with the kind of grin that could only belong to someone who was confident of who they were and where they were going. She only wished she was.

She kept on the road, every once in a while checking the rearview mirror. This Jeff Garrison fellow was a little too sure of himself, but otherwise probably harmless. However, after all the warnings she'd gotten from Lucy, she needed to make sure he wasn't following her. She was relieved when he finally turned off and she could concentrate on the road ahead. She came to the creek in less than a mile and stopped and studied her map. It said for her to continue on foot until she reached a giant boulder on the left side of the road with an arrow pointing right.

She got out and studied the creek. No need for boots. She could make it across by stepping on the stones. She took out her satchel, crossed without mishap, and continued up the road. Birds calling out and squirrels scampering through the underbrush kept her from feeling alone. She listened keenly as she trudged along. It was easy to recognize the chattering of a cardinal and the trill of a warbler. How she wished her Aunt Helen was with her now. Whether she had ever lived in these mountains or not, Holly knew she would love this place. Her aunt had studied all the birds outside their windows in Pittsboro and could recognize every call, every song.

Holly spotted a big boulder ahead and hastened on, wondering if that was the one on the map. When she finally reached it, she saw a big red arrow painted on it pointing to a foot path. A beat-up pick-up was parked to the side. It appeared that the road ended at this point. She turned up the path and hadn't gone far when she spotted the cabin.

She knocked at the door and waited for someone to come.

"Hello," she told the scruffy young man who opened the door. "I'm Nurse Holly. I've come to look after your wife and baby."

He stepped aside for her to enter. The room was sheathed with planks, but she could see daylight between the boards.

There was a dirt floor and chickens everywhere. They were perched on the chairs, the table, the shelves, with poop on everything. A young woman sat in a chair nursing her baby.

Overcome with disgust, Holly let her temper get the best of her. "I'm sorry, sir, but you can't have these chickens in this house with that baby!"

"What do you mean? That's how I make my living."

"You have to put them outside in coops."

He scratched behind his ear. "How can I do that? The hawks or foxes will get them."

"Well, I'm afraid you'll have to get rid of them anyway," insisted Holly. "This place isn't sanitary enough for a baby... for anyone. That baby's going to get sick!"

The woman barely whispered, "He does chicken fights on weekends, and it's the only cash money we get."

Holly looked at her and then on the beautiful, innocent infant suckling at her breast, and it almost broke her heart.

Tired from the long walk, Holly wanted to sit down, but with poop on everything she didn't dare. Instead, she leaned against a wall and thought.

"What if I can get you the money to buy lumber and supplies for a coop that the hawks and foxes can't get in?" she asked the man. "Will you build it? Can you build it?"

"Ma'am, I surely don't want my little girl gettin sick. If you can get the materials for me, I'll build it."

"Good." She dug a writing tablet from her bag, tore off a sheet, and handed it to him. "Draw out the coop and I'll take it to the lumberyard and find out how much it'll cost."

"I already know how much. I built one fer folks down the mountain. Materials ran a little under fifty dollars."

"Okay. I'll try to get it for you."

Holly looked around and couldn't find a crib. All she could see in the one-room cabin was a bed with two chickens perched on it. A galvanized tub that would do as a crib sat on the floor. She picked it up, and the woman told her someone had given it to her for bathing the baby. Holly quickly sterilized it with boiling water, then found some clean padding for the temporary crib.

She was reassured when the husband proved himself a carpenter by putting up a shelf for the baby's clean items. Hopefully it was high enough to be out of reach of the chickens.

HOLLY MANAGED TO visit two more patients that afternoon. On the drive home, she couldn't get the harrowing image of the baby in its mother's arms with chickens perched all around out of her head. Somehow, she'd have to find the money for the coop. There'd been no funds coming to her from the sale of her aunt's house, since her aunt's will stipulated that in the event of it being sold, the executors were only to release the proceeds to her once she reached the age of thirty or upon her marriage, whichever came first. The way Myrt had insisted on feeding her dinner every night was definitely saving her money, but it would only be fair to pay her for her board.

She approached the bridge leading into Bat Cave and swung onto River Road. The cat that had been sitting on the front door-step followed her as she went around to the back and walked through the overgrown garden. Yesterday, she had found tools in a shed at the rear, and tonight after dinner she would do some pruning.

She let the cat in through the kitchen door and smiled to see Myrt bustling around in the kitchen. A colorful salad sat on the table, and mouth-watering aromas wafted from the stove. That first day with Myrt, she would've sworn the woman hadn't so much as boiled an egg since her husband died. Holly couldn't help from thinking that her presence had reawakened the woman's nurturing instincts.

Holly rushed up the stairs, and after taking a quick shower, put on some jeans and a blouse. She strolled to the window and scanned the garden, anxious to tackle the rose arbor.

Back in the kitchen, she lifted the lid on a steaming pot to see what was cooking. Myrt shooed her away, telling her to get the butter out and fill the glasses with ice. All through dinner Holly enjoyed the ease of chatting with the kindly woman. Much like when she and her aunt would dine together.

"I have to figure out a way to come up with fifty dollars for one of my clients to get a chicken coop," Holly casually threw out as she explained the situation she had encountered that afternoon on her rounds.

"You could try the Episcopal Church in town or the Baptist Church right off the Chimney Rock Road. But, since these folks are up on Sugarloaf, you might want to start with the Mt. Moriah or Mountain Home churches up there."

"For such a small community, there sure are a lot of churches," said Holly as she helped herself to more stew.

"It's always been like that," said Myrt. "Back when I was a kid, there was no such thing as Social Services. In those days, it fell on the shoulders of the churches to provide for the poor and needy. Our priests and preachers would travel to big cities and conduct missions for clothing, toys, and bedding, then bring it all back and hand it out to those in need."

Myrt got up and brought a pie to the table while Holly cleared the dishes. Seated again and enjoying their dessert, Myrt continued, "Everybody knew what was going on in all the churches. If the Baptists were having doings, we'd go over there. If the Episcopal Church was throwing a dance or picnic, we'd join them. Then there were the circuit preachers with no church or denomination whatsoever—men who would study the Bible and go around on horseback preaching the word in the mountains.

"We didn't have TV or radio. Heck, most of us didn't have electricity. And if we needed to use a phone, we had to go to one of the big inns that had one. Poor roads... if there were any... kinda kept you close to home. So the only means folks had for socializing was the churches. They were the core of life back then. Where you might meet a possible beau, learn to read and write... pretty much everything."

After the dishes were done, Holly worked in the garden until dusk with Myrt sitting nearby with her cat in her lap reminiscing. In bed that night, Holly asked herself what she could have done better that day, as she had done every night since she started nursing. As usual, her temper came to mind. The way she had shouted at the woman's husband about the chickens seriously risked her being barred from the house. And then there was that fellow who changed her tire. Darn it! He was only trying to be helpful. How many times had she kicked herself for letting a smug little insinuation that she couldn't manage without a man's help bring out the worst in her?

She continued the ritual with her favorite way of ending the day. She asked herself what difference she had made to anyone's life. She buried her head in her pillow to suppress a giggle, remembering how, after dinner, she could barely fit a container of leftover salad into the formerly empty refrigerator. It touched Holly, thinking how Myrt's kind heart and generosity of spirit were the very things that were going to rescue her from her loneliness. Moving in with Myrt, Holly believed, had changed both of their lives for the better.

Then her heart warmed, thinking of the two little babies. There was no question she had positively impacted their lives. She was pretty sure the first one was asleep in his cradle with a full belly, while the one in the shack was lying in a clean crib. She wasn't earning as much money as she had in the hospital, but somehow that didn't matter. Her work in these mountains was paying her more by fulfilling a dream she'd had for as far back as she could remember. A dream that in her lifetime, she, herself, could make a difference.

CHAPTER SEVEN

Holly entered the elementary school building and poked her head in the office to let the secretary know she had arrived. The principal noticed her and waved for her to come into her office.

"I see a couple of the teachers in the first and second grade have set up a meeting with you after school today," said the woman. "You're new to this area and just getting your feet wet in public service, so I wanted to give you advanced warning. They're wanting to discuss the problem we have with children who smell."

"Thanks. I noticed it myself when I was giving the polio shots last week. A first grader's socks were wet with urine, and then I found out she wasn't even wearing underwear."

"We're a small community," said the principal, "with families that have been here for generations. The ones with roots in the mountains have always been hard working, God-fearing folk known for their tradition of helping one another. Over the generations, they've pulled themselves up by their bootstraps and are now among some of the state's biggest apple growers. They also contribute to society in hundreds of other ways.

"However, we still have a small segment of families that are living in distressed circumstances. Quite a few of their kids are bedwetters and don't have a change of underwear. They wet their pants at night and sleep in a urine saturated bed, often with no sheets. So, when they come to school, they smell, and the other kids make fun of them."

"That's so sad," said Holly.

"Tell me. Most of them are shy little girls. After being humiliated that way, the poor things don't want to come to school anymore."

Holly couldn't help thinking how well-suited the woman was for her position in the lower grades. She was accommodating, yet serious, like everyone's mom. "I'll look forward to talking to the teachers about it," said Holly. "There has to be something we can do."

Holly went to the nurse's room and prepared for an afternoon of eye examinations. A teacher had told her to pay close attention to one of the little girls. She was perplexed why the child hadn't been doing well in class even though she seemed to be bright and eager to learn. Holly was pleased when an examination solved the mystery. The girl was simply in need of glasses.

After two tedious hours of giving eye tests to a bunch of fidgety second graders, Holly finally had a moment to herself. She took out a piece of cornbread she'd saved from the lunch Myrt had made for her and sat down. All afternoon she'd been fighting off thinking about the poor little kids that were being teased about the way they smelled. As if it happened yesterday, she saw Joey Sullivan's sweaty red face inches from her nose and heard all the kids chanting in their horrible sing-songy voices. "Your mother didn't want you, your mother didn't want you."

The sudden entrance of the two teachers roused her from her thoughts. As they introduced themselves and chatted, Holly noticed how well-suited they were for their jobs, just like the principal. The older one exuded a competent, yet grandmotherly manner, and the other, a focused, youthful exuberance. The ice broken, they got down to the business at hand.

"It's an inherited condition," said the older one. "Most of these kids' parents did the same thing, and they don't see it as any big deal. 'I wet my bed. I smelled bad. So what,' they'll tell us."

"It breaks my heart to hear the names some of the kids call

them," said the younger one.

"We have to figure out a way to help these kids," said Holly. "Is there any kind of budget for dealing with this sort of thing?"

The teachers shook their heads and reluctantly offered that they were even having to buy a lot of their room supplies themselves.

The younger teacher looked pleadingly at Holly. "If you can either find the money or get a store to donate what we need, when the kids come in the morning, we could give the ones who smell bad some soap, a towel, and clean underwear and send them to the bathroom to wash their bottoms and change."

"We'd have to monitor the bathroom door so no one walks in on them," said the other one.

"Yes, we could do that," the younger one agreed. "Then we could take the soiled clothes home with us on Friday and bring everything back on Monday."

"How many kids are we talking about?" asked Holly.

A typed list with names, grades, and ages was quickly produced.

Holly studied it. "Three. That's not that many. Let's see. For the week we'll need fifteen each of towels, underwear, and socks. I'll see what I can do."

"Don't forget the soap and washcloths," one of them added.

On her way out, Holly stopped by the principal's office and filled her in on their plans.

"I wish you luck with this," she said. "Every extra dime we get, we have to plow into books and supplies."

HOLLY TOOK IN the sweeping view of the mountains from her bedroom as she slipped into a pair of jeans. Now nearing the end of March, the days had grown longer, and spring was casting promising veils of yellow and green on the forest trees. Aromas from the kitchen drifted upstairs.

"Dinner's ready," Myrt called up from the stairwell.

Holly looked forward to her evening meal with Myrt as she skipped down the stairs, when the woman she'd met at the post office suddenly appeared at the bottom and gave her a start.

"Well howdy-do," said Ella before leading her to the kitchen table where three places had been set. The postmaster pulled out a chair. "You set yourself right down, Missy."

The way Myrt was suppressing a smile as she put a steaming bowl of mashed potatoes on the table, Holly suspected Ella's appearance had something to do with her. With everyone seated, Myrt asked Ella to say grace. It surprised Holly, since they had never said grace at the table before.

As Ella came to the end of a rather long-winded prayer, she began to rattle off a litany of people she wanted blessed. As the names rolled out in an almost endless stream, Holly sneaked a look up at Myrt who was eyeing her back.

Finally hearing the "Amen," Holly started to reach for a platter of fried chicken when Ella slapped her hand.

"Not yet! I got somethin for ya. Didn't ya wonder why I was here?" Ella broke out in a wide, toothy grin, and handed Holly an envelope. Seeing the hesitation on Holly's face, she said, "Go on! Open it!"

Holly did as ordered and found five ten dollar bills inside.

"That there is from the Bat Cave Baptist Church's Good Neighbor Fund. My brother's wife is the pastor's cousin, and she told him about that poor baby livin with all those durn chickens. Seein you livin here, nice like, with Myrt, we decided we could trust you with the fifty dollars for that coop." She picked up the platter of chicken and offered it to Holly. "Now, help yourself, girl, and tell us about what you've been up to."

"I don't know how to thank you," said Holly. "This is going to mean a great deal to one helpless little baby."

"Never you mind about that. No need to thank me," said Ella. "You go on now, and tell us about your day."

Holly had no choice but to follow Ella's orders. The woman's solid confidence and rigid self-righteousness gave her the authority to command respect. Holly decided not to cast any gloom on what was turning out to be a rather interesting evening. The story of the chickens was a big enough dose of reality without going into children with bedwetting problems, or mothers who didn't have enough sense to know when their babies were hungry. Instead, she decided to tell them about solving the mystery of the little girl who needed glasses.

"So, what can you do about it?" asked Myrt, who as a former teacher was keenly interested.

"I sent her home with a note, asking her mother to call me." She reached for another piece of chicken. "I gave her this number. I hope it's okay. The girl told me they didn't have a phone, and her mother would have to wait until their father came home from work so he could drive her to a phone booth."

Myrt patted her hand. "Of course, it's all right, darlin."

"Well, what in God's name are ya gonna do if they don't have the money for glasses?" Ella asked.

"I'm pretty sure they don't. I plan to refer them to the Lion's Club. They'll make arrangements for a free exam and glasses."

Ella's toothy grin reappeared. "Well, how do ya like that? This gal's slick as a whistle."

Through the rest of the meal, Ella cheerfully related the latest town gossip as if it were her duty. The endless chatter about who was putting their property up for sale, how some woman's big toe was acting up again, and whose car Ella had seen towed past the post office amused Holly and gave her a soothing dose of banality.

As she sat barely listening to Ella go on about the sloppy way people were parking in front of the post office, Holly was glad she had avoided bringing the sadder realities of her work to the table. However, she was dead sure those two were aware of the darker side of things that went on in the county. The way they had gotten her the money for the coop showed they had the same compassion that drove her fellow nurses—a desire to reach out and help raise their fellow man up the ladder. It took a good deal of empathy for them, as well as the folks at the church, to look past the father who thoughtlessly endangered the health of a newborn by contaminating the house with chicken poop, and, instead, to think only of helping an innocent baby.

Holly caught a glimpse of Myrt nudging the woman.

Ella gave Myrt a quizzical look, then slapped her hand on the table. "Lord have mercy! Here I am runnin on at the mouth again. I almost forgot to tell ya!" She looked straight at Holly. "I think I found someone who knew of a woman named Baldwin."

Holly's heart jumped to her throat. "Who?"

"Hold your horses, girl. After Myrt told me about your lookin for Baldwins, I was askin around." She raised an eyebrow and stared at Holly over her glasses. "Discreetly, of course." Sure that she had everyone's rapt attention, she continued. "Well, I got to talkin with one of my box holders, and he thought he might've heard that name before. It's not common around here, ya know. His aunt, Annie Barnwell, who lived up on Slick Rock, used to do laundry for a lady nearby to her place. Way back during the first war when he was a kid. She used to tell him about the lady she worked for and a doctor woman who lived with her. The name 'Baldwin' definitely rang a bell with him. Annie moved away after her husband was drowned in the Great Flood, but still has folks around here."

Myrt squeezed Holly's hand. "I used to know Annie before she left this area. She has to be up there in age, probably in her eighties. But don't you worry none. I'll get a hold of her for you."

For Holly, that bit of news put a magical glow on an already memorable evening. The mere mention of a woman by the name of Baldwin made her feel somehow officially absorbed into this special mountain community where it seemed everyone— churches, schools, townspeople, charities—felt they were in it together. Yet, for the first time, she faced the possibility that at one time she might've been in the same dire need as some of the pitiful babies she'd visited that week.

As Ella was leaving, Holly hugged her, and for an instant, didn't want to let go.

HOLLY HAD NEVER asked anyone for money before and began to think it might be easier to get a discount from the store where she was going to buy everything. Her uniform should help. She had a fifty-dollar bill tucked in her wallet. No matter how little of a discount she got, that ought to cover it. She'd seen what looked like a lower-priced establishment on one of the streets off the main route in town. After going up and down a few streets, she finally spotted it and pulled into the parking lot.

As far as décor was concerned, it was a bare-bones operation, but the bins and racks were overflowing. She checked to make sure her badge was straight, then went up to the clerk at the counter.

"May I speak to the manager?"

The woman looked her up and down. "Bob's in the back. Let me see if I can get him out here."

She picked up a pager and "Code one wanted up front" echoed throughout the building.

Holly stood there thinking of what could be the worst thing that might happen, when a big, portly man, dripping sweat came down one of the aisles. Seeing Holly, he assumed he'd been summoned on her behalf.

"What can I do for you?"

Holly shared that she was a county public health nurse, all the time wishing the clerk wasn't standing there listening. A customer finally came to the counter, and the man asked Holly to follow him.

His office was no more than an enclosed cubby hole in the corner of the stock room. Holly took a chair and started anew. With the way he was riffling through the papers on his desk and jotting down notes, she worried he wasn't listening to her. An image of a little girl being shamed and taunted flashed through her brain and the importance of her mission took over.

"These poor kids, through no fault of their own, are being taunted every..." She stopped and closed her eyes tight to hold back her tears. It took a moment, but she finally got hold of herself. "I need to buy underwear and socks as well as hand towels and washcloths so they can get cleaned up and changed when they come in the morning." She swiped a tear from her cheek and barely squeaked out, "I'd really appreciate a discount. That way they won't smell so...." Her voice cracked, and she had to stop again. She looked up to see his eyes fixed on her.

"I'm sorry," she said. "I didn't mean to... Please forgive me. It's just that every time I picture those little first and second graders being humiliated... It's going to leave a permanent..." She stopped and crunched up her face to hold back a sob.

"Do you have a list?"

She took a moment to gather herself, then pulled the list from her purse and handed it to him.

He looked it over. "There's three of 'em?"

She nodded.

"Come back tomorrow morning before we open. I'll see what I can do."

HOLLY SHOWED UP at the store early the next morning. Instead of clipping her hair back in a neat ponytail, she'd taken great care in putting it in a severe looking bun, intent on erasing the image the manager must have of her after yesterday. Spotting the same clerk stocking a bin, she marched up to her and announced, "I have an appointment with Bob."

"He's not going to be in today."

"But..."

"Don't worry, honey, we got your stuff. I'll go get it."

She disappeared for a few moments, then came back with a large carton and plopped it on the counter.

"Here."

Holly pulled out her wallet. "How much is it?"

"Just take it. The owner's giving it to you."

Holly picked up a handful of washcloths on top, only to see more underneath.

"There's more than fifteen of these in there."

"What can I say. He told us to round up a bunch of seconds and to look for returns that had gotten too soiled to sell."

"Please tell him how very grateful I am," said Holly. "And I can see I need to thank you, too."

"That's okay, darlin. Bob's and my people are from back in the hills. We know where you're coming from."

CHAPTER EIGHT
1925

"Everybody has to have a birthday," Helen had insisted at lunch that afternoon. And since Lula had told her she was born during the Great Flood of 1916, it was established that the sixteenth of July would be her ninth. That night, Lula lay in bed excited over the party Helen was going to give in her honor and couldn't fall asleep.

Hearing Essie's loud voice coming from downstairs, it was apparent to Lula that she had yielded to her evil vice again and consumed too much alcohol. Lula fought the temptation, but finally succumbed to her vice, too. In order to eavesdrop on the conversation, she slipped out of bed and tiptoed into the hall that was open to the living room, careful to stay close to the wall so they couldn't see her from downstairs. She edged along until she reached the staircase, then crept down to the first landing where she could hear better. She sat down on a step and listened.

"Really, Helen," said Essie. "You're getting too attached to that child. Granny McDowell could come by any time and tell me she's taking her back to her kin. Now that one of her brothers has come off the mountain and is working for the newly built Salola Inn, there's no telling if she's going to be needed at home. Then, what's the poor thing going to do? Tell me!"

Lula pressed tight against the newel post as Essie rose from her easy chair and paced. Thankfully, she was too worked up to look up and notice her.

"Do you really think you're doing that dear little child any favors by teaching her to read and write? Geography? What in God's name is she going to do with geography! If they take her back, she's never going to fit in up there in that wilderness they always refer to as a colony. Helen, you have no idea how primitive their existence is. The few families that are left are still living like they're in the 1800s."

"It looks like you're more worried they'll take her back than I am," said Helen.

Essie took her empty glass to the sideboard and was about to reach for the whisky.

"You've already had two, and you know you've promised Father Phillips you wouldn't have more than that," said Helen.

Essie slammed her glass on the sideboard. "She's not your child, Helen, and she never will be. Every time we go up that mountain and get anywhere near what's left of that godforsaken settlement, she begs me to take her over there to visit with her folks. I only leave her with them long enough to go over and get some herbs and potions from Granny McDowell, and darn if she doesn't come away talking poorly again."

"I'd like to go up there and visit with her mother someday," said Helen. "To put her mind at ease. So she knows she's with people who love her."

"Ha! We both know you'd never make it. It's almost a day's climb."

"I'll take the buggy as far as it'll go, and walk the rest of the way with Lula." She thought for a moment. "And I'm going to do it before the summer is out." She rose. "I'm going up to bed." With that, she went over to the sideboard and picked up the whiskey.

Lula scampered up the stairs with Essie bellowing to Helen, "Go on! Take it! I've got more in the drugstore!"

Lula lay in bed thinking how wondrous it would be for her mother to meet Helen. Before the summer was out, at that. She hoped they could stay overnight since Billy Boy wouldn't be coming from the fields until sundown. When Essie took her up there in the spring to get more herbs, she knew her and her brother would have plenty of time to visit, since Granny McDowell was often paid with a jug of whisky and was sure to offer some to Essie.

She had to run high and low through the meadows looking for her brother, and when she finally found him, he gave her a good looking over and told her she sure dressed like the furriners he'd run into at the falls. By the grin on his face, she could tell he approved. She would always remember how he laughed when she lifted her dress and showed him her underwear. She had reached in her pocket for a piece of cornbread she saved from lunch to share with him, and the two of them went over and sat on a big rock to enjoy the treat.

"Big James went off the mountain," he told her. "Since their pa died, all the Garrisons are gone, too. Their ma is the only one left."

"I know Big James was off the mountain," said Lula. "I seen him working in the gardens at the Salola Inn when Essie was tendin to someone there. I couldn't get away to talk to him, but I know it was him."

"He puts aside a dollar ever moon and brings it to ma with coffee an sugar," said Billy.

They sat and held hands for a while not speaking, but Lula was sure her brother was itching to say something.

"I be owin a wonderful lot ta ye ifin ye could find me a place ta stay an be earnin two whole dollars like Big James."

"Do you think ma and pa can make do without you?"

"Now that Big James done gone, Luke's takin over." He scratched behind his ear. "He gets comfort in the old ways, an I don't rightly believe he'll ever be comin off this mountain. Nancy's gettin to the marryin age an askin James to find her work at the Salola Inn, too. Once I finish with the plowin, I'm aimin to leave and get some learnin so I can talk like ye. With all of us sendin a dollar, an less mouths ta feed, everthang at the homeplace should be jist fine."

Lula threw her arms around him. "It would be so good to

have you nearby. Don't you worry none. I'll be finding you a place and sending word up with the granny woman."

SUNDAYS WERE Lula's favorite day, but today would be even more special. Both Helen and Essie were confirmed members of the Episcopal Church, and they often invited the circuit riding priests for dinner when they came by to hold services in small nearby churches. Today, everyone in the household was looking forward to one of them coming to Edelweiss for dinner. They had rushed home from the Baptist church on Sugarloaf where Father Phillips was preaching, and Helen had been helping Katie in the kitchen a good deal of the afternoon.

It was Lula's job to set the table, but for this occasion, Helen was doing it herself. Wearing a lacy white dress with a skirt down to the floor, she flitted around the table enjoying the task. A damask tablecloth was taken from the sideboard drawer along with matching napkins. Then she went about setting the table with the fine china her grandmother had brought from England.

Lula came out of the kitchen with a vase of flowers she had picked from the garden. Helen beamed with approval and put it in the center of the table. Lula noticed the glass finger bowls Helen had placed beside the plates for the occasion. The first time she saw them, she had thought they were for drinking and took a sip. Essie had made a big fuss over it, but thankfully, since she had learned all the furriner's manners and ways, that sort of thing didn't happen at the dinner table anymore.

Essie came out of her room, and Lula couldn't take her eyes off her. It was one of the rare times she'd seen her in a long dress. Suddenly, Jack sat up, his ears perked. A sure sign some-one was coming up their road. He ran outside barking, and they all followed onto the porch. Father Phillips was making his way up the road on his saddle horse. As he neared, Lula was impressed with how well the animal was groomed, nothing like her father's mule.

Reaching the hitching post, the priest tipped his hat and greeted them with a cordial smile. Leather half-chaps that were as shiny as the horse were buckled around his legs and ran from his ankles to his knees. When the portly man dismounted, the stirrup straps squeaked so loud, Lula feared they would snap. After greeting Helen and Essie, it pleased Lula that he stooped down and said a few kindly words to her.

Refreshing cold lemonade was served, and Helen played her favorite Chopin pieces, that by now, Lula knew so well she had made up names for them. They were too beautiful to be simply identified by numbers. Then, as she had been anticipating all day, a delicious dinner followed. Moments after the priest finished saying grace, Katie rushed out from the kitchen with hot biscuits and poured cold tea while the chicken and dumplings were passed around.

Later, in the living room, talk centered on the need to build a church where regular Episcopal services could be held as well as a Sunday school.

"I preached at the Baptist church on Sixth Avenue in Hendersonville last Sunday and had dinner with the minister," said the priest. "That town is growing by leaps and bounds. One of his guests told me Southern Railway sold over 50,000 tickets to folks from Florida, Georgia, and South Carolina bound for Hendersonville this summer, and six trains are pulling into the town's Seventh Avenue station every day loaded with passengers."

"Gracious," Helen gasped. "How are they gonna put up all these people?"

"That's what I asked," he said, "and someone pointed out that the town's built dozens of boarding houses and rooming houses, and over ten hotels to accommodate them. It's a matter of time before folks start building in these mountains, too."

"Growth is already reaching us, Father," said Essie. "Inns with family accommodations are popping up all over." She reached over and picked up a brochure from a table and handed it to him. "That's from the Salola Inn right here in Edneyville. It opened this spring, 4,000 feet up on Sugarloaf Mountain."

"We're looking forward to going up there for lunch some day," said Helen.

He studied the brochure. "My, from the drawing, it looks like quite an undertaking. It says here it has three stories and twenty-five rooms. I see, they're charging less than the hotels in Hendersonville—$2 per day and $8 per week including meals." He handed the brochure back to Essie.

He took a sip of his coffee. "Now that the North Carolina cotton mills are making more yarn and cloth than they are in New England, we're seeing a lot of new wealth, and it looks like families can now afford to spend their summers here."

"You must agree with us, Father, that with all those folks coming to these mountains, there is even more need now for an Episcopal church here," said Essie.

"As I travel for church services around these mountains," said the priest, "I'm struck with the contrast between our towns and these remote mountain communities. It seems like these two cultures are running together like oil and water. Take the roads, for instance. It's still a challenge for hacks and buggies to make it up these rugged, unpaved mountain roads, while not fifteen miles away, those confounded Model Ts are spooking horses on Hendersonville's Main Street. In most areas I preach in, roads don't exist, just paths requiring travel by foot, horse, or mule.

"Yet, even though a lot of my flock live in abject poverty, I never fail to be touched by their yearning for education and a better life for their children."

"Oh, indeed, Father," said Helen.

"It's definitely a time for compassionate people to answer the need in these remote mountains for education, medical assistance, and basic necessities," added Father Phillips. "I'm afraid, the only way for these people to get help is for the churches and their congregations to rise to meet the need. Ladies, I agree with you. There is definitely a need here. I will make preparations to travel to New York and preach missions until I raise enough money for the materials and labor needed to build a church and school right here in Edneyville."

BY NOW, LULA had become quite helpful to Essie, and her knowledge of herbs was put to good use. Essie, a licensed pharmacist, had fled to the mountains years earlier, seeking solace after her husband committed suicide and left her penniless.

Thanks to Helen's generosity, she was provided with a place to live and a drugstore from which to earn a living. With her ability to lay in a supply of laudanum, morphine, and quinine, she was soon called on to help people who fell ill with no means of relief other than from the herbs and advice dispensed by granny doctors. Seeing a desperate need, and with no doctor for miles, she became a self-ordained physician ministering to the sick throughout the isolated mountains.

Through all kinds of weather, she scaled steep slopes and forded rushing creeks on horseback to make house calls. As a pharmacist, she had a deep respect for the knowledge the granny doctors had of the ingredients they harvested from the woodlands to put in their potions and elixirs, and she readily employed these remedies to help heal her patients.

On this day, a neighbor of a woman in labor came to Edelweiss asking her to come quickly to the McGraw place on Bearwallow Mountain. The woman's husband was concerned because it was his wife's first child and she was along in age. The house was reached by wagon road most of the way, so Essie, with Lula clinging to her with bare feet dangling, made good time as their horse galloped alongside the neighbor's.

The house and barns were grand for being in the mountains, thought Lula. As they pulled up to the hitching post, the husband came outside to greet them, appearing uncommonly upset.

"My wife's upstairs and there's no one to tend to her except my mother who has taken ill," the man told Essie as he helped Lula down. "A neighbor lady was fixin to help out, but has taken sick herself."

A blood curdling scream came from an upstairs window, and they all looked up.

Mr. McGraw ran his fingers through his hair in anguish. "She's been carryin on like that for a good while. My mother's so fearful she can't hardly help."

Essie hurried into the house with Lula hauling the bag behind her.

"Put on the kettles," Essie ordered.

Lula rushed to the kitchen and quickly found a poker, then

stoked what was left of the fire in the cookstove. Next, she searched through the wood box for some birch or cedar kindling that would go up fast. She put on two kettles of water, and satisfied she had a good fire going, put in a couple of dry split logs and opened all the vents before rushing up the stairs.

"In here," yelled Essie. "What took you so long?"

"The fire was out, but it's going good now."

"Help me get these sheets changed."

Lula got on her knees on the bed and rolled the woman onto her side to face her and saw her water had broken. Essie, on the other side of the bed, quickly bunched the sheet up tight against the woman and shouted, "Now roll her towards me." Lula rolled her over on her other side, then burrowed her hands under the woman and pulled out the soiled sheet. Then the whole procedure was repeated in order to put on a fresh one.

They tended to the woman's immediate needs, all the while hearing the chopping of wood outside. Had to be the poor husband working off his anxiety. As the hours went by, Essie grew concerned with the way the woman grew weaker every time her labor pains came.

It startled Lula when Essie abruptly rose from her chair and said, "Go fetch Mr. McGraw's mother. I'm gonna need her."

Lula sensed the gravity in her voice and rushed out of the room and down the hall, opening all the doors until she found the old woman rocking in her chair reading her Bible.

"You gotta come!" said Lula.

"I don't think I can stand seein her in such misery," the woman replied.

Lula gently took the Bible from her. "We're gonna need you." She helped the woman up and hurried her as much as she could back to the room.

"Go tell her husband to gather up the rest of their clean linens," said Essie, "then bring up two boiling kettles."

The pitiful woman's labor pains started up again, but she only had the strength to moan. Lula ran down the stairs and outside, but the husband wasn't there. She ran out to the barn. It was filled with barrels, but he was nowhere in sight. She started to leave when she thought she heard someone. She ran around a stack of barrels and found him on his knees praying.

"You gotta come right quick and round up some clean linens," she told him.

He looked up, anguish on his face. "I couldn't hear Molly screamin no more, so I thought she were dead."

"Well, she aint, so hurry. I gotta take up the water."

They rushed into the house, and Lula hurried up the stairs with two kettles. When she entered the room, she could see the old woman was soothing Molly who now lay with her knees bent in the air under a sheet.

Essie rolled up her sleeves as far as they would go. "Fill that basin with water," she ordered.

Lula did as told, then Essie tested the water with a finger before adding some cold water from a pitcher. She tested the water again and added more, then vigorously washed her hands and forearms. She took her hands out and held them up in the air.

"Pour everything out the window and put in fresh water," said Essie.

Once this was done, she dunked her hands and forearms into the freshly poured hot water for a few seconds and winced from pain. She quickly pulled her hands out and picked up a pressed and folded linen towel and wiped her hands. "Go downstairs and don't come in unless I call for you. Take the kettles with you and keep water going on the stove."

As Lula was closing the door, she heard Essie order the old woman to take the sheet off the woman's legs.

"This baby's breached, and I've got to get it out."

Lula ran down the stairs with the kettles and took them to the sink. She started working the handle of a pump, when Mr. McGraw took over. The room had become so warm from his stoking the cookstove, they had to go out on the porch to wait for news from upstairs.

After what seemed like forever, the shout of "Lula!" crashed through the quiet.

Lula and Mr. McGraw rushed up the steps and into the bedroom. Seeing Essie with one arm covered in blood and slapping a baby on the bottom, they froze. Suddenly the baby started wailing, and the father collapsed in a chair with his head in his hands, crying. The old woman clutched Molly's hand and rocked back and forth praising the Lord.

Essie swiftly cut off the umbilical cord, wrapped the baby in a small blanket, and gently put it in Mr. McGraw's arms. "Here's your son." She stood there as the man gazed at the pinched little face and let the tears flow freely into his beard. Then she took the bundle from him and handed it to the old woman, saying, "Hold him close and keep him warm." Then she went to the basin and washed. "Bring in the linens and plenty of hot water," she told the husband and Lula, "then I want you two to leave me to my work."

"Is Molly going to be all right?" he asked.

"Yes, now do as I said and be quick about it."

After taking everything upstairs, the husband made Lula and himself some tea, and they sat down. The man drummed his fingers on the table.

In an effort to calm his nerves, Lula asked, "Have you decided a name for the baby?"

"Benjamin runs in our family, so I guess if Molly approves, it'll be Benjamin."

Halfway through her tea, Lula finally worked up the courage to ask him the question that had been gnawing at her ever since she went in the barn looking for him.

"What do you have all them barrels for?"

"I'm a cooper. They're for our apple farmers, so they can ship em by express train from the Hendersonville station." He wrung his hands. "Can hardly keep up with the steady demand."

Lula became keenly interested. "Is it hard work," she asked, "makin them barrels?"

"It's plenty hard work. First, I have to rive out the oak staves and soak em. Once they're soaked enough and treated, I bind em into barrels with cured strips of hickory bark. Like I said, it's hard work, but the materials are all around here."

"With all the need for them, do you think you might be wantin a strong young man to be helpin you?" asked Lula.

80

"I sure do, but all the young uns around here are workin for their folk, mostly loggin."

"My brother, Billy Boy, would sure do good for you."

"How old is he?"

"I don't rightly know, but he's as big as you, and he plows all our fields with a mule."

"Where bouts does he live?"

"On Chimney Rock Mountain next to Sugarloaf."

"Do you suppose the doctor woman would speak well of him?" he asked.

"Yes. Granny McDowell, too."

"When do you think he can come round?"

"As soon as someone can get word up to him."

"Good. I'll talk to the doctor woman about it."

Molly's condition warranted that Essie stay the night to look after her, with Lula tending to the baby. It was now nightfall, and Lula lay on a cot. She'd fought off falling asleep ever since going down to the kitchen for a drink of water and finding Essie and Mr. McGraw sitting at the table talking and drinking whiskey. Knowing how mean-spirited Essie could get when she had too much, Lula thought it better if she kept herself fully dressed and awake. Her aunt Helen was finding it harder and harder to handle her when she was drunk. However, the next morning she awoke before dawn, realizing she had fallen asleep in spite of all her efforts to stay awake.

She tiptoed out of her room and down the hall to where Molly and the baby were sleeping. She opened the door and peeked in. The baby was bundled up next to his mother, and Essie was asleep on a straw tick mattress on the floor next to them. Lula shut the door with care, then tip-toed down to the kitchen. She fed the stove with more wood, then searched around for the makings for biscuits, gravy, and ham. She was putting on a big pot of coffee when she heard pounding outside and rushed to the porch. Seeing Mr. McGraw working in his barn, she went to tell him she'd have breakfast and coffee shortly.

"Good mornin to ya," he said as she walked in the barn.

She smiled to see him in such good spirits. "Your wife and

little boy are doing fine. I'll have breakfast with plenty of coffee for you right quick."

"Well, aren't you one helpful little gal," he exclaimed as he put his mallet down. "I had a talk with the doctor woman last night and am gonna take on Billy Boy. I'm aiming to pay a dollar for the first month, and if he proves hisself, two. I gave Mrs. Gordon a silver dollar for his first month, and she's agreed to send it to his ma with Granny McDowell to show I mean it."

"Much obliged, Mr. McGraw," said Lula. "You won't be sorry."

Essie and Lula tended to the mother and baby all day and stayed another night. The next morning, Essie announced that they would be leaving before the forenoon was done, but first she wanted to bathe Molly and wash her hair.

Lula fetched a kettle of hot water from the kitchen along with a large enamel pan. While Essie bathed Molly, Lula washed and changed the baby before putting him in his crib. Essie pulled Molly up to a sitting position and told Lula to climb up to the head of the bed so they could wash the woman's hair. Lula spread out her legs, put the large wash pan between them, and Essie poured in the water. Essie gently lowered Molly so her neck rested on a rolled-up towel and the pan's rim. Her matted, musky hair fell in the water. A look of sheer pleasure washed over Molly's face as Lula gently massaged her scalp, the magical scent of lavender soap erasing the tension of her agonizing labor. After her hair was rinsed, Lula lovingly combed Molly's hair and plaited it so it would be out of the way when she tended to the baby.

Later, outside at the barn, Essie sat astride her saddle and said goodbye to Mr. McGraw.

"I'll be dropping a barrel off at your drugstore the next time I'm passing by," he told her. Then he lifted Lula onto Brownie.

As Essie turned the horse and headed home, he called after them, "I'll be waitin on Billy Boy."

CHAPTER NINE

Helen and Essie talked endlessly about the fruits of Father Phillips' labors while casually enjoying a noon meal. His preaching in New York had brought in enough money for them to proceed with the Good Shepherd Mission they had dreamt of for years. With it, they purchased a site on Little Creek Road a mile or two above the Edney Inn, and many of the local mountain men were now hewing the logs needed to build the structure.

After the meal, Helen sat Lula down to study her multiplication tables while she practiced her scales and Essie read the days-old paper someone had left behind at the Edney Inn.

Jack's barking made everyone stop and look up. He ran out on the porch, the signal for all to follow. A horse-drawn wagon was coming up the road. Essie ran down and waved for the man to stop. They could see her talking to him, then pointing to the porch and drawing a circle in the air, indicating how he could go around and get back out.

The wagon pulled up to the porch and the driver quickly got off and filled a leather bucket with water from the trough and offered it to the horse. Seeing the wagon was filled with all kinds of boxes and wooden crates, Lula felt sorry that the poor horse had to struggle with such a heavy load up their steep, rugged trail for one of their small packages. The man finished with the horse, then pulled a piece of paper from his vest.

He put a foot up on the porch, pushed his wide-brimmed straw hat back on his head, and said, "Which one of you fine ladies is Helen Baldwin?"

Helen stepped up, and he handed her the bill of lading. She studied the paper and broke into a broad grin. "God Bless that man." She looked up at the anxious faces. "Father Phillips' preaching all over New York about the plight of some of our people has brought us all sorts of badly needed goods."

Everyone enthusiastically pitched in to get the shipment loaded onto the porch. The man obligingly opened the wood crates with a pry bar, then took the sandwich Katie had hastily put together for him and went on his way.

It was a glorious moment when items from the first crate were unpacked. Feather ticks, blankets, and colorful eiderdown quilts were wrapped around all kinds of cast iron pots, pans, and skillets. There were two big enamelware coffee pots and a stack of bowls made of the same material. With Katie busy folding the bedding and Essie stacking the kitchenware, Helen pushed aside the lid on another crate and began pulling out clothes. They appeared much too citified for Lula's taste, and she wondered if mountain folk would want to wear them. Helen pulled out a small red winter coat with a fur collar and examined it.

She turned to Lula saying, "Try it on, darling," and held it open for her.

The thought of putting her arms into the silky red lining was inconceivable to Lula.

"That coat's for someone grand," she said. "Folks would think I was gettin above my raising if they saw me in it."

"Nonsense, girl. You're as grand a child as there is," said Helen as she slipped Lula's arm into a sleeve. "Just as I thought. It fits you perfectly. You can wear it to church in the winter, and it'll keep you nice and warm."

Helen sorted the warm clothing into piles. The colorful array was breathtaking—mittens, wool scarves, all kinds and sizes of sweaters, coats, leggings, raincoats, gloves, shoes, and boots. Seeing them stacked in the living room, Katie was so overwhelmed by the generosity of the church-going folks in New

York, she covered her face with her hands and cried. Like Katie, Lula was also moved. These wonderful items would keep a lot of people warm that winter. She could almost feel their comfort.

Just when Lula couldn't imagine anything more marvelous, Helen reached in a box, and with two hands, pulled out a toy goat. It was affixed to a platform on wheels. Except for being only twenty inches tall, it looked almost real and reminded Lula of the goat she had kept as a pet up on the colony's plateau. Helen proudly placed it on the floor, and Lula got down on her knees to get a closer look. His glass eyes glittered in the sunlight. She gently fingered his horns, then the little brass bell on his fancy studded leather collar. She ran her hand lovingly over his long white fur, then looked up and smiled at Helen.

"It talks, too," said Helen. "I saw one in a store in Charleston." She gently pressed his head down, and it bleated appealingly.

Lula hugged it and didn't want to let go. With pleading eyes, she looked over at Essie who had been watching.

"You're much too old for that. That needs to go to a family with little ones," said Essie.

"Oh, please, please. Can't I have it?"

Helen came over and crouched down next to Lula. "Don't you want to see some poor little children enjoying this wonderful toy?"

"Can't I keep him for a little while?" Lula begged. "He looks like the dear little billy goat my pa gave me."

Helen look up at Essie. She would defer to her judgment since her work with the sick and needy put her in a position to know where most of these things were needed, including the toys. Essie rolled her eyes toward the ceiling and sighed, "All right, let her take it."

"There you go, sweetheart," said Helen. "You can keep it in your room until we come up with the perfect family for this precious little toy."

Suddenly, Jack shot out of the house barking and ran down the road to the drugstore. The clanging of the doorbell on the drugstore hut followed. Essie quit organizing the pots and pans and started down to tend to a customer. Lula continued to help Helen unload a crate, but kept an eye on the barn. In a short while, seeing Essie saddling Brownie, she rushed into the house for the satchel and ran to the barn with it.

Essie, already on her horse, reached down and pulled Lula up. "Old Gramma Byrne is needing me," she said, then took off in a gallop. They passed the man who had brought the summons, and Lula shouted him a howdy.

It was slower going once they reached the foot of Point Lookout Mountain and started the climb. It soon became dangerously steep, so they dismounted the horse and led it up on foot. They came to the edge of a small hollow and spotted the cabin below.

As they neared, dogs started barking. The commotion brought the old woman's elderly daughter rushing out to greet them.

"Bless you for comin so quickly," said the woman. "Ma's feelin mighty poorly."

Essie tied Brownie to a hitching post, and they went in. An old woman lay on a small cot next to the fireplace in the small one-room cabin. Essie took her hand.

"I can hardly eat no more," the ghostly thin woman said. She patted her bloated stomach. "An it gets to hurtin real bad." Her face suddenly twisted in pain, and her bonny fingers dug into the quilt.

Essie gently pulled the quilt back, then lifted the woman's dress. Her stomach looked like a barrel that was about to burst and was as yellow as the woman's face. Lula had been helping Essie for more than two years, and she had never seen anything like it.

"Please get me a glass of water," Essie told the daughter.

While the woman went to fetch it, Essie took out a bottle of laudanum. When the daughter returned with a tin cup filled with water, Essie poured in some of the drug, lifted the woman's head, and said, "Drink this. It'll ease your pain."

Seeing the woman had soiled herself, the three of them got her washed and the bedding changed.

Essie gave the daughter the bottle and said, "Give her a tablespoon for pain." Essie studied the pitiful woman, now asleep. She shook her head. "I don't think you're gonna need more, but if you do, send word. And, no matter, if I'm happening to be passing nearby, I'll stop in."

The grateful daughter insisted they take some tea before they were off or she'd be shamed. Essie and Lula went out onto the porch and waited for it to brew.

Essie lit her pipe and took a deep drag.

"Why didn't you do more for that poor old woman?" Lula asked as Essie slowly blew out the smoke.

"Because there's nothing I or anyone else can do for her."

Lula snapped, "Whenever things looked hopeless, Granny McDowell would always call for the power of prayer and chant Bible verses, and when that didn't work, she'd put a sharp knife in their bed to cut the pain."

"I do believe in the power of prayer, Lula, but the notion about the knife is nonsense. You have to put all these mountains myths out of your head."

The daughter came onto the porch with tea and two small pieces of cornbread. She pulled the bottle of laudanum from her apron pocket and fingered it nervously.

"My ma's been doctorin folks for most her eighty-two years. There's no tellin how many babies she's delivered in these parts. When I was a young un, I fell on a rock and cut my lip clear open, and she done sewed it up with needle and thread. Did the same for my pa when our oxen tore open his leg with its horn. I sure do wish I could be more useful for her comfortin now."

"Don't worry," said Essie, "you'll be doing just fine administering that medicine I gave you. That and prayer is all anyone can do for her now."

THE BUILDING OF the mission they would call the Good Shepherd School moved along rapidly over the summer, and Helen and Essie couldn't wait to finally have a place to hold regular Sunday church services. Father Phillips had already hired a qualified woman to teach grades one to seven during four months of the winter. Benches would hold four to six children, of whom they already had over fifty signed up. On days Essie didn't need Brownie for her doctoring, Helen drove out in her buggy to see the progress and took Lula along.

Lula had enjoyed watching the men notch the logs and lay them in a large square. When the walls reached eight feet in height and the men were getting ready to put on the rived wood roof, Lula had managed to reach the top by climbing up the notched ends. The plain front had a narrow door, and the sides a small window each. Now that the structure was almost completed, everyone looked forward to the day the church would hold its first service.

Two weeks later, Lula stood in front of the tall mirror at the end of the upstairs hallway. She wanted to look her best for the Good Shepherd's first service. Two long golden braids lay over the front of the navy blue dress that went a short way below her knees and had come in one of the boxes from New York. Lula marveled at the way the white grosgrain ribbon ran along the dress's neck. Even the low-hanging sash was trimmed with the elegant ribbon.

Helen had allowed her to pick out three dresses. This one was for church, and the other two were for the school she would be attending in Hendersonville. The awful row Essie'd had with Helen over her going to school in town surfaced as she stared at herself in the mirror and remembered.

"What on earth is possessing you!" Essie had shouted. "She's nothing but a poor mountain girl who's never gonna fit in with the likes of the pampered brats at that fancy school. Send her to the Good Shepherd where she belongs. Helen, she's not the same as you, and she's never gonna be!"

Lula posed her feet in several positions so she could get a good look at the black leather shoes and white stockings that went to her knees that Helen had bought for her in town. Since she went barefoot most of the time, no matter how hard she looked at the shoes, she couldn't get used to seeing them on her feet. She actually looked like the girls pictured in the magazines Helen was always thumbing through.

Helen called for her to come downstairs, and Lula gave the

toy goat she had named Billy a hug. It had stood in an honored place in her bedroom since the day it arrived. Lula dared not ask for any of the dolls or stuffed animals that were in the boxes from New York for fear that Helen and Essie would 'find the perfect child' for Billy.

Hearing Helen call out again, she ran down the stairs and out to the buggy. Helen had arranged for a photographer to come by the church and take a picture of the congregation. Lula had never had her picture taken before and wondered how it all was going to happen. They boarded the buggy and stopped by Katie's house to get her little sister, Karen, who Helen had made sure had a Sunday dress, too.

Their buggy had a front seat for two, and the floor extended three feet in the back and was boxed in. Both Lula and Karen, who was a year younger, sat in the box with their feet extended underneath the front seat. The two girls were enjoying the ride until Brownie made a sudden start and their heads bumped against the seats.

Hearing the girls yelp, Essie, who was driving, hollered, "I'll let out a shout before I take the whip out of the stock, then you girls sit tight and you won't bump your heads."

The two girls couldn't see ahead, but they were enjoying the scenery as it passed. There were plenty of rough places, uphill climbs, and sudden downhill runs, along with an occasional crossing of a stream.

Seeing a deep creek, Essie called back, "We're going through water ahead that'll be up to Brownie's belly, so stand up and hold on to the back of the seat or you'll get your bottoms wet."

"Hold on to my hands," shouted Helen, turning around. "I don't want you girls losing your balance and falling out."

The girls giggled as they rocked and bounced through the stream.

As they neared the church, they began passing families making their way from the valley on foot. Most of them were carrying large lunch baskets. Lula couldn't help noticing that many wore clothing and shoes that had come from out of the large wooden boxes from New York. The buggy's top had shaded the seats, but little shade fell on the girls, and by the end of the nearly two-mile journey, they were hot and anxious to get off.

The churchyard buzzed with activity. Folks put their baskets on tables made of planks set on sawhorses outside in the shade. Essie pulled up next to two other buggies and tied Brownie to the long hitching post. The horse quickly availed itself of a drink from the trough. While Essie and Helen engaged in conversation with Father Phillips and his wife, Karen, who seemed to know everyone, wove in and out of the crowd pulling Lula along, as she said hello to friends and neighbors.

Lula spotted a family from up on Sugarloaf that Granny McDowell had sold her herbs to, and she ran to greet them. The mother wore a simple, but modern looking dress, and the six children were all neatly dressed and wearing shoes. Lula suddenly filled with joy, knowing that Helen and Essie's good work had aided the folks up on her mountain. If it weren't for all the proper clothes, the family would've been too ashamed of their meager means to come to church.

Something from the corner of her eye drew her attention and caused her to look over. It was Big James! She ran and jumped in his arms and wrapped her legs around him. He whirled around with her, laughing and throwing his head back.

He set her down with a big grin, "Well, I'll be hogtied. If it aint my baby sister all growed up."

Lula almost cried when she saw that her sister Nancy was with him. Nancy, who was shy like their mother, seemed mortified by all the fuss the two were making. She stood head bowed, with her hands clutched in front of her. She was plainly dressed in a long-sleeve white blouse and long skirt, but neat and proper. James seemed eager for Lula to introduce him to Essie, who was a bit of a celebrity and highly respected by area folk due to all her doctoring and missionary work, but Nancy had to be coaxed along. Finally, it was Helen and Essie who found them.

After introductions, Helen said, "I'm so glad you two are joining with us in prayer today. I do hope you can have dinner with us some evening."

"We be right proud, ma'am," said James.

"Well, how about next Sunday. You can follow us home from church."

As James agreed, the church bell rang, and Father Phillips made an announcement.

"Everyone line up in front of the building so our photographer can take a picture."

Lula went and stood between her brother and Nancy in the third row, but the photographer pulled her out and had her stand up front with the other children. While he went around repositioning folks to tighten up the cluster, Lula remembered Essie constantly talking about community. She always supposed Essie was referring to how her people in the colony felt. Standing here with so many friendly folk and two of her kin, she felt connected and believed this was what Essie would call a community.

The picture taken, everyone poured into the church. Not having enough benches for all to be seated, Lula stood at the back between James and Nancy. They held her hands during the service, except when everyone got to singing and clapping.

Father Phillips' fiery sermon brought back the words Lula had heard Essie say to another priest who had come for dinner. "His preaching will scare hell out of people," she had said. "He'll preach a sinner right into a corner, leaving them no options but to get right with God."

Like James and Nancy, Lula hadn't been baptized, but Helen had spoken of it several times and said she would talk to her mother about it when they made a trip to the colony. Lula could hardly wait for this to happen. After listening to Father Phillips, she figured the sooner she was saved, the better.

WHEN MOTHERS who lived on the road spied a wagon loaded with crates and boxes making a turn onto the lane that led to Edelweiss, it was only a short time before their porch was swarming with neighbors come to see what had arrived from New York. With all the added work the regular shipments created, Katie would often bring her sister, Karen, to the house to help with sorting. After these rushes were over, on days when Essie wasn't going out doctoring and Lula's lessons were done,

Helen would let the girls read *The Sunbonnet Babies' Primer.* Lula always wanted to read the part of Baby Mary, while Karen preferred Baby Molly.

On days when Karen came over, she was invited to eat at the table with Lula. On this day, with all the road work going on, all Helen and Essie talked about over the luncheon meal was the poor condition of the roads.

"It's high time the county did something about that nasty buggy trail to Bat Cave and Chimney Rock. It doesn't deserve the honor of being called a road. It's full of ruts and rocks, and in wet weather my buggy wheels sink nearly to the axle in mud," Helen complained.

"The last time I was in Hendersonville, there were all kinds of rumors about automobiles being brought in and people actually buying them," said Essie. "That's what's putting pressure on the county to fix the roads. And rather than pay some of our poor farmers for an honest day's work, they're using chain gang labor."

"Think about all those surreys from Hendersonville that pass by on Sundays," said Helen. "They're filled with young folks out for a day of sightseeing and picnicking in Chimney Rock. Mable Jervis in Bat Cave was telling me she's been getting a good deal of business in her store from tourists coming up from Rutherfordton or who have come through the gorge from Asheville to visit the bat cave. I hear they're even planning on putting down a hard surface on parts of the Hickory Nut Gap Road."

A big boom sounded and rattled all the china in the cabinet.

"There they go again with that dynamite," said Helen as they rose to clear the dishes. "You girls go out and play and stay away from that convict labor."

The two girls ran excitedly out the door. They played in the creek until another dynamite blast went off. Sounding as if it were coming from the road below them, they ran to the bank that ran along the Chimney Rock Road and looked down at all the activity. They could see men in striped black and white suits chained together from one ankle. A man, who looked to be guarding the prisoners, carried a rifle. Lula looked down one side of the road and up the other. She could see they'd been blasting the massive rocks that the old road had to weave around, causing it to cross the creek in two locations. It was clear they were straightening the road, and the rock below them was still in the way.

The girls sat down and watched a prisoner dunk a gunny sack into a pail of water to soak, and then wrap it around a spike. Then he held the spike upright as two other prisoners, with alternating blows, drove it into the stone with heavy hammers, letting out a grunt with each blow. Soon smoke rose from the wet sack.

A guard finally yelled, "Stop," then inspected the hole. He pulled a stick of dynamite from a leather satchel and stuck it in, then yelled for everyone to scatter. The prisoners scuttled as best they could and crouched behind boulders. After seeing everyone safely hidden, the guard yelled, "Blast" as he ran for cover. Even though Lula and Karen were at least fifty feet above, they ran until they heard the terrifying noise and felt the tremor under their feet. Lula swung around and saw rocks flying through the air.

The girls quickly returned to the bank and looked down. The huge granite mass was splintered. Convicts busily cleared the smaller pieces and heaved the larger ones over the side of the new stretch of road. As Lula watched them toil in the searing heat, Father Phillips' fiery words ran through her head. "Sinners will burn in the fires of hell for all eternity." Working like that sure looked like hell to her. She hoped they could go visit her mother soon, so she could be baptized and saved from sin.

CHAPTER TEN
1960

Holly knocked on the trailer door, and the girl shouted for her to come in. Without the baby screaming, the place seemed eerily quiet except for the droning of the TV. Holly could see the baby contently sucking on its bottle in its mother's arms as she sat on the couch watching a soap opera. Holly measured and weighed the baby, then swelled with pride as she noted in her file that this was the second week in a row it had put on weight.

As Holly was leaving in her car, the girl's mother pulled up next to her. Holly rolled down her window to say hello.

"Thank heavens for you," the woman said. "It took a smart young thing to figure a way for my little girl to know when to feed her baby. She may be slow, but once she learns something, she never forgets it."

Holly smiled and said she would check back in a week. As she continued to her next appointment, she couldn't get that little baby out of her thoughts. When that girl runs out of the formula the clinic had given her, she was sure to start using Carnation powdered milk mixed with water, and that baby wasn't going to continue to thrive. Her supervisor had told her that was why some parents started their babies on soft food as soon as they could. Unfortunately, it was often white food without any iron, like potatoes, gravies, biscuits, and grits. Some mothers were putting their infants to sleep with their bottle, only to have the sugar in the milk rot their teeth. By the time their permanent ones came in, their baby teeth were rotted out.

Something had to be done to give these babies and children from poor families access to nutritious food at a time in their growth cycle that would positively affect them for the rest of their lives, thought Holly. Pregnant women, too. When she was in school, she'd heard that the nurses' organizations were advocating for state and federal programs that would address this problem. If only it would happen, and happen soon.

As she neared the road to her next appointment, she grew anxious to see if the materials for the chicken coop had arrived. She'd never be able to face Ella if something had happened to the fifty dollars she had rushed over to them the day after Ella gave it to her.

The road being muddier than before, she put on her boots before wading across the creek, then trudged up the road. She reached the rock with the red arrow and noticed the pickup wasn't there. She took the path to the cabin, and spotting it ahead, searched for signs of chickens running freely. There weren't any. Hopeful, her eyes shot up to the open window where two had roosted the last time she was there. She smiled when she saw there were none.

She went onto the rock stoop, kicked off her boots, and quickly put on her oxfords. As she was about to knock, the woman opened the door wearing a broad grin.

"They're in the coop!" she announced, and the two hugged in triumph. It made Holly happy to see that all evidence of the chickens had been removed from the cabin. After weighing and measuring the baby girl, Holly sat down with the mother and told her how the free clinic could help her family in the future.

On the walk back to her car, it occurred to her that a public health nurse had to have a special empathy, something beyond what normal people would have. Seeing what an overwhelming mess some people were in, you couldn't blame anyone for judging the situation as hopeless and turning their back to it. In order to succeed in public health, you had to have what it took to look beyond the mess and suppress the urge to be judgmental. You had to let your innate concern for another human take over and do whatever you could to help, even if it were no more than finding money for a chicken coop.

IT HAD BEEN raining for a week, and Holly was more nervous than ever as she made her way down the mountain road. She wondered if she would ever get over her fear of going around a one-lane blind curve with a wall of granite on one side and a hundred foot drop on the other. She eased her car around the rock face, and as she had dreaded, saw a pickup coming around the curve ahead. The truck stopped and she gave her rearview mirror a quick glance. There was no way she could back up. The truck door swung open. Of all people, it was the Garrison fellow again.

He waved at her, shouting, "Don't back up! I'll do it!"

He got back into his truck and slowly backed around the curve with Holly following a good twenty feet behind. Hitting the straightaway, he pulled into what looked like a path. Considering it common decency to stop and thank him, she stopped in front of his truck, opened the door, and with one leg standing on the ground, threw a wave and called out "Thank you!"

He stuck his head out of his window, and with a smile, shouted back, "No problem. Don't want the territory's nurse falling off a cliff."

She jumped back in her car and drove off wondering how she should take that remark.

Her next stop was on a trail off Sugarloaf Road. No pavement, no gravel, just a muddy path with a crooked sign saying Jason Road. Nailed on a tree next to it was a sign with a shotgun drawn on it, along with "KEEP OUT!" She picked up the file and checked the instructions. It definitely said she was supposed to stop there today, so she forged ahead. Every twenty feet or so, she'd spot another warning sign nailed on a tree. One with "We Shoot at First Sight" was scrawled in red to look like it was dripping in blood.

She continued for a distance in the dense woods when a pickup came speeding around a curve and slammed on its brakes right in front of her, blocking her way. A man got out, yelling "You get the hell outta here!" He pulled out a shotgun and pointed it straight at her. She quickly put the car in reverse and started backing up. Trembling with fear and with her knees knocking, she weaved from side to side on the narrow path until she finally made it to a place where she could turn around.

She drove as fast as she dared on the rugged trail, and when she reached the main road, drove up a distance and pulled over to let her heart stop racing. Looking in the rearview mirror, she saw the truck shoot out of the woods and speed in the opposite direction.

She sat there for a while, thinking about the client she was supposed to visit. She'd met her at the clinic before the baby was born. Even then, the woman seemed undernourished. She was dressed like a hippie, and Holly worried that she might be doing drugs. When the hospital notified the clinic that the baby was born slightly premature and underweight, Holly was relieved that it wasn't suffering from something much worse.

When her heart finally stopped racing, Holly thought about the baby. She'd only been making rounds for a couple of months, but knew enough of the conditions in some of these cabins to fear for its life. A lot of times, it only took a little bit of help to make a huge difference. The formula she had packed for the baby's bottles might be the only thing keeping this newborn from dire consequences. Yet, she couldn't ignore the advice the nurse who turned this mountain district over to her had given her.

"Being a public health nurse can be dangerous," Lucy had said. "I prayed a lot. Sometimes, I felt God watching over me. Holly, you have to learn that if you hear a voice in the back of your head telling you 'don't go there,' then for God's sake, don't."

Those words rang in her head, but ringing out even louder was the thought of something tragic happening to the baby if she postponed this visit. Armed with resolution, she started the car, turned around, and drove back onto the dirt lane. Every time she spotted a sign, she had second thoughts, but the picture of a help-less baby screaming for nourishment kept her going. She reached the cabin without incident and was surprised to find three pick-ups parked in front. She ignored the voice in the back of her head telling her not to go there, and, aflame with purpose, grabbed her satchel and knocked on the door.

A scruffy man opened it and looked her over. "Who the hell are you?"

Out of the corner of her eye, Holly could see people in the dark living room passed out. It was obvious they were doing drugs. A shiver went down her spine. She was definitely in a dangerous situation and had better convince the man fast that she wasn't from law enforcement.

"I'm Nurse Holly and I've come to take care of the woman of the house and her new baby."

"You're a nurse?"

"Yes."

"I'm the husband." He grabbed her arm and pulled her into the house, then dragged her over to a man with blood gushing from a fresh stab wound to his arm.

"Then take care of this!"

"I don't have any bandages. I just came to see your wife and baby."

Hearing the commotion, the wife came running from the bed-room and stood between him and Holly.

"Let her go," the woman begged.

Holly spotted a towel, pulled herself free, and quickly wrapped it around the injured man's arm.

"Somebody has to take him to the emergency room right now!" she demanded.

Getting an order from a young woman confused the husband for a moment, then he quickly roused the other two men.

"Get out! I'm taking Butch to the emergency room!"

Everyone took off in short order, leaving Holly alone with the mother.

"I know I said to come by today, but you should've moved on when you saw all those trucks," the woman said.

"I can see that now," said Holly while helping the woman back to her bed. She spent the next two hours tending to the baby, making up a supply of bottles, and cooking something for the woman to eat.

"Do you have somewhere to go until you're back on your feet?" asked Holly. "I'll take you there right now."

"No."

"How about your parents?"

"They're Mennonites in Pennsylvania. They forbid me to marry him, and the last time I asked for help, they said, 'You made your bed, now lie in it.'"

"How about friends?"

"Nobody in this town."

"Okay. I'll come back tomorrow."

"You can't. You've met him. He doesn't trust anyone."

"Well, if you care about your baby, and I know you do, you'll convince him that I'm here to nurse you and his son."

"You sure are stubborn," the woman said. "If you're crazy enough to come, make it early in the morning. Nobody's here then, and he sleeps til noon. His truck is black. If you see more parked out there, keep going."

BY THE TIME Saturday rolled around, Holly was lying in bed thinking she'd had about as much excitement as she could stand. She glanced at her clock and was amazed to see she had slept until ten. Smelling bacon frying, she jumped out of bed and ran down the stairs in her pajamas. Myrt automatically poured her a cup of coffee and put it on the table. Holly couldn't resist the urge to give her a hug.

"Now, now, young lady. You sit yourself right down and eat your breakfast," said Myrt as she grabbed a plate. She filled it with scrambled eggs and bacon and put it on the table in front of Holly. "It's about time you got up. We're gonna be busy today."

"Are we?" said Holly, buttering a piece of toast.

"Annie Barnwell's cousin walked into the post office straight off this morning. She'd heard I'd been looking for Annie, and told Ella she'd been visiting her in Salisbury and brought her back with her. Annie's gonna stay for a couple days, then her son is coming to take her to Georgia to visit with his family. She said you and I could come over anytime this afternoon."

A few hours later, Holly, wearing a skirt and blouse, gave herself a final look in her bedroom mirror, then grabbed her purse and started for the stairs. She stopped and thought for a moment, then went back to her room, picked up the small framed photo of her aunt from her dresser, and put it in her purse. Myrt was waiting for her downstairs, and to her surprise, so was Ella.

"You're pretty lucky the post office closes at noon on Saturday," Ella told her. "Now I can come along to help."

They all got in Myrt's Chevy Impala, and she drove down the road to Route 64.

"My dear William bought me this car two months before he passed," she quietly murmured. "Every time I drive it, I'm thinkin he's up there watchin me all proud of himself."

Holly, who had a client on Slick Rock Road where Annie's cousin lived, knew it would be to their right, and was surprised when Myrt made a left turn onto the Edney Inn Road.

"Where in tarnation are ya goin?" yelled Ella.

"Want to show Holly where I was raised," she said.

They went over a bridge and up the road a bit when she pulled aside next to a log cabin.

"That's where I was raised, and my father before me. It's all done over and added on to, but still pretty much how I remember it." Then she pointed to a big stone house a few hundred yards ahead. "That's where the old Edney Inn used to stand before it burnt to the ground back in the 30s.

"That's where my dad met my mother. Both his parents worked for the Edneys so it was natural for him to work there, too. My mother had come down from the hills at fourteen after both her parents died with fever, and she worked there as a maid. When she turned seventeen, my father asked her if she wanted to marry him." Myrt laughed and looked in the rearview mirror at Holly. "She told him, 'I sure do!' The marriage lasted sixty-two years," Myrt added proudly as she turned around and headed back to Route 64.

"When I was a kid, this was only known as the Chimney Rock Road," Myrt added. "Used to walk barefoot to the grocery store in Bat Cave for penny candy."

The car continued for a quarter of a mile, then swung onto Slick Rock Road. After another mile, Myrt pulled into a long driveway leading to a large brick house surrounded by a nicely groomed lawn.

"This is where Annie's cousin lives," said Myrt.

A door opened, and a big Bernese Mountain Dog came bounding out. An elderly woman at the door yelled for it to come back, then welcomed the three into the house.

"Annie's in the living room. Go right in, and I'll make y'all some tea."

Like old friends who hadn't seen each other for years, Myrt, Ella, and Annie fell into animated conversation while Holly smiled and looked on. Listening to them talk about each other's first, second, and third cousins, it became evident to Holly that all the old timers in these mountains were related to each other. When she thought about it, it only made sense. When they were growing up, the sheer isolation of the region dictated that most of the people they came in contact with were family, neighbors, or fellow churchgoers, and when it came time to choose a partner, he or she came from that same pool.

Holly had always thought it a little sad that she and her aunt never really had a family bigger than the two of them and Doris. There were always letters from cousins in far off places and occasional visits from distant relatives, but try as they may, with only the three of them, they never could create the same flamboyantly joyous holiday atmosphere always portrayed in movies and magazines. Instead, times like Christmas always made them feel a little lonely. Looking around Annie's cousin's house, family photos were on every available flat surface in the room, something always missing from her Pittsboro home.

All the pictures, as well as the three women's joyful remembrances, suddenly brought back all the longings, all the frustrating not-knowing, all the feelings of being abandoned by someone she yearned to know and love. She quickly gulped back a wave of melancholy, a remedy that by now came naturally to her. It was time to put all that behind her, she told herself. She was here in these mountains to track down the only clue she'd had of who she might be, and the woman sitting two feet from her might have the answer.

Myrt squeezed her hand and woke her from her thoughts. "Go on, sweetheart, tell Annie what you're lookin for."

"I was adopted by Helen Baldwin," Holly offered. "She was a teacher and passed away at eighty last year. She always told me she had no idea of where I came from and that I was an orphan. My birth certificate says I was born in Raleigh, but all the adoption records are sealed. I grew up referring to her as my aunt since she was never married."

"How can I help you?"

"Well, it's hard to say. My aunt was hardly a recluse, but she kept much of her past from me. I always thought it was strange, but I loved her dearly and knew enough not to ask questions she was never going to answer." Holly wrung her hands and continued. "I knew she was born in Columbia, South Carolina, so I sent the paper her death notice. One of her distant cousins showed up at her funeral, and he told me she once lived in the mountains near Bat Cave. I know that's not much, but it's all I have."

Annie scratched behind her ear. "You say her name was Helen Baldwin?"

"Yes."

Annie sat thinking. "I don't rightly know. It sounds familiar, but I can't hardly remember anything these days." She shook her head. "No. I don't think I know anyone by that name."

"Nonsense!" Ella said. "That nephew of yours told me he remembers you tellin him stories about a woman you used to do laundry for with that name."

"He did?"

Ella nodded.

"It was Paulie," Myrt interjected.

"Oh, that boy was quite a lad. Quite a storyteller, too," said Annie.

"Annie! You gotta get your head clear," Ella demanded. "Paulie said she lived with another woman who did doctorin. Now I want you to think real hard. This dear little thing has come all the way to these here mountains lookin fer kin. Think of it. She could be your's or my blood."

Holly could see that the pressure Ella was putting on the woman was making her nervous. She took one of Annie's hands and gently patted it. "That's all right, Annie. I understand if you can't remember. Don't let it worry you."

"Fiddlesticks! Where's that picture you told me you brought," said Ella.

Worried about Annie, Holly reluctantly pulled it out of her purse.

Ella grabbed it from her hand. "Here! Take a good look at this," she said as she thrust it in Annie's face.

Annie put on the glasses hanging from around her neck and stared at the picture, then looked up at Ella. "Paulie said she lived with a woman who did doctorin?"

"Yes."

Annie thought for a moment. "There *was* a doctor woman. Way back. She did all she rightly could for my poor Edward after he went tumbling down the mountain durin the Great Flood. Those were plenty hard times. I lost Edward, our cabin, all the stock, everything we done had. The doctor woman fixed it for me so as to earn money to go to Salisbury to be with my daughter by doin wash for this fancy lady she boarded with."

The mention of a fancy lady piqued Holly's interest. "Do you remember the lady's name?" she urged.

"No. I don't rightly think I do."

"Please, take another look at the picture," Holly pleaded.

Annie took a long look and shook her head. Discouraged, Holly reached for the picture frame. Annie suddenly took it from her grasp and looked hard at it.

"Now I remember. She had me wash all sorts of fine things for the table. Never saw such fancy things before. Napkins and tablecloths all lacy like. Her place was too high on the ridge to get the floodin, but she had me wash and press everything just the same. She was kindly enough, but too fussy."

"Did anyone else live with them?" asked Holly.

"Not that I saw. But I was only there for a couple of weeks."

"Do you remember the woman's name? Was it Helen Baldwin?" pressed Holly.

Annie took off her glasses and rubbed her eyes. "Lordy me. I'm afraid that's all the rememberin I got."

"Where was this house?" asked Holly.

"Right up there on the ridge above the Chimney Rock Road across from Little Fork Mountain. Tween here and the Edney Inn Road."

Annie's cousin came in with tea and a tray of cookies, and after a bit more gossip, the three got up to leave. Annie insisted on walking them to the door even though she needed two canes to manage it.

At the door, Annie pressed Holly's hand. "I'm so sorry I couldn't help you none darlin, but all I remember is washin and ironin those fancy linens and cryin over my dear Edward while she played on a big ole piana like nothin was wrong."

"Piano?" said Holly. "Tell me! What kind of piano?"

"Not like anythin usual. A big piana. Long and wide, and I swear it was mahogany."

The three got back in the Impala. Myrt looked back at Holly and saw tears running freely down her cheeks.

"Don't cry darlin. We'll find her," she said.

"We already have. That was my aunt's grand piano."

CHAPTER ELEVEN
1929

After seven months in Hendersonville, Lula, who was now thirteen, was delighted to be back at Edelweiss listening to the sound of Helen at her piano. The upright at the boarding house had sounded so tinny, her aunt couldn't bear to play it.

Once Helen finished her favorite etude, Essie and Helen sat in the living room catching up on gossip while Lula cuddled up on a sofa with a book and Katie brought in tea and biscuits hot out of the oven.

It wasn't long before Lula had to listen to Essie carry on again about how foolish it was for Helen to send her to a private school and take rooms in Hendersonville for the winter.

"You can hardly expect me to spend the winter huddled up in front of the fireplace," said Helen. "Plus the child needs a proper education if she's going to be a teacher. And then, if she goes to Asheville Normal for two years, she'll earn a Class A teaching certificate. By the way, Essie, she's too old to be riding all over the county on that horse with you this summer."

"What are you talking about?" Essie protested. "She's my right arm. Teacher? That's absurd! That girl was born to be a nurse."

"I'll not have you dragging her all over these mountains and exposing her to fever," said Helen. "Besides, she's reached womanhood, and it isn't proper."

"I suggest you think on that, my friend. If she doesn't have work with me, they'll be wanting her back home."

"Nonsense," said Helen. "Her mother has refused the money for Lula's helping you for years. Besides, when I visit her mother this summer, I plan on making permanent arrangements."

"I can imagine what those arrangements are!" Essie lashed out. "*Aunt Helen?* You think I didn't know what you were up to when you told Lula to call you that?"

"Really, Essie. How else was she going to explain me to the girls at school?"

Lula lay on the couch listening and remembering all the harsh partings the two old friends had each fall, yet, she wasn't concerned. Every time they were resettled in Edelweiss in the spring, they were so content to be back together again, it only took a couple of days for the rift to be healed.

The next day, Katie discovered another empty whiskey bottle under the couch.

"People who live like Essie will not inherit the Kingdom of God," Katie fussed to Lula. "Miss Helen should close the place for the winter instead of letting that woman stay on while you two are gone. It's a wonder she hasn't burned the place down."

The two Feist dogs a mountain man had given Essie in trade for her services started scratching at the door, a sure sign Helen and Essie were coming up from the drugstore. The dogs were a replacement for Jack, who hadn't made it through the winter. Essie had named the two rat terriers, Remus and Romulus.

Katie had come early that morning and started a fire in the cookstove as well as the living room fireplace to chase away the spring chill. The warm hearth reminded Lula of the cozy times in front of the fire with her family up in the colony. She ached from missing them so much, and she was looking forward to going up on the plateau with Helen once they were settled. Over the years, Helen had managed several visits with her mother, but each time the arduous trek had taken its toll. Lula was relieved when Essie mentioned that loggers had made a wagon road over the winter that would allow them to go a good portion of the way by buggy.

After lunch, Essie left with Remus and Romulus to work in her drugstore, and Helen practiced her scales on the piano. Lula finished helping Katie with the dishes and came out of the kitchen eating a scone. She strolled over to the window and looked out on Little Fork Mountain, remembering the biscuits Helen had served her the day she arrived at Edelweiss. As much as she had hungered for the last one left on the plate, as a stranger in the house, she thought she'd be overstepping if she took it.

The odd feeling she sometimes felt flowed over her. She had one foot in one world and the other in another, a pupa clinging to a stem about to become a butterfly. Sometimes on school outings in Hendersonville, the girls would see a mountain family on Main Street and make fun of the poorly dressed, barefoot little children. Lula was overwhelmed with a feeling of hypocrisy. What would her friends say if they knew she had once been one of those "poor little children."

Lula and Helen heard the two dogs yapping down at the drugstore and rushed out the door to the porch. A buggy was coming up the lane. Lula, seeing her sister, Nancy, riding with a young fellow in a jacket and tie, was struck with fear. The last time Nancy had appeared out of nowhere, she had brought news of her father's death.

The driver pulled up to the porch, then got down and tied the reins to the hitching post before politely helping Nancy from the buggy. Lula was stunned to see her sister dressed like the ladies in town with a hem that only went down to her calves. And instead of a sunbonnet, she had on the kind of snugly fitting hat that Helen called a cloche. Nancy's dress was simple and her hat rather plain in comparison to the elaborately decorated ones that Helen had; yet, her classic features and flawless complexion were as easy on the eye as ever. Lula began to suspect her news wouldn't be the tragic sort this time.

"Welcome to Edelweiss," Helen sang out to Nancy who had come for dinner on several occasions along with her brother

James. Lula ran up and gave her a hug.

Nancy blushed as she told Helen, "This is Cecil Robertson. We've been to see Mr. Justice who done married us."

Lula, still with one arm around her, looked up at her sister in amazement.

"Well, how wonderful of you to come and tell us the good news," said Helen. "Here, come in. You must take lunch with us."

"Thank you, ma'am," said Cecil, "but we just came to say our goodbyes. We've got a train to catch."

"You go on in with Miss Baldwin, Cecil," said Nancy. "I want to set a while on the porch with Lula."

Helen could see Nancy wanted a few minutes alone with her sister, so she took Cecil by the arm and led him inside and chatted away while Nancy and Lula sat down on a bench.

"Yesterday, Cecil got a letter from his older brother," Nancy told Lula. "It had been sent a few weeks back, but was slow in gettin here. His brother started a welding shop in Pittsburg a while back, and it's doin so good he wants Cecil to come help him."

"I still can't believe you're married!" Lula exclaimed.

Nancy blushed. "We've been steppin out together, him workin at Salola like me. Right after he read the letter, he came searching for me and asked for my hand." She smoothed the line of the dress. "Does it look proper on me?"

"It's lovely," said Lula. "But not as lovely as you."

Nance turned her head away and blushed. She nervously felt the cloche with both hands. "Mrs. Williams, whose husband owns the Salola, gave me this dress and the hat, too. She said I couldn't be goin on a train to Pittsburg dressed like a granny woman. She also lent us her buggy to come tell ya. Her and her husband done come from the colony when they were younguns, and she meant to help us."

"What about Ma?" asked Lula.

"Aint got time to go up there. Mrs. Williams let us use the inn's telephone to call Cecil's brother to say we is comin, and he said to get on the next train. It wouldn't be right proper for an unmarried woman to be goin alone with a man, so we got hitched this morning. Cecil gave Mr. Justice a dollar for doin it."

Nancy squeezed Lula's hands as if she were finding it hard to go on. "I got more to tell ya." She looked steadily at Lula. "We're takin Billy Boy with us."

The welled up tears in Lula's eyes spilled over.

"Don't you go frettin. He's been wantin to go. Heard there's plenty of work in the steel mills."

"Can I go with you to get him and say my goodbyes?" asked Lula.

"We already been there askin him if he aims to come. He's got to go with Mr. McGraw to deliver a load of barrels and is gonna meet us at the train station in Hendersonville. That's why he ain't with us to say goodbye to ya. Lula, now that Big James has gone to Raleigh, it'll be up to you to go tell Ma."

Lula sniffled and nodded.

Nancy rose. "It's gettin on. I better fetch Cecil."

The two went in and found Cecil alone in the living room. Helen came rushing in with a wrapped package and handed it to Nancy.

"Here, darling. It's a set of sheets I brought from France. I want you to have them."

Nancy took the gift and bowed her head. Cecil took Nancy's arm and said, "Thank you muchly for the gift, ma'am, but we got to be gettin along iffen we're gonna make that train."

"Not before we have a toast," Helen gaily sang out. She went to the china cabinet and took out four of her cherished crystal liqueur glasses and put them on the sideboard. Then she opened a cupboard door and brought out a bottle of cognac. She poured some water in one and barely an ounce of cognac in each of the other three. She handed the cognac to the newlyweds and the water to Lula, then took up a glass herself and raised it saying, "May God bless this union."

Nancy's hand shook as she raised her glass and looked into Cecil's eyes. Seeing Helen drink down her cognac, they both emptied their glasses. The strong spirit sent Nancy into a cough-ing fit. Lula quickly poured her a glass of water and Cecil encouraged her to drink it down. The four of them laughed happily, though Lula was having mixed emotions.

Lula stood on the porch and watched their buggy bump down the lane. It was almost seven years since she had stood barefoot watching Granny McDowell disappear down that same lane. She was struck with how much her life had changed since then and wanted to fall on her knees and cry for the family she had lost too soon. Her sister's cloche-covered head grew smaller as the buggy wobbled away. Tears rolled down Lula's cheeks, and she wondered if she would ever see her sister again. Big James, Billy Boy, Nancy, and she... fledglings flung into the wind.

THE SUN YET to rise, Helen and Lula were asleep when they were awakened by a ruckus downstairs. They ran to the balcony and looked down into the living room. Two men stood over a man lying on the couch. Essie was administering to him.

One of the men looked up at Helen. "There's been an accident. With all the rain we've been havin, his wagon slid off the bank and tipped over on em. We had to shoot the horse."

"Who is he?" Helen called down.

"One of the Freemans from up on the Hickory Nut Gap Road. He was headed to Hendersonville. We wanted to get him to the hospital, but the roads are so washed out, we figured he'd bleed to death before we got there."

Lula ran back into her room, quickly dressed, and ran down the stairs.

Essie, noticing her hurriedly clearing the table, said, "Good." She turned to the two men. "Let's get him on the table."

Lula, knowing Essie would need hot water to wash her hands, ran into the kitchen and put on two kettles of water and a pot of coffee. The way Essie was teetering, Lula figured she'd been drinking all night again and needed something to sober her up. By the time she came back in the living room, the man's leg was exposed with a bone sticking out.

"Go fetch me two pieces of wood like I showed you when we fixed that man's leg at the Flack Hotel, then bring in the hot water," slurred Essie.

Helen, who had come downstairs, followed Lula into the kitchen.

"I'll go get the wood," Lula told her. "You can take in the water and a couple of basins." As Lula ran out the kitchen door, she called out, "We're gonna need clean rags, too." She rifled through the wood pile until she found two strong slats the right size, then rushed them back to the living room.

Essie handed Helen a bottle. "Be ready to give him some when I tell you."

Lula's eyes widened. The bottle of carbolic acid Essie had given Helen would poison him. Lula snatched the bottle from Helen, exchanging it with a bottle of laudanum. It was obvious Essie was too drunk to continue.

"Why don't you sit down, Essie," cajoled Lula. "You've shown me how to do this so many times, I can take care of it."

Essie stalked toward her. "Wadda ya mean? I'm more than capable..."

One of the men grabbed Essie as she started to fall.

"Excuse me, Ma'am, but I think you need to set yourself down," he said as he led her toward the couch.

Essie yanked her arm away and began to teeter. She grabbed the couch and caught her balance, turned, and tottered to her bedroom mumbling profanities.

Lula glanced over at the two men as she finished washing her hands. "Hold him tight. I need to set that fracture." She looked at Helen. "Okay. Give him a big swig of the laudanum."

Once that was done, she doused the wound with carbolic acid before starting to pull. The man screamed in agony while the bone was slowly eased back into place. Lula eyed Helen, whose face was the color of fireplace ashes. Clearing her head of anything other than the task at hand, Lula sutured and wrapped the wound in gauze, then secured the splint with strips of rags. As soon as it was over, Helen collapsed on the couch fanning herself.

"This should hold him til you get him to the hospital," Lula announced as she finished the splint.

Once the man was taken away, Lula went in the kitchen and

filled a tub with cold water and put in all the bloody towels and rags to soak. She came back into the living room to see Helen shaking her head as she picked up a glass and an empty bottle of whisky.

"No matter how much she fights her temptation, or how many times she repents and promises Father Phillips she will abstain, she hits the bottle every chance she gets." Helen sighed. "I'll make us some breakfast."

Lula followed her to the kitchen, filled a pail with hot water, and put in some 20 Mule Team Borax along with a scrub brush. After she finished cleaning the living room, she emptied the pail over the front porch railing and sat down to rest. She smiled to herself. Never was she more happy and content than when she helped someone who was ill or injured. Somehow, she had to convince Helen she was born to be a nurse, not a teacher.

"HELP ME GET IT over the rug," Helen directed as she and Lula dragged the steamer trunk out of the closet at the end of the upstairs hall. When they finally wrestled it into Helen's room, she pulled up a stool and plopped down next to the enormous wood chest plastered with travel decals from nearly every country in Europe.

"Come here, dear," she said. "I want to show you some of the places I've been."

Lula pointed to a label with a white star on a red flag. "This one's pretty."

"Oh, yes! That's from the White Star Line. That was from my first trip to Europe on the RMS Olympic."

"What's this one for? It looks like it's at the seashore."

"Oh, my, yes! The Hotel Le Royal on the Côte d'Azur."

Seeing her so animated, Lula grew excited about the trip she was planning for the both of them.

"Now darling, I do hate keeping you out of school this fall, but the trip will cost us so much less at this time of year. I'll get your course books and teach you your lessons in Europe, and when we get home for Christmas, you'll be able to start school at the New Year and be not a day behind."

Helen pulled a key from her pocket and unlocked the trunk, then lifted the lid and examined a tray of compartments on top.

"I've written to my agent in New York and asked him to find us proper but modest lodgings for three weeks in Ireland and three weeks in Switzerland. I told him to get us places off the beaten path, rather than where most of the tourists go. This will let us get acquainted with the local people at a greatly reduced cost. Of course, we'll stop off in London and Paris and try to steal a visit to Rome."

"You do like to travel, don't you, Aunt Helen?"

"I surely do. Think of it. It's how I discovered this wonderful place. During my last trip abroad, I made some friends at the Hotel du Louvre in Paris, and they mentioned that the summers in the Appalachian Mountains of North Carolina were cool and free of mosquitoes. They told me the Edney Inn was a real haven for summer visitors at unbelievably low prices, so when I came back home, I sent them a letter of inquiry.

"Being a spinster lady with no income other than from my inheritance, I always find low prices to be of great interest. They were quick to reply that my board would be seven dollars a week, and if I brought a dog, it could stay at no extra charge and eat table scraps. Their letter said they ran a hack to Hendersonville to meet the Carolina Special and bring their guests back, as well as a wagon for the trunks. I decided I could easily afford to stay for the following summer and wrote back to them by return mail.

"Once I got here, I discovered that this area on Hendersonville's north border abounded in boarding houses—the Salola, Esmeralda, Glen Eden, Slick Rock, Mountainview, and Bee Hive inns, and the Lowrance and Flack hotels. And once I met Essie, I had a friend to visit and dine with in these wonderful places."

Helen slapped her knees and rose. "Let's go down and make some tea, then we can search through the atlas for all the places we'll visit."

Lula was amused by Helen's almost giddy spirits as she arranged a tray with tea and cookies and took them to the table in the living room.

"We must stop in New York for a couple of days to buy clothes. We don't need too much, but they must be fashionable." She thought for a moment. "But first, we need to pay a visit to your mother, and then we have to go about getting your passport."

"Essie said you're going to ask my mother if you can be my legal guardian. Is that true?"

"Yes, darling. It is."

"She'll still be my mother, won't she?"

"Of course, darling. Nothing will ever change that. However, your mother and I are in agreement about your future. Since you're living with me, and I'm providing for your education, it will work out better if I'm authorized to give permission for you when required."

Helen reached over and took Lula's hand. "I was proud of the way you took care of that Freeman fellow," she said as she squeezed it, "and your mother would be, too."

Lula took a deep breath and sat straight up in her chair, beaming with pride.

"Indeed," said Helen. "Essie's been telling me for years that you were simply born to be a nurse, and I finally saw it for myself. When we get back from our trip, I'm going to look into seeing what's required for you to attend a hospital nursing school."

CHAPTER TWELVE

L ula was stunned as she watched Helen descend the staircase in a pair of slacks. The legs flared out at the bottom,
and two rows of buttons lined either side of the top of the front.
It reminded Lula of the uniforms sailors wore in a picture she'd
seen in one of Helen's *Saturday Evening Posts*.

"Heavens to Betsy," Katie blurted out, almost dropping the
dish she was holding.

"Don't look so shocked, Katie," said Helen. "I plan to do a
good deal of hiking with Lula in the Alps and need the appropri-
ate outfit. And it's the perfect thing for me to wear on my hike to
visit Lula's mother." She slowly turned around for everyone to
see. "It's what all the French and Swiss are wearing in St.
Moritz. I ordered a pair for you, too, Lula. They're on your
dresser."

Essie put down the newspaper she had been reading and
studied Helen's new outfit. "Next, you're going to be asking me
to teach you to ride Brownie."

Helen laughed her sweet, light lilt. "No, my friend. Next, I'm
going to get myself one of those automobiles. I understand they
don't need to be cranked anymore and are easy for ladies to
drive."

"I wouldn't be so anxious to spend that stock money," said
Essie. She picked up the paper she brought home from the Edney
Inn. "Listen to this," she said, then read, "More people are bor-

rowing and speculating today than ever in our history. Sooner or later a crash is coming, and it may be horrific. Wise are those investors who now get out of debt and reef their sails."

"Nonsense," said Helen. "My brother would never risk a penny of my inheritance."

"The *New York Times* is not to be ignored, Helen. I'd reconsider this trip if I were you."

"Well, my brother writes that the outlook for the fall months seems brighter than at any time in our history, and he urges me to take advantage of this prosperity and enjoy myself. Besides, I'm going to be fifty this Christmas, and this might be the last opportunity for me to enjoy a grand tour."

"When are we going to see my mother?" asked Lula.

"Tomorrow, if Essie can spare Brownie."

"I'll get him hitched to the buggy in the morning, so we can set out around seven," said Essie.

"You're going up there with us?" asked Lula, excited.

"No. Now that Granny McDowell has passed, there's nothing left there for me. The buggy will make it all the way up to Gus Gibson's house and sawmill on the new logging trail. I'll let you two off on the path to the colony before we get to his place. Then I'll go on past Gus' house and stop in and see old Carrie Sutter. Her husband's ailing. Afterwards, I'll visit with Gus and his wife until you make your way down again."

THE BUGGY ROCKED and bumped on the rugged, winding wagon trail.

"What on earth happened to this footpath?" cried Helen.

"The loggers did it," hollered Essie. "They've been snaking out crossties for railroad tracks and sledding out chestnut bark for the tanning industry all winter. One day, I watched them load everything onto a long wagon drawn by a team of oxen so they could take them to the railroad station for shipment by freight. It was quite an undertaking."

It had been well over an hour since they left Edelweiss when Essie stopped the buggy at a beaten footpath. "This is where you two get off," she said. She pointed to a house on the road ahead.

"That's the Gibson place. Look for me there when you come back."

The two got off and assembled their bundles, then Helen glanced at her new wristwatch.

"It's almost nine," she called up to Essie. "We should be there by one and back by five."

"Are you sure you can carry that?" Helen asked Lula as Essie drove off.

"It's not heavy," said Lula as she slung a sack over her shoulder. "Just the throw I knitted for my mother and the sweater I bought in town for Luke."

Helen seemed to be enjoying the trek more than usual with the trail being much shorter and the air much drier than when they had come up in past summers. After a rather long and steep stretch, hot and sweaty, they were grateful to reach a familiar resting spot next to a stream with a series of small waterfalls.

"Is it all right if I take off my shoes and go barefoot in the water?" Lula asked.

"Yes. This'll be a good place to rest and have our lunch."

Lula sloshed around in the stream picking up pebbles while Helen took a checkered tablecloth from her basket and spread it on the ground. They ate their sandwiches listening to the pleasant sound of water tumbling over moss-covered rocks. Every once in a while, a bird sang out and they'd scan the trees for it. They sat so still listening, a rabbit peeked from under a fern and skittered across the path.

Lula reached over and picked a small white flower waving in a clump of green.

"Here," she said, handing it to Helen.

She took it and said, "How beautiful."

"It's the flower of the bloodroot."

"You miss this place, don't you, darling?" said Helen. She took a moment to study the surroundings. "I don't blame you. It's beautiful."

Refreshed, they continued their hike. It saddened Lula when they came to the cabin where Granny McDowell always stopped to trade. Smoke no longer rose from the chimney. Vines were already trying to erase the small abode, and what was left of the fence, leaned ready to collapse. Lula missed visiting with the woman's two girls and wondered what had become of them.

Hours later, when they reached the outer edge of the plateau, Lula was surprised to see Helen still in high spirits after the strenuous climb. More than a dozen times, Lula had to either pull her up or push her over an obstacle. The enthusiastic way she was forging ahead convinced Lula that she was on a mission. She couldn't help thinking it had something to do with the argument she'd overheard between Helen and Essie last night; the one about her guardianship.

The closer they got to her family's cabin, the faster Lula walked. Soon she was at a full run. Seeing her mother in her long skirt and bonnet hoeing in her garden, she almost burst with love. Tears stung her eyes. The old hound noticed her first and began barking. She saw her mother glance up, shading her eyes with her hand. Even from this distance, Lula could tell by her smile when her mamma recognized her. Lula dropped her sack and ran into her arms.

"Ye be here with the doctor woman?" she asked as she lovingly chased stray locks from Lula's face.

"No. Helen brought me."

Helen emerged from the thicket and started across the meadow.

"Lordy, she's in breeches jist like the doctor woman," said her mother in surprise. She took a step back to get a good look at her daughter. "Land sake! Yer wearin breeches, too, and all growed up."

"I measure five-foot two inches, now," said Lula.

Hattie hugged Lula again. "No matter what yer wearin, the sight of ye tis good fer sore eyes."

Lula retrieved her sack, pulled out a light blue throw, and showed it to her mother. "I made this for you. It took me all winter."

Her mother rubbed it against her cheek. "Be soft as kitten fur."

Helen finally reached them, and the warm way the two

women greeted each other filled Lula with joy. Ever since Helen's first visit with her mother four years ago when she was nine, the two women had developed a special bond.

"Come inside and rest a spell," said her mother as she took Lula and Helen by their hands.

The minute Lula entered the cabin, the glow of the hearth, the smell of beans and pork belly cooking on the fire, all of it, made her feel safe and warm and cloaked in love. Never had Lula heard a harsh word spoken within these walls, unlike Edelweiss where Essie made terrible scenes when she was out of her mind with whisky.

"Can I git ye somethin ta eat?" asked her mother.

"Thank you, Hattie, but we ate on the way up," said Helen.

"Then I'll make some tea."

"I'll make it, Momma," said Lula. She quickly took three tin cups from the shelf and placed them on the table. Finding the jar where her mother kept her tea, she put some in every cup while Helen got settled.

"It be a true pleasure to be settin with ye an my Lula, Miss Baldwin," said Hattie.

"Now Hattie, how many times do I have to beg you to call me, Helen."

Her mother blushed. "I feel it be too familiar, a fine lady like ye."

"Oh, Hattie, I'm not one hair on my head finer than you."

Lula finished pouring hot water in the cups and was about to sit down when her mother said, "Please be fetchin the cornbread, child. It be in the larder."

Lula brought the cornbread to the table and sat down, then took her mother's hand. "Momma, I brought news about Nancy and Billy Boy."

"I already knowed," said her mother. "Mrs. Whitfield went down to the Salola fer tradin her honey an chestnuts, an heard tell." She reached to the center of the table and pulled a small envelop from under a bowl. "She brought me this, too. It be a letter from Nancy. Went to the place she worked, seein we got no address." She lowered her lids, embarrassed she couldn't read. "I be hopin ye be comin by to tell me what it speaks bout."

Lula picked it up. "Momma, you haven't even opened it."

"Didn't want to hurt it none."

Lula carefully opened the envelope and pulled out a small letter. Folded inside were five dollar bills. She handed them to her mother.

"Well, I'll be," said Hattie. "I keep tellin em to keep their earnins so as they can make their way an not be in need."

Lula took up the letter and studied it. "Billy Boy wrote it, Momma." Lula looked over at Helen. "Mrs. McGraw taught him how to read and write."

"Well, go head an tell it to me," implored Hattie.

Lula began reading. "I got to Pittsburg on a train with Nancy and Cecil Robertson. Mr. Justice done legally married them. Cecil works for his brother and I have me a job at the steel mill. The work is hard and fearful and the pay plenty good. I keep money out for room and board, and Nancy holds the rest for me. She works for the boarding house I stay at. This town is dirty and noisy, and I miss the mountains, but I sure am glad I came. Billy Boy McWade."

Hattie reached for the letter and turned away to put it and the money in a tin. Lula knew her mother didn't want anyone to see her wipe her tears.

"Nancy told me Ned and Jake were working for a logger and were going off to Haywood County with them," said Lula as her mother returned to the table.

"Done knowed that, too. They came an said their goodbyes." She smiled wistfully. "Your pa, God rest his soul, would be proud seein all ye chillen doin so good fer yournselves."

"Where's Luke?" asked Lula.

"In the back field. Tryin to dig it up good fore sowin time."

Lula pulled the sweater from her sack. "Look what I brought him, Momma."

Her mother took up the sweater and caressed it. "Sho is fine. He be a heap pleased, needin such fer poor weather."

Helen reached in her basket, took out a package, and handed it to Hattie with a warm smile.

Hattie blushed and bowed her head humbly. "Thank ye muchly."

"Open it, Momma!"

Hattie carefully untied the string, then unfolded the paper to reveal a beautiful wool shawl. Lula jumped up and put it around her mother's shoulders.

"I helped Helen pick it out, Momma. It looks beautiful on you."

Hattie ran her hand down its tassels. "It pleasures me greatly," she said. Then she rose, went to the cupboard, and brought out a small package. She handed it to Helen. "I knowed ye'd be a comin ventually, so I made this fer ye."

Helen opened the cloth, pulled out a strung necklace, and held it up. "My. It's absolutely lovely." She put it around her neck and arranged it across her chest.

"I done saved up apple seeds special an sewed them in that string with fine silk thread Nancy brung me."

Helen grasped Hattie's hand. "Thank you so much, Hattie. I'll cherish it forever."

A feeling of contentment fell on them as they drank their tea. The door was open, and the sweet smell of irises blooming at the doorstep wafted in as they sat and enjoyed each other's company for another hour.

"Momma, can I take a cutting of your rose bush for Helen's garden? She'll love that it's sweet smelling and lusciously pink."

"I kin rightly do better. Got one started," said Hattie. "Figured Nancy'd be gettin married an be needin one fer her kitchen garden. Being she's gone, you might be takin it yerself when it's time to be leavin."

Helen looked over at Lula. "Why don't you go see if you can find your brother. He'll be upset if we have to leave without saying hello."

"Can't I stay?" pleaded Lula.

"Now, Lula Mae, ye do as ye be bid," said Hattie.

Lula stood behind her mother, put her arms tightly around her, and nestled her chin on her shoulder. "I never want to let you go," said Lula.

"Now, now." She patted Lula's arm. "Get a goin, like ye be bid."

Lula sighed and ran from the cabin into the sunshine. Spotting Luke leading their mule to the barn, she ran up to him.

"It's good ye come. Ma's been pinin fer ye," said Luke.

"I brought you a sweater. It's in the cabin."

"I do hope yer not runnin all over tarnation in them breeches," he said.

Lula laughed. "No. Just to hike up the mountain."

He took off the mule's hitch and hung it in the barn.

"How are you doing without Billy Boy and Big James?" asked Lula as she helped him give the mule some water and feed.

Not getting an answer, Lula said, "It's too bad Ned and Jake slipped off to go logging. I hope it's not too hard on you, all alone."

"I hain't alone. I got a hired hand."

"The same one you had when pa was sick?"

Luke nodded. "As fer Ned an Jake, they were so itchin to go, they twernt worth what it took to feed em."

He picked up a hoe and handed it to Lula, then grabbed one for himself. Lula followed him to the garden her mother had been hoeing, and the two of them finished every row without uttering a word. With that done, they went to the well, and Luke brought up some water. He took the ladle from its nail, dipped it in the bucket, and offered it to Lula. She took a long drink and handed it back, all the while aware she was under his gaze.

"What?" she asked when she could stand it no longer.

"Yer growed to be a right fine maid," said Luke.

Lula laughed and put an arm around his waist, burying her face in his side. He patted her on the head like her father always did, and she knew she pleased him.

"Let's go in. I'm hankerin for some food," he said.

As they entered the cabin, Lula noticed Helen twisting the lid onto her ink pen, before quickly putting it into her basket along with a piece of paper. The minute Hattie saw Luke follow Lula in, she jumped up, hurried to the hearth with a large bowl, and started dishing up some beans. Like most mountain women, she was accustomed to waiting on her menfolk.

"Lula, you take Miss Helen to the west side of the barn wheres I got the new rose bush laid by, while I rustle up vittles fer Luke.

After Helen exchanged greetings with her brother, Lula rose and went outside with her.

"First, I want to show you the bush it came from," said Lula. She took Helen to the east side of the cabin and pointed to a large, winding rose, already ablaze with plush pink blooms. "Come smell," Lula said as she offered one to Helen.

"How absolutely wonderful," said Helen.

"This rose bush came from England over a hundred years ago and has been kept going by our family ever since. Every winter, we bend it down and bury it, to be sure it makes it through the cold."

Lula led Helen to the barn, when a man came out. He was unkempt and stared at Lula for a longer moment than he should have before his gaze dropped to the ground. Lula said a fleeting hello and continued to the side of the barn to get the rose bush.

"Who was that?" whispered Helen.

"Luke's hired hand."

Keenly aware that Lula's blossoming womanhood was becoming apparent, Helen said, "I didn't like the way he looked at you."

"Don't worry. I stay clear of him when I'm up here."

Helen glanced at her watch. "Good heavens! It's already three-thirty. We'd better get going."

"Oh, can't we stay longer?" begged Lula. "You know the trip's always shorter going down."

"Let's not risk putting Essie in one of her moods," Helen said, making a slight face. "She'll be wanting to get back to Edelweiss, and you know how agitated she gets if we keep her from her liquid refreshments."

Lula laughed. "I wouldn't worry too much about that, Aunt Helen. Gus Gibson and his clan have had the biggest still in these mountains for as far back as I can remember. I bet she's sitting on his porch right now with a glass of whisky in her hand."

They returned to the cabin and Helen settled the small rose bush in her basket.

Hattie handed her a cloth-wrapped package. "Here be corn-bread an dried apples fer yer journey."

The three hugged and kept repeating their goodbyes, until Helen finally coaxed Lula on their way. Walking through the meadow, Lula kept looking back at her mother who stood with her faithful hound at her side watching them disappear over the horizon.

As they descended into the forest at the edge of the plateau, Lula was overcome with longing. More than anything in the world, she wanted Luke and her mother to come off the mountain. There was great opportunity in the valley for honest, hard-working men like her brother.

Suddenly the hopelessness of that dream stabbed her heart, for in all her travels with Essie, she'd come to know mountain folk like Luke. They were comfortable with their farming way of life and content to live in harmony with the land. Yet, how she wished her brother wasn't so proud of being withdrawn from the world below, unable to see any use for change and unwilling to embrace it. As for her mother, Lula was determined, that one day when she had a home and a family to share with her, she would bring her down to the valley to live out her days in comfort.

CHAPTER THIRTEEN

The noisy tooting of a horn outside the Edelweiss cabin made Lula scamper so quickly downstairs from her bedroom, she stubbed her toe. She sat on a step for a moment rubbing it, then jumped up and raced out the door with Essie right on her heels. Helen had been threatening to buy an automobile all summer, but actually seeing her driving one took Lula's breath away.

Essie puffed on her corncob pipe while circling the dark blue steel box. It sat on four whitewall tires, rumbling a noisy purr and belching out exhaust.

"What do you think?" Helen called out to Lula through her open window.

"It's... it's... Darn it! What do those flapper girls always say?" asked Lula.

"It's the bee's knees!" Helen sang out, laughing.

Lula ran around to the other side and fumbled with the door until she finally opened it. She slipped onto the leather seat and looked around.

"There's only room for two," she observed.

"There's a rumble seat in back for two more."

"I gotta see that!" Lula jumped out and ran to the back. She strained to twist a lever behind the rear window.

"Wait up. I'll get it for you," said Essie. She swiftly turned the handle and lifted, unfolding a sleek leather seat.

Helen laughed seeing Lula climb up in her bare feet and slide in. "You're a little monkey!" she called out.

Lula quickly climbed down and joined Essie who was inspecting the spare tire and luggage trunk sitting on a small platform on the back.

The two of them strolled around the car and ended at the driver's side. Essie put a foot on the running board and looked in at Helen. "Well, are you gonna let it run all day?"

"I had to take a minute to thank the Lord for getting me here unharmed," said Helen as she turned off the engine. "I went straight off the road lest I hit Ben Stuart's horse. It took the both of us to figure out how to back it out of there. After I got going again, I was praying so loud not to miss our lane that everyone who lives on the road was sure to have heard me. If I'd of passed it by, I don't know how I'd ever get back home."

"Who taught you how to drive it?" asked Lula.

"Oh that poor young man. He kept telling me I was going to strip the gears smooth. By the time I knew how to get it to stop and go again, we were already on the Chimney Rock Road, so I slammed on the brakes and ordered him out. When he said he needed to get back to the agency, I told him to walk!" She threw her head back and laughed. "Good Lord! I'll have to bake him some cookies and beg his forgiveness."

Essie and Lula helped her out, and they all tumbled onto the porch, laughing.

"I don't remember ever being in such high spirits," Helen said as she collapsed on a rocking chair.

"We've had an exciting day here too," said Lula. "Mr. Flack came by with a telegram and a letter for you. I'll go fetch them."

"I'm glad to hear someone's in good humor," said Essie as she paced the porch. "When I went to the Edney Inn for lunch, the place was buzzing with fearful rumors."

"Rumors?" said Helen as she fanned herself.

"The news from New York isn't good. The recession's gotten worse, and the brokerage houses are urging people not to liquidate their stocks."

Lula came running back out with the telegram and letter.

Helen studied them. "How odd. They're both from my brother."

"Read the telegram first," said Essie.

Helen's face paled as she read.

Finally, she looked up. "My brother says for me to stop all spending and withdraw my money from the bank. He said he sent me a letter explaining everything but was afraid it might arrive too late."

Essie picked the letter off Helen's lap, tore it open, and handed it to her.

"Read it!"

Helen took it and read, then sat staring off in the distance.

"Well, aren't you going to tell us what it says?" asked Essie.

"He says our stocks were plunging, and he was advised to sell everything. The dollar yield was less than a quarter of what they had been. He's put everything in gold and instructed me to cancel my trip."

She seemed dazed as she continued. "I thought the manager was acting strange when I went to the bank this morning to withdraw the seven hundred dollars for the automobile. When I ordered the travelers checks for our trip, he seemed hesitant for a moment. I asked if anything was wrong, and he went to great pains to assure me all was well. However, while I sat waiting for them to make up the checks, I remember thinking there were quite a few people lined up at the windows."

"How much do you have in the bank," asked Essie.

"I don't know exactly. At least two thousand."

"Well, it's past three, so they're closed. Now you'll have to wait until Monday."

"I must send a letter to my travel agent tomorrow morning."

"It'll be faster if you go up to the Edney Inn on your way back from the bank on Monday and phone him."

"Yes. I'll do that," said Helen.

Watching Helen pull herself up from the rocker as if it took all her strength, almost broke Lula's heart. That summer she'd been like a young girl, happily packing and gaily jabbering about their trip; now, as she slowly walked into the house with her usual straight-backed dignity, she looked every bit the refined, settled, fifty-year-old spinster.

Later, Lula peeled potatoes and carrots while Helen worked on the chicken and dumplings. With Katie out of town for a wedding, they'd been cooking together for the past few nights.

"I'll be telling Katie we won't be needing her again next summer," said Helen. "That way, she'll have plenty of time to secure work for next year."

They worked in silence until Helen said, "Thank God my aunt convinced me to earn a teaching certificate. Oh, how my mother carried on against it. She insisted I'd end up a spinster if I did." She reached in her apron pocket for a hanky and wiped her eyes. "I've got to go see if your school will hire me as a teacher. At the very least, I should be able to earn your tuition. That way we can continue spending our winters at the boarding house. I swear, I'll freeze to death if we have to stay here over the winter. I don't know how Essie does it." Helen stopped what she was doing and turned to Lula. "Do you think we can raise some chickens... maybe a pig?"

"It'll be fun," chirped Lula. "We can do that next spring. I can make us a bigger garden, too, on that sunny patch out front."

While Helen was busy with the chicken, Lula went in the dining room and set the table. She came back to find Helen seated at the kitchen table appearing dazed. Lula went to her side and put an arm around her shoulder. Helen grasped her hand and squeezed.

"It was a wonderful dream," said Helen. "I've already been to Europe three times. This time was for you."

"You can still take me on the tour," said Lula. "We'll read all your books and go there in our minds. Nobody describes a place better than you."

Helen strained to look into Lula's eyes. After a long, thoughtful moment, she smiled. "All right. We'll start on that trip tonight when I tuck you in."

"Paris!" cried Lula, throwing her arms in the air. "Tonight I want to go to Paris!"

"No, no, no," sang Helen, shaking her head. She lifted a

brow. "Tonight, we're going to sail for the port of Southampton with first class accommodations on the Olympic."

LULA HAD NEVER seen Helen in such a determined state. The day before, she drove to the Edney Inn and back several times so she'd have the courage to drive into Hendersonville that day to talk with the director of the Fassifern School for Girls. She'd been gone for most of the day, and it was getting late, worrying Lula. She heard the dogs yapping and ran to the porch to see the car coming up the lane. Helen pulled up, and when Lula ran down to open her door, she was stunned to see the bedraggled state her aunt was in.

"Are you all right, Aunt Helen?

"Yes, darling. Let's get dinner ready."

As they prepared the meal and put it on the table, Lula could see Helen was still in the purposeful mood in which she'd started the day. Essie had more than her usual dose of whiskey during dinner and was showing her meaner side before they were half-way through the meal.

"I've taken a teaching position at Fassifern," announced Helen.

"I knew you'd come up with some way to keep Lula in that school!" scoffed Essie. "I suggest you go out and sell that car, too!"

"No. I consider it a gift from God," Helen said. "If I hadn't gone out and bought it that morning, not only would I have lost all the money I had on deposit at the bank, I also would have lost the seven hundred dollars I paid for it."

Lula sensed it was going to be another night that didn't turn out too well. After the dishes were all washed and put away, Helen whispered to Lula that it might be a good idea for her to go to bed early, and that she wouldn't be coming up to say good night since she had business to discuss with Essie.

Lula lay in bed listening to the sounds of the night. The katy-dids clicked away even though it was late in the summer. She listened for the whippoorwill, but feared it was too early and hoped she could stay awake long enough to hear it. How she missed all the sounds of the mountains the months they were in town.

It seemed like only a blink of an eye, but by the dewy feeling in the air, Lula knew it had to be late when Essie's shrill voice coming from downstairs woke her.

"What do you mean, I can't stay here for the winter!"

This news shook Lula wide awake. She leapt out of bed, snuck onto the balcony, and made her way to the landing, all the while dreading the thought of having to confess her vile sin of eavesdropping to Father Phillips again.

"With what's happened with the stock market, my brother can only send me a fraction of what I've been receiving, and I absolutely must rent Edelweiss for the winter. I've talked with Father Phillips, and thank God, he's found someone to rent the place," said Helen.

Essie went to the sideboard, poured herself a drink of whiskey, and gulped it down.

"That's your fourth drink tonight," said Helen.

"What am I going to do with Brownie? You're already refusing to pay for your half of his upkeep. And what about the drugstore?!"

"Without the herbs from Granny McDowell, and with the sporadic hours you've been keeping, people hardly come to it anymore," responded Helen. "Then there's the improved roads. You know as well as I do that a lot of folks are finding it easier to go to Hendersonville to get their medicines and see doctors."

Essie flung her glass across the room. It smashed against the wall, splintering into a thousand pieces, making Lula flinch.

"Get a hold of yourself, Essie," Helen sternly ordered. "Carrie Sutter will let you stay with her up on Sugarloaf over the winter. I spoke with her about it today, and she said now that her husband has passed she'd welcome the company."

In her most soothing voice, Helen added, "Essie, with all your charity work and the way you've helped all the mountain people, I was proud to offer you a place to stay and sell your medications, but my situation has drastically changed. I am no longer a wealthy woman. My brother has written that our tenants are having difficulty paying their rents, and many of their stores are being boarded up. He tells me not to count on any more than what he is currently sending me. And, surely, you can't expect me to pay for a horse that I don't need or don't use. Besides, you shouldn't be riding at your age and with your problem with alcohol."

"My problem with alcohol! You have a lot of nerve! I'm a saint next to you! I wouldn't dream of stealing someone's child! We both know the minute you laid eyes on Lula you wanted her for your very own little girl. And now that you're her guardian, she might as well be!"

Lula sat on the stair landing listening to the same vicious accusations from Essie she'd heard over and over again throughout the years whenever she was in a drunken state and Helen lectured her about it. It puzzled her that Essie, who was known and respected throughout the mountains, who would do anything, make any kind of sacrifice to help someone who was sick, could let herself sink to this pitiful condition.

Lula didn't understand as much about people as Helen did, but she did know that two of the people she dearly loved were trapped in a web of their own making. Her brother Luke was caught in his blind refusal to see any value in the results of inevitable change, and Essie was drowning from her inability to free herself from the temptation of alcohol. It depressed Lula that Essie always made things even worse by soiling a friend's good intentions in order to make her misdeeds look minor by comparison.

Essie continued yelling her accusations, sending Romulus cowering under the couch, but Remus gently pawed at her leg as if he wanted her to stop. She glared at him in anger and kicked him against the fireplace.

His yelp and pitiful whimpering were more than Lula could stand. She ran down the stairs to comfort the poor animal. Helen was already crouching down to lift him from the hearth when Essie grabbed her arm. Lula dashed across the room, but before she reached Helen, Essie had flung her to the floor.

"Keep your hands off my dog!" shrieked Essie. "It's one thing you're not gonna take from me!"

Essie went to the sideboard and poured herself another drink. When she turned to see Lula helping Helen up, she slammed her glass down, ran over, and slapped Lula's face with enough force to make her lose her footing. Helen, now on her knees, clutched Lula in fear. Essie pulled her leg back and was about to kick Helen when Lula lunged at her.

The two of them struggled on the floor with Lula on top, trying to hold Essie down. Without warning, Essie stopped fighting and her eyes became wide and fixed. Lula looked up to see Helen pointing the barrel of a shotgun straight at Essie's chest.

"Get up, Lula," Helen ordered.

Lula gave Essie a quick glance. Terror was written across her face. Essie's fingers slowly released her, and Lula scrambled to her feet, trying to catch her breath.

"Get out." Helen said as she deliberately stepped forward to put herself between Lula and Essie. "Now." The stone-cold tone of her voice frightened Lula. She was sure if Essie lunged at her, Helen would pull the trigger.

Essie groped to get up, but kept falling over. Lula, crying openly, helped her to her feet and over to the couch. Essie dropped her head into her hands, wailing and begging for forgiveness like she had done countless times in the past. Only, this time was the first time she had ever struck either one of them.

Helen put the shotgun down at her side and stared at Essie for a moment. "Let's get her into bed," she finally said.

It was a struggle for them to wrestle Essie to her bedroom. Her arms flayed and she kept falling to her knees, pitifully asking the Lord to forgive her. Then, suddenly, she slipped from their grip and landed on the floor with a thud. Lula froze. Essie didn't move. Lula bent over her and listened to her breathe before looking up at Helen.

"It's all right. She's just passed out."

Helen grasped Essie from under her arms and Lula lifted her feet, and they dragged her onto the bed.

"I'll take it from here," said Helen. "You go to sleep, darling."

Lula left Essie's bedroom, but couldn't go upstairs without straightening the living room. There was no telling who might show up early the next morning. After a while, Helen came out and the two finished up.

"You're a good girl, Lula. I should've known you wouldn't leave us in a mess."

Finally, the two went up the stairs, their arms around each other's waist. At Lula's door, Helen kissed her tenderly on the forehead and said goodnight.

Lula slipped between the sheets and put her head on the pillow. She watched the lace curtains ruffle in the gentle breeze. Her racing heart gradually slowed as she listened to the repetitive beat of "whip-poor-will, whip-poor-will," coming from outside. She remembered how Billy Boy had told her that only the males sang out. Lula loved the way it sweetly trilled the "will" part of the call. She'd never laid eyes on the bird, knowing only what Billy Boy had told her, yet, she had been listening to its calls in the darkness of the night for as long as she could remember. She drew solace from the haunting tune—a comforting song from an old friend on this sad night.

Her tear-soaked pillow stuck to her cheek. She hadn't cried like this since her first night at Edelweiss when Essie had too much to drink and was mean to her. Helen's dead serious statement of "Get out" echoed in her brain. She was never going to forget those final words, or that moment, or the pitifully sad faces they all wore, for the three of them at that instant realized this tragic event had ended an unforgettable era. It was a time that had been filled with love for each other and a joyful feeling of sisterhood as together they cared for each other and the poor folk in the mountains. Tears ran freely and her heart ached. Lula knew Helen wasn't going to allow Essie to remain under her roof.

CHAPTER FOURTEEN
1933

The Fassifern School stressed three qualities they considered indispensable for an accomplished young lady—personality, charm, and graciousness. Lula's Aunt Helen possessed these attributes in abundance; and over the past four years, they had propelled her to the rank of the school's favorite teacher.

Because seventeen-year-old Lula was one of the few day students at the school, she didn't have the advantage of joining in nightly bedroom gab sessions that bonded girls for life. It could have been a handicap to her status at the school, but between having the popular French teacher as her aunt and her own ability to project an extraordinary aura of empathy to all she met, Lula had more than fit in. She was roundly liked.

"DO YOU WANT ME to drive you to the hospital?" Helen asked.

"No. It's only five blocks. I'll walk," Lula answered as she put on her coat.

Helen shook her head, "I don't know why I let you volunteer. You're spending more time every weekend at Patton Memorial than you are with me."

Lula hugged her. "I'm not simply pushing a cart around and

offering patients books and magazines, Aunt Helen. When the flu was raging through town, they let me help with the patients."

"Really, Lula. You're going to be graduating in a couple of months, and we still have to sew you a dress for the May Day Parade. I'm sure you'll be one of the Queen's most beautiful attendants." She pressed Lula's nose with her finger. "And you, my dear, had better start looking for a beau for the Junior-Senior Ball at the Grove Park Inn." She threw a hand in the air. "Oh my, we'll need a dress for that, too."

"I hope we hear from the Wesley Long Hospital soon," said Lula.

"Oh, you needn't worry about that." Helen pulled Lula's cloche tight around her head. "Once they read the reference letter from Patton's nursing director and see all the awards you've been given at Fassifern, they'll be thrilled to have you." She opened the door to their one-bedroom suite at the Waverly Inn and went down to the entrance hall with her. "Now, off with you."

Helen watched Lula for a while, then closed the door and fretted. When she'd helped Lula button her coat, she'd noticed that Lula's figure was getting more womanly, making the coat snug. Helen shook her head. The little dear knew she needed a new one, but knowing her aunt's circumstances, she was determined to make do. How she would like to buy that child the kind of clothes the other Fassifern girls had, but since the stock market crash, she was barely existing on her salary and the meager stipend her brother was sending.

She looked around the small suite. It wasn't elegant like the mansion she was raised in, but thanks to the rent from Edelweiss, she was lucky to have it. It had almost broken her heart those four years back, telling Essie she couldn't spend the winter at Edelweiss, and then to have to ask her to move out entirely, but a recent letter from Carrie Sutter, telling her that she and Essie were still enjoying each other's company, gave her peace of mind.

THE BRISK, COLD air hit Lula the minute she stepped onto the porch. It went with her mood. She was braced and excited about her future. Now that Helen was arranging to send her to nursing school in the fall, all her years at Fassifern seemed suddenly worthwhile. Although she never truly felt like she belonged there, the school was an important bridge to achieving her dream of becoming a nurse.

She reached the two-story brick building set back from the street and raced up its steps and down the hall to the nurse's room. She quickly hung up her coat and took off her hat. She was already wearing her uniform but needed to put on her cap. A nurse opened the door and walked in, giving Lula a quick glimpse of a gurney in the hall carrying a moaning man.

"What's wrong with him?" she asked the nurse.

"He's got a compound fracture."

The blood curdling scream Lula had heard as she reset Mr. Freeman's bone came back to her, making her grimace.

"Don't worry," said the nurse. "Before they reset it, they'll put him to sleep with ether, and he won't feel a thing."

"Ether," Lula repeated to herself. Another new word. She wondered if she'd find out how ether worked at nursing school. All the new procedures and medicines she was learning about excited her much more than the dozens of social events she was obliged to engage in at Fassifern. If they weren't so important to Helen, she'd have had none of it. If she'd had her choice, she would've gone to a public high school.

She was elated every time she recognized one of the herbal medicines the hospital was using. They weren't simply names of plants; they were precious memories. She knew what they looked like, what they smelled like, and where and how they grew.

Patients suffering from heart failure were being treated with digitalis, the same herb that Granny McDowell would utilize for the malady. Only, Granny called the sickness dropsy and treated it with tea made from the very foxglove flowers Lula had gathered on the mountainside.

She found her cart, took a few moments to straighten the books and magazines, and headed down the hall. She peeked into a room, and the woman in the bed waved at her with a big smile.

"I've been lookin for my little angel," the woman said. "I missed you all week."

Lula cheerfully found her some magazines and chatted amicably while she poured her fresh water and fluffed up her pillow. As she wheeled her cart out of the room, Lula felt the happiest she'd been since she was there the Saturday before.

The days she ran barefoot toting Granny McDowell's herbs and poultices were now long gone, as were the years she clung to Essie as they galloped on Brownie along rugged footpaths and wagon roads to aid the mountaineers. Yet, as she roamed the halls of the hospital, that same exhilaration of being part of a force for healing came flooding back to her and filled her with contentment. This is where she belonged. This is what she was meant to do.

EVER SINCE SHE met William McClure at Fassifern's St. Patrick's Day dance, Lula began looking forward to the Monday trips downtown where students from the Blue Ridge School for Boys strolled along Main Street hoping for a chance to talk with Fassifern girls.

Lula hurried from her class to the school's porch and looked around for her cadre of friends. They were mostly from wealthy families, who in spite of the Depression, had hung on to enough of their money to afford sending their daughters to prestigious Fassifern. The girls in her circle were willing to overlook the fact that she lacked the credentials to be considered of their social rank; however, it was obvious to all at the school that her aunt, Miss Helen Baldwin, did.

Spying her friends sitting on the railing, laughing and talking, Lula made her way through the gathered throng as their four chaperones emerged from the grand hall.

One of them clapped her hands to get everyone's attention. "Ladies, please get in formation."

Lula scrambled to be situated with her friends on the long driveway leading down the hill to the street from the school's imposing cluster of colonial buildings. As they marched in twos, her friend, Frannie, always eager to be with her, squeezed her hand and giggled. "Do you think your darling Mr. McClure will be there?"

"He's hardly *my* Mr. McClure. I only talked to him once at the St. Patrick's Day dance," said Lula.

Frannie giggled. "For almost two hours!"

"I was only being sociable. Since he wants to be a doctor, we had a lot in common."

"Did you tell him about your family?"

The question made Lula frown. "No, but I most certainly will if I ever talk to him again and he asks."

With the weather being unusually warm for April, Lula took pleasure in the four-block walk to Main Street. She didn't have money to spend on the kinds of trinkets the other girls bought, but she was always willing to browse in the stores with her friends and make favorable comments whenever they purchased anything.

Finally, one of the chaperones said, "Those of you who want to get ice cream and sodas follow me."

Lula and her friends rushed to line up behind the woman and march to the Economy Drug Store on Fifth and Main. Lula scanned the tables and counter as she entered. As usual, the girls who were considered the 'elites' had already gotten seats at the tables next to the boys from the Blue Ridge Academy and were already engaged in conversation with them. Lula and three of her friends settled down at the last empty table.

Frannie nudged her. "Did you see him?"

"Please, Frannie, don't make a fuss," Lula whispered.

Frannie nudged her again. "He's behind you."

They ordered ice cream sodas and were chatting away when Frannie, who kept looking over her shoulder, whispered to Lula, "I think he's got a crush on our lil ole May Queen, Elizabeth Whitcomb."

Lula casually sipped on her soda, hoping Frannie would stop her badgering, when the bell on the door jingled, causing Lula to look over. A woman in a granny bonnet and long skirt had come in. She was toting a large basket, and a small child clung to her skirt. The girls at the elite table snickered and pointed at them. The child couldn't help noticing and buried her face in her mother's skirt. Lula felt her ears burn.

One of the ladies serving at the counter scurried to the back for the owner. Lula's heart broke at the sight of the woman with bowed head and the little girl hugging her at her skirt. Lula could see there were eggs in the basket. The woman must've come down from the mountain to sell them. Lula rose from her chair and went over and smiled at the woman, then she crouched down next to the child, pulled a peppermint stick she'd bought at a store from her pocket, and said, "This is for you."

The child took it and smiled shyly. The owner came out and transferred the eggs from the basket to a large bowl. Lula stayed crouched, smiling at the child who licked the candy. The owner paid for the eggs and thanked the woman, who, as she turned to leave, gave Lula a slight curtsy and a "Thank ye."

Lula rose and opened the door for them. She started back to her table with everyone staring at her.

"Egad! Don't touch me!" cried Elizabeth as Lula brushed against her chair. "You've got to be covered with that child's germs! Ooh! And those dreadful rags they were wearing!"

Listening to the girls giggle, the blood rose in Lula's cheeks and her heartbeat drummed in her ears as she glared at Elizabeth.

"Remember the Fassifern creed?" Lula said. *I will look up, and laugh, and love, and lift.* We're supposed to lift people. There was nothing funny about those two. They needed to be lifted, not made fun of."

Lula made her way to her table, grabbed the sweater from her wire-backed chair, and told her friends, "I'll wait for you outside."

Lula was looking in the window of the next store trying to appear casual when someone tapped her on the shoulder. She turned to see the tall, dark-haired William McClure.

"You were very kind to that little girl. I totally agree with what you said to Elizabeth. Her behavior was frightful."

"No. I'm afraid I was too outspoken. It's always been one of my failings."

"My mother would've done the same thing," he said. "She was a suffragette ever since her college days, and so was my grandmother."

Lula noticed the crowd of Fassifern girls spilling out of the drugstore with their chaperone.

"I have to get in line," she told him.

When she turned to go, he called after her, "I'll see you at the dance you girls are throwing for the Blue Ridge seniors Saturday afternoon!"

After her last class that afternoon, Lula met up with Helen in the east parlor. As part of Helen's salary at Fassifern, she and Lula enjoyed lunch and dinner Monday through Friday in the school's dining hall.

"I had a chance to re-read the letter from the Wesley Long Hospital and study all the information they sent us," said Helen as they sat in the parlor waiting for the dining room to open. She perused the hospital's brochure, reading parts of it aloud. "After three years, you'll get a diploma and be eligible to take the State Board examination for your R.N. degree. I like that they're affiliated with North Carolina College for Women. It'll give you the added advantage of college work while you're learning a profession."

She turned to Lula. "Darling, are you sure you want to do this? Their rules are quite stringent." She peered at Lula over her glasses. "We both know what an independent spirit you are." Not getting a comment from Lula, she continued reading. "You'll only be free one-half hour each week and for five hours on Sunday. The rest of the time, you'll be on duty from 7 in the morning until 7 at night, and they're only allowing you a half hour for meals."

Lula, still embarrassed about the encounter at the drugstore, was only half listening. By now, what had happened at the Economy must have spread through the dormitories like wildfire.

"They're not going to charge tuition," Helen continued, "and will be giving you a monthly allowance of ten dollars the first year, twelve the second, and fifteen the third. You'll be getting your room and board and laundry, but we're going to have to pay for your uniforms and books."

Helen put the brochure in her purse. "It said they want you to come to Greensboro for a personal interview. If you're absolutely sure you want to do this, I'll arrange it."

Lula looked squarely at her aunt. "I'm absolutely sure."

The parlor was filling up, and soon the doors opened to the dining hall. Helen, got up and went in since she served as a proctor, rotating to different tables for each meal. Lula started in alone and noticed everyone was looking at her. She'd been going to Fassifern since she was nine and, by now, could read the mood in the room as clearly as words on a page. The way some of the younger girls were smiling and winking at her was a clear sign the air was thick with approval.

Frannie, all fidgety and excited, was already at their usual table, motioning for Lula to come sit next to her.

"Did your aunt tell you what happened to Elizabeth?" she whispered.

"No."

"Well, one of the chaperones told Dr. Sevier what happened in the drugstore, and he called her in for a conference. She has to write two letters of apology for her unladylike behavior, one to the owner of the Economy and another one for her to give to that woman the next time she comes in." Frannie squealed loud enough to get a nudge from the girl next to her. "Wait til you hear this: She can't go to the dance we're giving for the Blue Ridge seniors next week!"

After dinner, Helen and Lula walked together to their boarding house.

"Aunt Helen," said Lula.

"Yes."

"I know by now you've heard about what happened at the Economy. Thanks for not coming down on me for being so outspoken. I wish I could keep from losing my temper the way I do. I want you to know that I'll try harder not to in the future."

"Oh, I hardly hold out hope for that, Lula Mae," responded

Helen. "Remember, I was the one who had to yank the knife and fork out of the ham that first night you came to Edelweiss."

"HOW DO I look?" Lula asked her aunt as she twirled around, making her full skirt swing.

"Gracious, girl. I've never seen you so excited about one of Fassifern's dances." She looked into Lula's eyes. "Is there some beau you're looking forward to seeing?"

Lula, pretending she didn't hear her, twisted her ankle back and forth to get a better look at her shoes. "I hope I don't break my neck in these."

"Oh, they're not that high," her aunt laughed. "Besides, with the straps, they should stay nice and snug." Helen picked up a brush and started running it through Lula's bobbed hair. Her golden waves glistened. "I think you should let your hair grow out. I read in *Vogue* that longer hair was going to be in style this fall. You've got enough natural curl that it should be easy for you to maintain while at school. Come on, it's time to go."

They straightened the room and left in their car. Helen stopped at the top of Fassifern's driveway. "I'll pick you up at six. We've been invited to dinner at the Hendersonville Country Club, so don't go nibbling too much. And don't forget, you'll be needing a date for the Junior-Senior Ball."

Robust singing made them turn their heads. The bus from Blue Ridge was coming up the driveway. Lula said a quick good-bye to her aunt and hurried up the staircase to the broad veranda flanking both sides of the main entrance.

She was surprised to see the elites, who in spite of the absence of their most prominent member, were happily laughing and waving at the boys as they spilled out of the bus.

Frannie waved Lula over. "I looked over the records they're going to play. All fox trots and waltzes. You know, Paul White-man and his Orchestra stuff."

Another girl piped up, "Can't wait to get back to New York. Everyone on Long Island is crazy about swing jazz."

The whole afternoon on the porch, Lula kept looking for William, but he never appeared. After she danced with the third

Blue Ridge boy, she worked up the courage to ask him where he was.

"He's packing to go home to Bar Harbor. His grandfather's ill."

"Maine?" Lula asked.

The boy nodded.

"What about graduation?"

"He finished all his courses, except for a couple of papers he has to write. He'll mail them in, and they'll send him his diploma."

"I'm surprised they're letting him do that."

"Two of his brothers have graduated from Blue Ridge, and his dad went to Davidson with Dr. Sevier's son, so he's pretty well connected."

Disappointed, Lula strolled over to the porch railing and gazed down the driveway. A car coming up caught her eye. It stopped at the bottom of the staircase to unload someone. William jumped out, stunning her. He saw her and waved as he took the steps two at a time, calling out to her. He was breathless by the time he reached her.

"They're taking me to the train station, but I made them stop here." He handed her a piece of paper. "Here's my address. Can I have yours? I'd like to write to you."

CHAPTER FIFTEEN

Helen sat pumping the treadle of the sewing machine in the middle of the living room at Edelweiss. They had moved back to the mountains after Lula's graduation, and all their time was now spent preparing Lula for nursing school.

Lula read aloud from the school's manual. "The school uniform must be worn on duty. White oxfords with rubber heels and white hose are worn. A net must be worn over the hair at all times. The uniform must not be worn off the hospital grounds. Jewelry must not be worn on duty."

"Lord have mercy," remarked Helen under her breath as she listened to Lula read the hospital's rules and regulations. "That place sounds like a nunnery!"

"Probationers must be in bed with lights out at 10 p.m. Late permission will be granted once a week until 11 p.m." Lula continued.

"Good heavens! When am I ever going to see you?" said Helen. "I'm tempted to buy a house in Greensboro and quit teaching at Fassifern."

"Can you afford to do that?"

"Now that my brother has passed away, since he never married, I'm to inherit everything he had. The depression took its toll on his estate, as it did mine, but I figure once all is settled and his trustee sells most of his holdings, I should be able to buy a comfortable winter house. I've decided to keep his downtown properties. My father used to tell me that the value of land will always go up if you wait long enough. This pitiful economy won't last forever." She finished sewing a long seam on Lula's uniform skirt, then slowly shook her head and gazed ahead. "I was always careful with the money my mother left me, but I never expected to see such hard times. It's been a struggle, but somehow we made it."

"Getting a winter house would be really keen, Aunt Helen!" exclaimed Lula. "I hope it'll have running water and a flush toilet like the boarding house."

"Really, Lula. Of course, it will. Now go on and read me some more of that edict."

"Breakfast is 6:30 to 7:30; Lunch 12:00 to 1:00; Dinner 5:30 to 6:30." Lula laughed. "Here's one I know you'll approve of: Nurses must leave their rooms in good condition when going on duty. Beds must be made; all clothes and shoes must be put away; rooms must be open for inspection at all times. Dishes and silver from the dining room must not be taken to rooms."

"Does it say anything about your laundry?" asked Helen as she started to attach the skirt to the uniform's top.

"Collars and cuffs collected Monday at 7 a.m. Beds are stripped and bed linen ready for the laundry on Wednesday morning. Uniforms and personal laundry are put in a striped ticking bag, which the student must provide, and be ready for laundry Friday morning."

"That calls for me to run into town for more material," said Helen.

"Gee, they sound prudish," said Lula, making a face. "Listen to this, "Nurses are requested not to appear in bathrooms or corridors without wearing a robe or kimono."

"Can you take visitors to your room?"

"Let's see," said Lula. "Here it is. Visitors are not to be taken to the nurses' rooms or shown through the hospital without permission of the Superintendent of Nurses. Visitors are to be entertained in the living room or on the porch of the Nurses Home." Lula let out a shriek. "I can't believe it! Students are not permitted to have charge accounts."

"Well, of course not! What eighteen-year-old has a charge account!"

"All the girls at Fassifern. That's who!"

"Well, you know as well as I that there's not a one of them who will ever earn a living."

"I don't know about that, Aunt Helen. Marsha Evers is going to Bryn Mawr and wants to be a professor, and Lucy Benson is going to Vassar. She's planning on being a doctor like her father. He says they have a good science department."

"Lula, I do love hearing about the courageous women of tomorrow, but do you think you can put those papers down and cut out those aprons?"

Lula perked up her head. "Someone's coming up the lane."

She rushed to the window and saw it was Mr. Flack, the mailman.

"He must have a package for us," she said as she ran out to greet him.

Lula brought back a small box and some mail and gave them to Helen.

"Look. There's a letter for you, Lula," said Helen as she handed it to her.

Lula took it and slid down on a couch. She glanced up and saw Helen was looking on. Lula smiled. "It's from William McClure."

"That's nice," said Helen. She started casually unwrapping her package, but Lula knew her aunt was pleased.

Lula took out the letter with trembling hands and read. "I can't believe it!" she gushed. "He says his mother wants us to come up to Bar Harbor and spend a week with them!" She clutched the letter to her chest. "Oh, Aunt Helen, please can we go?!"

"My word, Lula. I imagine we can, but first we've got to finish all your outfits for school. Let's talk about it tonight, and you can write back to him tomorrow. I understand nights are cooler in Maine in the summer. If we decide to go, we'll have to choose our clothes carefully."

Except for taking a break for lunch, Lula and Helen spent the day working on her three blue and white stripe cotton uniforms. Helen studied the hospital's sewing instructions. "They want the hems on the uniforms and aprons exactly eleven inches from the floor." She rolled her eyes. "Lula, put on those dreadful oxfords, while I fetch the measuring stick."

With Lula standing on a box, Helen finished pinning the hem, then stood back and took a good look at her.

"Sakes alive, you're as pretty as a peach." She took out her hanky and dabbed at her eyes. Bittersweet tears had been threatening to fall all morning. "And that's saying something with you in that drab, unstylish dress." She clapped her hands. "What am I doing, standing here crying. Hurry and take it off so I can finish the hem." She started to help Lula out of the dress.

"Wait! I want to look in the mirror upstairs," Lula cried out.

"Go ahead," Helen said, then followed her up.

Lula stared at herself in the full-length mirror with tears running freely down her cheeks. Helen handed her the hanky.

Lula looked at her pleadingly. "I know we went to see my momma last week, but can we please go up again tomorrow?"

"Darling, it's too soon for me to make that hike. My knees won't stand it."

"Then let me go by myself. It won't be the first time. Please, Aunt Helen. I want my mother to see me in my uniform. I won't be able to visit her again til next summer, and this is how I want her to picture me whenever she thinks of me. My mamma knows little of the outside world, but once she sees me wearing this uniform, she'll understand why I can't be up there on the mountain with her. She'll know I'm on a journey; that I'm on a mission."

Helen sighed. "I understand, darling. I suppose you can go in the morning."

"Can I *please* stay overnight?"

"You might as well. I'll take you up to the trailhead and meet you there on Tuesday. We can't keep asking Gus Gibson to bring you home. If you leave your mother by noon, you should be back around three."

"Can I take a pair of the white hose to put on?"

Helen put an arm around her as they started for the stairs.

"Yes. And you can wear the new slacks I bought you. You might as well wear the new watch, too. That way you'll be sure to get back down in time." She laughed. "Not the hair net, though."

"Oh, no, Aunt Helen. When I introduce Nurse Lula to my mother, she's going to be dressed in the dead-serious uniform that meets every requirement of Wesley Long Hospital."

Helen laughed. "I'm beginning to think this whole thing is dead serious—uniforms, aprons, a watch with a second hand, cuffs, collars, white hose, and those awful white oxfords. Good gracious, child, I doubt Florence Nightingale herself had to go through such a rigmarole."

THE ROAD TO GUS Gibson's place was improved enough to make the ride up in Helen's car enjoyable. Helen stopped at the trailhead, and they sat quietly until a Carolina wren sitting on a fencepost let out a trill and broke the silence.

"Are you gonna visit Essie while you're up here?" Lula finally asked.

"I'll go on up to Carrie Sutter's place and see if she's there. The last time I tried, no one was home."

"Do you think she's still boarding with her?"

"I know she is. The pastor at Mt. Moriah told me so," said Helen. Her nails clicked as she drummed them on the steering wheel. "Not a day goes by that I don't worry about her."

"Me, too. If she's there, please tell her I love her."

"I will, and you do the same for me with your mom." She gave Lula a peck on the cheek. "Go on now and remember tomorrow at three. I'll be waiting. And if the weather turns bad, stay another day."

Lula got out, slung her pack over her shoulder, and waved as she set off into the woods. She was making good time and enjoying the coolness of the early morning. The climb became much steeper, and she smiled remembering how, at seven, she had to pull Granny McDowell up the steeper grades much of the way home. She laughed, remembering how she'd had to sometimes get behind and push Granny's rump until she made it. She admitted to herself that she was a feisty, determined little creature of the mountains and made up her mind to be as intent in the practice of nursing.

After a few hours trudging uphill, she finally arrived at her favorite section of the trip. The high bald cliff with its breathtaking view of the valley was a perfect place to sit down and rest. She took out the sandwich Helen had packed for her and ate, thinking that in a couple of months she would be starting a new life, but knowing that a part of her would always be of this time and this place.

She sat solemnly reflecting on the changes she'd witnessed in her short life, changes that no one could ever reverse. The way the modern world was closing in on her beloved mountaintop reminded her of the hawk she had seen one afternoon. It had swooped down on a timber rattler as it lay sunning itself. The hawk fluffed out its feathers and menacingly dug its deadly talons into the snake. She could still see the serpent writhe straight up into the air in anguish, and after an agonizing moment, drop back down to the ground. Then the hawk squeezed more fiercely, making it writhe even higher. When the snake could struggle no longer and lay motionless, the hawk flew off with it limply dangling from its talons.

It saddened Lula to realize that her cherished community, like the snake, didn't stand a chance once the outside world got its grip on it. Even the bottom of the narrow footpath on which she had made her way down the mountain with old Granny McDowell those ten years past had been transformed into a road on which trucks and motor cars could easily travel.

The massive cliffs to the colony's north had once walled off the world burgeoning in the gorge below. But now, from the very spot her brother had taken her for her first look at the world beyond, she could look down and see elaborately dressed people trek up the rock-lined trails and climb the stairs that had conquered the mountain. Once these sightseers reached the top of Falls Creek, awestruck, they'd watch the water tumble over the cliff.

These days, when the handful of children that were still living in the colony saw their first glimpse of the scene below the falls, they would see, not merely four or five buildings, but dozens in what could rightly be called a village, as well as cottages sprinkled along both sides of the gorge. Instead of the carts she'd seen pulled by horses and mules, they would marvel at the automobiles swirling along the road like bumble bees, stopping at lean-tos and the rustic little shops clustered in the village.

Life, as it had been lived for generations on top of the mountain, would soon be gone forever. Even now, back in town, they referred to it as the Lost Colony. The ancient ways they'd clung to for over a hundred and fifty years were becoming a thing of the past. Folks like her brother Luke were trying to escape from the modern world just like the timber rattler tried to escape from the hawk, but change would win in the end. The thought made her sad.

Over the years, she had witnessed the colony's parents hunger for their children to acquire the learning they'd never had and yearn for a better way of life for them. A few years back, a woman from the village of Chimney Rock made the treacherous journey up the mountain from below the falls, so she could teach school for four months one summer. Appreciative folks carefully cut the grass and weeds away from the sides of a foot path to keep the dew from wetting her feet as she traversed it daily from the nearby house where she boarded.

Billy Boy and Nancy, and her other three brothers all had that same hunger and had set out to satisfy it. Now, it was her turn.

LULA MADE GOOD time getting to the plateau. As tired as she was, the minute their cabin came into view, she filled with energy and ran the rest of the way. No one was about, but smoke rose from the chimney. Breathless, she flung the door open. Stunned to see her mother on a cot at the hearth with her faithful hound lying at her side, Lula rushed over.

"What's wrong, Momma? Why are you in bed?"

Hattie sat up. "Don't ye be afeared child. My bones twer givin me a fit, an I be warmin em up. Now tell me what done brought ye so soon."

Lula quickly made her mother a cup of tea and placed it on a stool next to her.

"How come there's no pots cooking on the hearth?" asked Lula.

"Luke be gone over Sugarloaf Mountain, so I gave the ole pot a rest."

The two laughed, then Lula said, "I have a surprise for you, Momma. Drink your tea." She got up and skipped behind the cot out of her mother's line of vision. "Now don't you peek."

"Jumpin Jehoshaphat, girl. Yer a twirl."

Lula quickly shed her clothes, carefully put on the stockings, and proceeded to don the complete uniform.

"Close your eyes, Momma, and don't open them until I tell you to." When she stood in front of her mother, her back ramrod straight and head held high just like Helen, she whispered, "Open your eyes."

Hattie clasped her hands in awe. "Praise the Lord, ye be a doctor woman."

Lula slowly turned around. "Do I look like those pictures I showed you?"

"Ye sho nuff do."

After her mother's thorough inspection of her uniform, Lula said, "I better get everything off and put away." She carefully took off the hairnet. "Where's the hired hand. I didn't see a soul when I came up."

"Luke got rid a Zeb."

"Has he gone off the mountain?"

"No. He be stayin in the McDuffy's old cabin. He twas a good worker an abided by the Good Book til he got hisself afflicted with that evil moonshine. Now, he got hisself a still, an plenty a men folks are showin up to buy his whisky."

"Where did Luke go?" asked Lula while fixing a pot of beans and fatback.

"That ol mule finally died an he be oer the mountain to fetch another."

Lula could see the wood pile was low. With the hired hand gone and the mule dead, it was apparent her mother had taken on a lot more work. Probably the reason she was resting mid-afternoon.

"I'm going outside to get some wood," she told Hattie.

"Don't be troublin yerself. Luke will see to it."

Lula fluffed up her mother's pillow and told her to rest, then started bringing in the wood. After stacking the final load, she saw her mother had fallen asleep. She had better check the barn and see to the chickens and pigs.

Lula found that the stock had already been fed and eggs collected, but her mother's garden needed weeding. A short time with the hoe soon had the rows neat and tidy. An eerie quiet made her look around. She knew enough to be wary, for a lurking bear or coyote could have scared off all the birds. Seeing nothing unusual, she stood leaning on the hoe remembering the sounds of her childhood—everyone screaming as Billy Boy ran through the garden chasing a pig that escaped from its pen; the incessant chopping of firewood; Big James playing the mournful Scottish ballad on his tin whistle as everyone sat at the hearth listening to her mother somberly sing *Sweet William on his deathbed lay, fer love a Barbry Allen.*

After supper, Lula sat with her mother in front of the fire. Her mother put a hand in hers, and Lula, feeling the roughness, took it up and studied it in the flickering light. The coarse, thick, twisted fingers told of more hardship than most women would ever know. Then she remembered the softness of Helen's hands when she ran them affectionately down her face. These two women were so different, yet clung to one thing in common. They both loved her as their own. Tears welled in Lula's eyes. Somehow, and at a time unknown to her, the two had come to an understanding that they would share her. Like herself, they had accepted that they were at a moment in time that had to span one hundred and fifty years in one generation; a time when the old way of life had to bow to the new.

Lula rose and found her mother's coffee tin. She spooned some into the smoke-blackened pot, poured in water, and hung it on a hook over the hot coals. "I know you like coffee after dinner, Momma. I do too."

Evening coolness settled on the cabin, and the two pulled their chairs close to the hearth. The distinctive smell of smoke from burning oak and hickory brought Lula's memories flooding back. She could see her father puffing on his corncob pipe as he gazed in the fire, content to be surrounded by his family and pleased that he was able to provide for them.

"This ol place is near onto two-hundred yars, I reckon," said Hattie. "I knowed, after Luke, it will be forgotten, an vines will swaller it like they have so many others." Hattie looked around the cabin. Shadows cast by the fire danced on the walls. "Put some apple wood to the fire," she told Lula. "The flame be brighter an full a colors."

"That's right, Momma." Lula laughed, for she knew what her mother would say next.

"It be so, cuz the fairies dance in apple wood flames."

THE NEXT MORNING, Lula stood a chunk of wood up on the stump and picked up the axe. She split it with one blow and tossed it on the pile. Her mother emerged from the cabin as Lula set another one in place.

"Gittin late. Ye not be keepin Miss Helen awaitin," she said.

Lula put the axe on the porch and started gathering up the wood. "As soon as I get these in the house, Momma. I don't want you running out before Luke gets home."

Once it was done, Lula brushed herself off and gave her mother a warm hug. "I wish I could put you in my sack and take you with me."

Hattie turned her head, but not fast enough to hide her tears.

"Git, afore I fall to pieces."

Lula threw the sack over her shoulder and started across the meadow, every once in a while, looking back and throwing a wave. Lula reached the thicket satisfied that her mother had seen her in her uniform and had understood. Content that her mother would now be able to think of her as Nurse Lula, she was filled with hope in the future that lay in front of her. Then she thought about the trip to visit William McClure and his family and danced down the path.

CHAPTER SIXTEEN

Helen drove past Carrie Sutter's house and was happy to see the old black Ford Father Philips had sold to Essie parked in the yard. She patted the basket of scones she'd brought for her. Good, she thought. When Lula comes down from visiting her mother, the two of them could stop by and have a nice visit with their old friend. She turned around in Gus Gibson's yard and went back down to the trailhead to wait.

She sat in her car watching two sparrows chase each other in and out of the thicket. The cloudless North Carolina blue sky and the sweet smell of a newly mowed meadow exhilarated her. Anxious to see Lula, she glanced at her watch every few minutes.

By the time three-thirty rolled around, her mind was in a turmoil, thinking of all kinds of mishaps that might've happened on the rugged trail. How could she have let her precious Lula climb that treacherous mountain by herself. Did she even make it up to see her mother? No! Don't let your imagination run wild, she told herself. Something trivial like a twisted ankle could've slowed her down.

Her eyes stayed glued to the clearing, and her breathing grew more rapid with every passing second. Calm down, she told herself. Maybe Hattie was sick, and Lula had decided to stay behind for another day. No. Lula would never leave her waiting and wondering. She would've sent word with her brother.

She kept checking her watch. If Lula didn't show up soon, she'd have to do something. But what? She wasn't strong enough to bring Lula down the mountain by herself if she were hurt. Thank God for Essie! The Lord must've made sure to have her handy. She quickly got out of the car and set out on foot for Carrie Sutter's cabin, leaving the car behind so Lula would know she was nearby in case she came from out of the woods.

Remus and Romulus started barking as she approached the cabin. The door flew open, and Essie stood with pipe in hand looking surprised. Helen, relieved to see her sober, quickly told her about Lula.

"Of course, I'll go with you," said Essie. "If she broke a leg or got hurt, she has enough sense to sit and wait for someone to come get her. Though I suspect we're going to run into her on the way." She studied Helen. "You can't make it up the mountain in that skirt. Come in and change into a pair of my britches while I pack my bag. If she has a broken leg, I'll need rags for the splint."

By the time they made their way to the car, Essie could see Helen was out of breath and disappointed at not finding Lula.

"I think you should sit here and wait," said Essie. "I'll go up and look for her and send word down if we plan to stay up in the colony."

"No! I can't just sit here."

"All right, but you need to keep up. If she's hurt, we have to get her back down before nightfall."

They set out and were making good time, but as the terrain grew steeper, Helen began slowing Essie down.

"Why don't you wait for us here," Essie told her.

"No. I'll lose my mind waiting." Helen hurried ahead. "Let's go."

Essie put a hand on her shoulder. "Calm down, Helen. She's a strong girl, and she knows these mountains."

"Yes, of course she does."

They started up again and hit a slow but steady pace. Essie stopped and pointed to a bald cliff in the distance. "That's the halfway point. The colony's over the next ridge."

The path became narrower between two massive drifts of rhododendrons. Essie looked over her shoulder to see Helen below, taking a rest before tackling a huge boulder. Essie turned and started up again, when something caught her eye. She looked back and scanned the thicket, then cautiously pushed a low hanging hemlock limb aside and caught her breath.

Helen yelled from below, "I'm afraid I'm going to need some help getting up this boulder."

"Stay there and sit a while. I'll be right down," Essie shouted back.

HELEN SAT DOWN on a rock and tried to slow her breathing. Both she and Essie were in their mid-fifties, but she'd never been as athletic, and the climb was taking more out of her. On top of that, she was in a panic and hyperventilating. She had to calm down or she wouldn't be able to go on. She sat erect taking long, slow breaths. After what seemed too long for Essie to be gone, she shouted out for her.

How strange. No answer. Sensing something was wrong, she studied the boulder. There was no way she could pull herself up on it, so she reached up and grabbed a small tree next to it and pulled herself up enough to get a toehold on the rock, then, using every ounce of strength she could muster, grabbed the tree hand-over-hand until she was on top of the rock.

She stood up and froze. Essie was coming with Lula slung over her shoulder. Why was the child wearing her uniform? The woods started to spin, and Helen leaned against a tree to keep from falling. Her head cleared as Essie neared. She had never seen a graver expression on her friend's face.

"Is she...?"

"No. It's a concussion."

Helen gasped in horror as Lula's lithe, fair arms and golden hair swayed with Essie's deliberate steps as she passed.

"Go get her sack. I left it on the trail," Essie commanded. "Look around and make sure nothing's been left behind."

Helen stumbled forward along the path, afraid she might faint or scream until she tripped over Lula's sack. Feverishly, she searched the long grass, then lifted a hemlock bough and looked underneath. It was dark, but lying on the ground were the slacks she had bought Lula. She picked them up and couldn't comprehend the torn, soiled item. At first, she thought the pinkish bundle on the ground was a pile of leaves, then she reached for it, and the hair on the back of her neck stood up. It was Lula's underwear.

Clutching it to her chest, she fell to her knees and let out a blood curdling scream. Then, an anger like she had never felt before seized her. That's what took Essie so long! She was putting Lula's uniform on her naked body! She jumped up, put everything in the sack and started back down, stoically putting one foot ahead of the other until she caught up with Essie.

When they finally reached safer ground, Essie gently slid Lula off her shoulder and carried her in her arms.

Seeing the blood on Lula's skirt, Helen bit her fist to stop a scream.

As they neared the trailhead, Essie asked if Helen had a blanket in her car.

"In the back, in the rumble seat," she responded.

"I want you to go get it and bring it to me. I don't want anyone to see her like this."

Helen hurried to the car, retrieved the blanket, and ran back into the woods.

"Now spread it on the ground," ordered Essie.

Helen quickly obeyed, then watched Essie lovingly lay Lula down. She wrapped her in the blanket, then covered her blood-smeared face before gently lifting her again.

"Now get the door."

Once Helen had the car door open, Essie swiftly emerged from the woods and slid in with Lula in her arms.

"Drive home," ordered Essie once Helen was behind the wheel.

"You're not making sense. She needs to go to the hospital, and we need to call the sheriff."

"You're the one not making sense, Helen. You know as well as I that rape is always considered the woman's fault. They'll only blame it on her and look at her with disdain. Worse yet, once this gets out, she can forget about becoming a nurse... and you can count on it getting out. We need to take care of this amongst ourselves, or she'll be scarred for life. God help me, I've seen it happen dozens of times."

"What about the person who did this to her?" asked Helen.

"Nothing! That's what! I'm pretty sure it's that Zeb who used to work for her brother. Remember, you told me you didn't like the way he looked at her. If she accuses him, the sheriff will say it was her fault and sweep it under the rug. That's just the way it is. Now, let's go!"

CHAPTER SEVENTEEN

Helen finished folding the apron and put it in the box with all the other items Lula had been planning to take to school. She picked up the envelope addressed to William McClure and tucked it in the box, then buried her face in her hands and sobbed. Hearing Essie's footsteps on the stairs, she quickly wiped her eyes with her lacy hanky and looked up.

Essie descended the stairs, strolled over to the box, and fingered the apron.

"Did you tell her what happened to her?" asked Helen.

"Yes. But she already knew." She lit her corncob pipe and took a puff. "You know, after all she's been through, her biggest fear was that her mother might find out. I assured her you and I are the only ones who will ever know." Her brows furrowed. "Why are you putting everything in a box?"

"Well, she'll hardly be in condition to go to school in September. I still have to get down on my knees every night and pray to God she'll come out of this."

Essie puffed on her pipe and paced. "I don't know. Going off to that hospital might be the best thing for her. Her schedule will be so full, she won't have a minute to think about anything else."

"What are you talking about?" said Helen. "You haven't been able to leave that girl's side for the past three days, and that school starts in less than three months."

"If she doesn't move on with her life, and you keep her here,

159

she'll never get over it," said Essie. "I've seen it happen."

"I'm not planning on keeping her here. I've written to my brother's trustee and told him not to sell the family's summer place on Sullivan's Island. When she's on her feet again, I'm taking her there to spend a few weeks." Helen gazed off in space. "That place has healing powers." She came out of her trance and flipped her hand in the air. "Maybe we can do some shopping in Charleston, too. The change will do her good."

"A couple weeks walking on the beach might help," said Essie, "but she needs more than a shopping spree on King Street to get over this. She needs to concentrate on her future."

The squeak of an opening door made them both glance up. Lula, looking frail, appeared at the balcony railing in her nightgown.

"Aunt Helen, Essie's right. I need to go to school and get on with my life."

Lula's sudden appearance stunned Helen, but only for a moment.

"Of course, if that's what you want, darling, but it certainly won't hurt to go to the beach for a couple of weeks."

"DO YOU THINK she's going to be all right back there?" Helen asked Essie as she turned and waved at Lula who was settled in the rumble seat.

"Yes, or I wouldn't have put her there," said Essie as she pulled onto the Chimney Rock Road. "When is the train getting to Charleston?"

"Not until seven-thirty tonight."

They came around a steep curve, and the line of stopped wagons and cars disappeared around the mountain. A man who was pacing next to his car came up to Essie's window and looked in.

"A horse got spooked and backed up. Their wagon's been hanging off the road ahead, but I think they've unloaded it enough by now to pull it out. It shouldn't be too much longer."

Helen glanced anxiously at her watch. Their train was scheduled to leave at nine-thirty. Just as she was about to give up on getting there in time, the vehicles ahead started moving.

As Essie pulled up to Hendersonville's Seventh Avenue station, a conductor's voice boomed, "All aboard the Carolina Special. Next stop Spartanburg."

Lula and Helen hurriedly got out and assembled their carry-ons, while Essie found someone to load their suitcases onto the train.

"Send me a telegram when you know when you're coming back, and I'll pick you up in your car," Essie shouted to Helen who was waving goodbye from the train's window.

They quickly found a seat, and the train lurched forward. Startled, Lula let out a muffled cry. Helen put her hand in Lula's, and squeezed. When Lula gave her a reassuring smile, Helen put an arm around her, pulled her near, and tenderly murmured, "My darling Lula Mae."

The almost ten-hour trip that stopped at almost every little town in South Carolina was broken up with sightseeing from the observation car and two trips to the dining compartment. By the time the train reached Charleston, they were both happy to be on solid ground again.

Lula gaped in awe as Helen rushed her through Union Station. She'd never seen such a huge indoor space. Her first breath of air outside told her why so many people from Charleston spent their summers in the mountains. The air was as thick and sticky as honey. She could feel sweat running down both her front and back while waiting for Helen to hire one of the dozens of motorized and horse driven hacks waiting at the station. A foghorn blasted, making Lula jump. She looked around and could see a vast waterfront nearby.

Their luggage was finally loaded on a horse-drawn surrey, and it started its clip-clopping journey on the wide brick-paved street. A nearby trolley rang its bell and startled Lula, but seeing it filled with cheerful passengers, she smiled with relief.

She clutched Helen's hand while staring wide-eyed at all the new sights passing by as the hack made its way through the heart of downtown. Even at this hour, the sidewalks overflowed with people. The smell of food being grilled, fried, and baked in the dozens of restaurants lining the street lingered in the thick, humid air. As foreign as it was, the scene stirred Lula.

Just past downtown, the hack pulled onto the Cooper River Bridge. Lula strained from her seat to see the bay to the east, the sun on its journey toward the horizon to the west, and the downtown behind them slowly starting to light up.

Once over the nearly three-mile long iron span, the terrain grew lush and the road to the island, dusty. It surprised Lula when Helen told the hack's driver to stop in front of an old, weathered beach house. It stood on stilts, starkly surrounded by sand. Helen jumped out of the hack, hurriedly paid the driver, and ran up the steps to the porch. After retrieving a key from a ledge and unlocking the door, Helen flung it open with a delighted flourish.

Lula, somewhat stunned by Helen's eagerness, helped the driver carry the luggage up to the porch, then stood looking over the railing at the expansive marsh glistening orange in the sunset. She entered the house and found it more sparse and rustic than Edelweiss. Mementos from the ocean were scattered about— shells, sand dollars, an ancient oar hanging on the wall. The sound of doors being flung open echoed down the hall as her aunt went from room to room.

"Just as I remember it!" Helen proclaimed as she picked up Lula's suitcase and took it into a bedroom. She pulled up a shutter and hooked it onto the ceiling, revealing a screened opening.

Hearing the sound of crashing waves, Lula rushed over and looked out, but all she could see was moonlight flickering off the ocean waves.

"Help me lift all the shutters and get some air in here," said Helen as she raced from one room to the next.

It was obvious to Lula that her aunt was thrilled to be at her family's beach house. That night, as Lula lay on the cast iron bed listening to the waves break on the shore, she was convinced that this weather-beaten old place was going to tell her more about Helen than anything else ever had.

Lula had been up since sunrise exploring the beach. As she neared the house, she saw her aunt waving to her and hurried along. Cupping the shells she'd collected in her blouse, she ran up the steps to the porch.

"I managed to get the gas stove going, so I've made coffee, and we have the hardboiled eggs and scones I brought," Helen announced.

Lula was hungrier that she'd been for days and was in the middle of her second scone when someone knocked at the kitchen door. They both got up to see who it was.

An elderly man with a deeply-tanned face and thick white hair that stood out like a lion's mane smiled at them.

"I'm Bobby Walters, but folks around here call me Bubba. Mr. Kingston sent word by phone to Archie's that you'd be needing groceries." He was hanging onto tongs gripping a big block of ice. "I brought this for you. Yesterday, I cleaned out your water barrel and had it filled. The water man won't be around again til next Monday, so watch how much you use. I also cleaned the rain barrel on the roof so you can take a shower."

"Well thank you kindly, Bubba," said Helen.

"Mr. Kingston says we're supposed to take good care of you."

"How thoughtful!" cried Helen. "I swear we might've starved to death if you hadn't shown up." She pointed to the oak icebox. "Please put the ice in there." She looked at Lula. "We must thank the Lord for my brother's trustee seeing to us like this. Get your shoes on, Lula. Bubba's going to take us to Archie's to get our groceries."

"I'd really like to stay here, if it's all right with you."

"If that's what you want, dear. We'll be back in no time at all," said Helen as she scurried out with Bubba.

Lula cleared the table, then strolled out to the back porch and gazed at the marsh. A boy of around twelve was fishing on the dock. She went down and crossed the dirt road, causing him to look up and wave.

She meandered over to him and said, "Can I look in your bucket?"

"Yes, Ma'am."

Lula laughed. It was the first time anyone had called her Ma'am. She liked the way he stretched out his words as did Helen and the Fassifern girls from the deep South. He tied up his rod and placed it on the dock, then dug out a net bag from his pack.

"I'm gonna get me some oysters next," he said.

"Oh, can I go with you?"

"Not dressed like that, you can't."

She looked at her skirt. "It's okay if it gets wet." She held onto a post as she took off one shoe and sock, and then the other. "There! Let's go."

"WELL, IT'S ABOUT time you came back," said Helen as Lula peeked in the door.

Lula curled her finger and motioned for the boy to follow her. Helen stood with her fists on her hips, curious to see what Lula was up to.

"Aunt Helen, this is Royal Fillmore. Royal, meet my aunt."

He held up a bag of oysters. "A dozen of these are yours."

Helen clasped her hands. "Wonderful! We'll have them tonight."

"Do you want to go out with me again tomorrow?" Royal asked Lula. "I'll get my uncle's boat and take you to a bigger bed. Archie pays good money for fresh oysters."

Lula gave him an enthusiastic yes, while Helen, who had been glaring at her wet skirt, added, "And she'll be dressed appropriately."

That night, after Helen found a pair of britches in one of the drawers and cut them at the knees for Lula to wear, they sat on the porch rocking.

"Did you come here often when you were young?" Lula asked.

"All my life, up until my mother's death. The summer heat in Columbia is unbearable, so we spent them here at the beach. My father would come on weekends, and a woman who had been born a slave on a nearby plantation did all the cooking and cleaning. She taught me how to grill, fry, and bake every kind of seafood, and my brother taught me how to catch it."

Lula and Royal fell into a pleasurable routine of fishing every morning. They'd spear flounder in the shallows, trap blue crabs from the pier at the tip of the island, and reel in spot tail bass and speckled trout from the boat in the estuary. Every night, Lula was amazed as she sat on a stool watching Helen broil fish, whip up shrimp and grits, or lovingly prepare a Low Country Boil with shrimp that came off ocean-going boats, and that Archie gave them in trade.

Afternoons were spent casually reading in the breezy shade of the porch with occasional strolls along the beach. Lula relished the evenings when she and Helen would rock on the porch watching the waves come in and the sky turn various hues of pink and blue as the sun sank behind them. Lula discovered a particular freedom in the darkness of the night when no one could see into her eyes or read the expression on her face or see the tears streaming down her cheeks. Where words hung starkly in space for but a moment before evaporating into nothingness.

Nearing the end of their stay, Lula didn't want to let these days of mindless joy end, yet knew it was time to talk about things that had been left unsaid as the two rocked on the porch.

As darkness cloaked them, Lula said, "Do you think I can ever get married?"

The sweet, lyrical voice she'd fallen in love with when she'd first heard it at the age of seven rose from the night and caressed her. "Of course, you can. Things like this have happened throughout the ages, and life has gone on."

"I hope so, Aunt Helen. It just about broke my heart to write to William declining his and his mother's invitation for us to visit them in Maine." She let out a pitiful sob. "Will I ever stop feeling sullied, Aunt Helen?"

"Yes, darling, you will. Remember, rape has nothing to do with sex. It's always about power. Power to inflict cruel control over someone else who's weaker." Helen reached and squeezed Lula's hand. "You're the same beautiful person you've always been."

The peacefulness one only hears at the beach in the night

slowly fell over them. No gulls calling, no children laughing in the surf, only the soft, sudsy sound of waves licking the beach.

"Aunt Helen, why didn't you ever fall in love and get married?"

"Oh, I was very much in love at one time, but my brother wouldn't let me marry him. He said Arthur wasn't good enough for a Baldwin, but I knew he felt it was my place to remain in the home and take care of my ailing mother. And that's what I did... for years and years. Up until my thirty-fifth birthday when my mother died."

Helen became quiet for a while, "Those were hard years. Arthur married another girl from the same social circle in Columbia, and every time I heard about the birth of another one of his children, it about broke my heart."

"Why didn't you run off with him?"

"He wanted to, but I didn't dare. Back then, it was unheard of for a girl in society to marry without consent. There were long engagements, announcements in the paper, the gathering of a trousseau, and exchange of a dowry. I was too accepting of what was expected." She laughed. "Oh, how my brother regretted what he did to me! Arthur ended up one of the richest and most respected men in South Carolina."

"Is that why you never talked about your only sibling or visited him?"

Helen nodded. "Seeing him would only remind me of that heartbreaking part of my life. After my mother passed, I wanted to run as far away from Columbia and all the sad memories as I could. I'd either travel abroad or spend time in Florida or New York. It wasn't until I heard about the Edney Inn that I visited the mountains. I fell in love with it and bought Edelweiss, the only place I could ever call my own."

"Did you ever forgive your brother?"

"Yes. Hate and resentment do nothing but eat you up. I let it go and got on with my life."

"That's what I want to do, Aunt Helen. Let what happened to me go and get on with my life."

CHAPTER EIGHTEEN

"Can I set the table with your mother's china?" Lula called up to Helen who was in her room getting dressed.

Helen leaned over the balcony. "You sure are in a lather over this dinner. Go ahead, and use the good linens, too."

Lula finished setting the table, then thought for a moment and put out three fingerbowls. She quickly gathered up odds and ends left from the last of the sewing of her uniforms for school and put them away.

Helen came down the stairs in a stylish new dress with a hem to her mid-calf, remarking how nice the table looked.

"Essie's going to be pleased with you making a big fuss over her," she said.

"I want it to be like old times," said Lula as she rearranged a place setting.

"I don't know how I'm going to survive your being away at school in Greensboro," said Helen.

The sound of a car and barking made the two rush out to the porch.

"Good Lord, she's brought those two dogs!" Helen declared.

The minute Essie pulled up, Remus and Romulus leapt out the car's window and ran into the house, almost knocking Helen over.

After warm greetings all around, Helen said, "Let's sit a while on the porch." She carried out a tray from the house, poured two glasses of sherry, and one that was watered down for Lula.

"A toast to our beloved Nurse Lula," said Essie as she raised her glass, seemingly enjoying her warm reception.

Lula sat barely sipping her drink and listening to the two women. Now that Essie wasn't living with them anymore and Helen rarely mixed with the locals on her own, she was anxious to get caught up on all the gossip.

Lula was amused with the way Essie's tales enthralled Helen. Lula had always considered Helen as perfect of a woman as could be, however she couldn't help but notice how she had always openly indulged in her one vice with her friend. With all Essie's charity work and doctoring, no gossip got past her; and no detail of this news was too insignificant to be devoured by Helen.

Helen finally pulled herself away to get dinner on the table.

"I'll help," offered Lula.

"No, we mustn't leave guests sitting by themselves," said Helen as she left the two on the porch.

The minute Helen was out of sight, Lula picked up the bottle of sherry and refilled Essie's empty glass with a wink. After years of riding all over the mountains with her, and seeing her throw down several shots of whiskey at every stop, Lula knew a couple drinks of sherry would have no effect. That done, Lula got right to the business at hand.

"I'll be at the hospital until next summer," said Lula, "and I wanted to ask you to look in on my momma when you can. She seemed so tired and worn this summer."

Essie finished off her drink, poured herself another, and swiftly drank it down. "As you know, I don't have Brownie anymore so I don't get out as much. However, from time to time I'm called upon to go up to the colony. So, don't you worry. When I do, I'll stop in and visit her."

Helen appeared at the door and announced that dinner was on the table. She whisked up the bottle of sherry and told everyone to bring their glass to the table, where she refilled Essie's.

"There now, Essie. That makes two drinks, just like you

promised Father Phillips."

With everyone seated, Essie pointed to the big, bronzed, roasted chicken sitting on a platter. "Is that Sheba or Desdemona?"

"Oh, really, Essie! Now, how am I going to carve it?" fussed Helen.

Lula pulled the platter near and picked up the carving knife and fork. "I'll do it, Aunt Helen." She grinned at Essie. "It's Desdemona. We ate Sheba last week."

"I thought it was her," said Essie. "After taking care of them for those two weeks you two were at the beach, I kinda got attached to them."

Helen fanned her face with her hand. "Stop, you two. You're making me feel like a cold-blooded murderer."

"Aunt Helen," Lula said in her most reassuring tone, "you'll be moving to the boarding house for the winter, and you could hardly expect your renter to take care of them. You had no choice."

The food was passed with Essie distracting Helen from the fate of Sheba and Desdemona with a juicy bit of gossip. Without warning, Lula jumped from the table, ran out on the porch, and retched over the railing.

Hearing her, Helen said, "See what you've gone and done, Essie. All that talk of eating my two dear pets has turned her stomach."

Essie went outside and handed Lula a napkin, then put an arm around her waist and walked her into the house. "Come upstairs and let me take a look at you. There's a fever going around."

After Essie led Lula upstairs, Helen sat at the table for a while sipping her sherry, concerned about Lula. Suddenly, a heart-wrenching cry shot through the air. Helen jumped up and ran up the stairs as Lula sobbed, "No! No! No!"

She ran into the room to see Lula thrashing on the bed crying and kicking. She rushed to her side and took her in her arms, then looked anxiously at Essie.

"Lula's with child," Essie whispered. "I'll go get my bag."

Helen held Lula in her arms, gently rocking her and softly cooing, "Lula Mae. My darling Lula Mae" until the cries finally subsided into heartbreaking whimpers.

Essie came back upstairs holding a glass.

"Help her sit up," she said.

Helen did as told and wiped away Lula's tears as Essie managed to get her to drink most of what was in the glass.

"That ought to help her sleep for a while. She needs her rest."

Helen gently lay Lula on the bed and covered her with a blanket. After Essie's urging, Helen followed her downstairs.

Helen sat at the table in a daze while Essie ate.

"So what are you going to do?" Essie asked as she reached for another roll. Getting no answer, she said, "In a couple of months when she begins to show, you'll have to do something."

The only response she was getting from Helen was sniffles and nose blowing.

"Pregnancy out of marriage is no stranger in these mountains," Essie continued. "They either have a shotgun wedding or make the culprit provide for the child. But this case is different." She shook her head. "If her brother finds out Zeb raped Lula, he's gonna kill that bastard and keep Lula up in the colony with the child."

Helen dropped her head in her hand and sobbed openly.

"Then again, you can always keep her here and raise the baby. A good deal of the folks will be sympathetic and kindly, but she'll always be considered ruined. This kind of thing threatens their whole social order. She'll probably get married someday to some widower with a batch of kids, or some nice man who loves her for herself... but definitely not an up-and-comer from the Blue Ridge School for Boys like I'm sure you were hoping for."

Essie reached over and poured the rest of the sherry in her glass. "If you want my opinion, I'd take her to the home for unwed mothers the Catholics operate in Raleigh. They'll arrange for an adoption in a good home."

Helen looked up at her, incredulity on her face. "Give Lula's baby to a stranger?"

"Well," said Essie, frustrated at not getting anywhere with Helen, "there's always Granny Bloom up on Burnshirt Mountain. She's been putting an end to this kind of problem as long as I've been in these mountains." Essie finished off her drink and put the glass on the table with a thud. "It can be dangerous, but I'll stay up there with her for the two days she'll be laid up and make sure nothing goes wrong."

They both looked up as Lula descended the stairs in her stocking feet. She came to the table, pulled out a chair, and sat down. She reached for a roll, picked up a knife, and started buttering it, almost seeming like herself as she spoke.

"You don't have to make sure nothing goes wrong, Essie. Nothing's going to go wrong at Granny Bloom's, because I'm going to have this baby." She turned and looked at Helen. "And, don't worry, Aunt Helen, we're not giving it to a stranger."

CHAPTER NINETEEN
1961

"All right, girls. Go behind the screen and turn your blouses around so the buttons are behind you. That way I can examine your backs," said Holly to the three bubbly fifth graders.

They scampered behind the screen laughing and jostling each other. Patsy Burrows was the first to come bouncing out, gracefully pirouetting around the room. Holly rolled her eyes. And they're not even teenagers yet, she said to herself.

Since Patsy was obviously wound up, Holly decided to examine the other two first. Holly noted on their charts that both girls had excellent posture, but upon studying Patsy's back, she had immediate concerns. Her shoulders were uneven and shoulder blades too prominent. She also seemed to be leaning toward one side.

"Patsy, I want you to bend over and touch your toes," said Holly.

The raised hump protruding from her back as she bent over was a classic indicator of scoliosis of the spine.

"Okay, girls, get dressed," said Holly. She pulled Patsy aside and was careful not to sound overly concerned. "I'm going to write your parents a note, and I need you to give it to them tonight. Can you do that for me?"

"Is anything wrong, Miss Baldwin?"

"Nothing that can't be fixed. You get dressed now, and someone will bring you the note before you go home."

After the girls left, Holly sat down and wrote to Patsy's parents. Something had to be done about the girl's scoliosis or she could end up permanently deformed. Holly finished making her notes as the next child appeared at her door.

Two hours later and with all the exams completed, Holly went by the office. She had to drop off the note, and she also wanted to see if Sally Hunt, the school secretary, was having any luck finding out if her aunt had ever taught in the Henderson County schools.

Sally greeted her with a smile as she entered the office.

"Here's a note for Patsy Burrows to take to her parents," said Holly. "I'm trying to set up a time for a home visit. Please let me know when they get back to us."

Sally took the envelope. "By the way, I heard from my friend at the board of education. There's no record of a Helen Baldwin ever teaching for the county."

"How about any students with the Baldwin name?"

"No. Nothing there either."

Holly thanked her and left, disappointed at coming up against another dead end.

RAIN PELTED her windshield so hard Holly could barely see ten yards ahead. She'd turn right around if the new mother she was going to see didn't need the baby formula so badly. The young woman's newborn wasn't thriving. Holly was certain it was because the woman's breast milk wasn't nourishing enough. During Holly's visit the day before, the girl hardly had the strength to get out of bed.

Turning off the main road, she drove up a muddy path to the cabin. Rivers of water streamed across the grassless yard. She changed to boots, grabbed the formula from her front seat, and sloshed her way to the covered porch. She knocked on the door, but the rain pounding on the tin roof was so loud she could barely hear the bid for her to enter.

"Thank heavens you're here," moaned the young woman. "I've been hopin you'd come."

Holly looked around the room. It was obvious that no one had been there to help the girl."I thought your mother was coming."

"She can't til tomorrow, and my man couldn't get off work."

The kitchen was in disarray, but the diapers hanging from a clothesline zigzagging around the cabin testified to the girl's determination to take care of her baby. Holly found an apron and began sterilizing bottles and preparing enough formula to get the baby through to the next day. With enough done to tide the girl over until her mother arrived, Holly dashed back to her car.

Her tires kept spinning on the washed-out driveway, but she finally made it onto the road. The windshield wipers thunked back and forth at full speed, and the defrost blasted, yet, she still could barely see through the window. Creeping along, almost blind, she made her way down the mountain. Suddenly, blurry headlights glared in her rearview mirror, and the vehicle hit her bumper. She gripped the steering wheel and fought off panic. The vehicle suddenly appeared on her left and inched closer. Afraid it was going to hit her, she veered to the right and rumbled off the road into a ditch. Her heart thumped in her chest as she watched the vehicle's rear lights disappear into the grey mist.

Once the rain stopped, she tried to back out of the ditch, but the wheels kept spinning. She stepped out and saw she'd dug herself into a rut. She'd have to wait until someone came by to help her. She stood for a while wondering why anyone would try to run her off the road, when a pickup came by and a man stuck his head out the window.

"You needin help, Ma'am?"

"I ran into the ditch and can't get out."

He slid down from his truck and studied the situation. "This is gonna take a tractor. I just passed the Garrison place. Saw Jeff hauling apple crates to his orchard. I'll go get him."

Before she could say anything, he jumped in his truck, turned around, and drove back. Fifteen minutes later, the man slowed as he passed and yelled out the window that Jeff was on his way.

She heard the tractor well before it appeared on the horizon. Her heart rate sped at the thought of seeing him again, and she tried to squelch the feeling. She liked the man, but knew he'd probably have some sort of 'damsel in distress' comment, and she wasn't in the mood for it.

As the tractor neared, she saw his shirt was wet with sweat and clung to his broad chest in a way she couldn't ignore. He had to be thinking she was becoming a nuisance by the brisk way he turned the tractor around, backed it up, and jumped off without giving her more than a nod and a smile. Wasting no time, he dragged a chain from the toolbox, attached it to the tractor, and dragged out a tarp. Tossing it on the muddy ground behind her car, he lay on his back and ducked under the back end to hook up the chain, Holly couldn't resist studying his impressive physique.

He scooted out and folded away the tarp.

"Hop in and put it in neutral," he hollered as he swung back on the tractor. "And keep your foot off the brakes."

She got into the car, aware he was watching her. He quickly pulled her car out and took the chain off. As he came up to her window, she braced for the wisecrack she knew was coming.

He put a hand on her open window and leaned in. His manly scent wafted in, and she bit her lip as heat shot through her. She hated herself for stealing a glance to see if he was wearing a wedding ring.

"You should be all set now," he said.

She looked straight ahead, afraid he'd read how she felt if he met her eyes.

"Thanks for helping me out," she said, still gazing ahead.

"No problem. Those cloudbursts make it tough to drive around here. The roads get slippery."

She wanted to tell him about the truck that kept edging her over, but thought better of it. Except for a long, sharp cry from a bird, all was quiet as she sat waiting for him to take his hands off her car.

She finally broke the silence. "Can I pay you this time for your service?"

"I have a better idea. How about letting me take you out some night?"

Darn it, she said to herself. He's being so nice, and she didn't want him to be. Now wasn't the time to get involved with anyone. She was getting close to an answer and had to keep her mind on finding her mother.

"Well, what do you say?" he asked.

"I'll think about it."

He took his hands off her car and backed away.

Regretting her awkward response, she glanced up at him. "I suppose you want my phone number."

He folded his arms and grinned. "I already have it."

She looked at him in disbelief.

"My cousin's the school secretary."

"Sally? She's your cousin?"

"Yep."

He looked so pleased with that fact, that she had to bite back a smile. How was she supposed to answer that? Unable to come up with something, she thanked him again and pulled away.

So he had her phone number. He wouldn't have gone through the trouble of getting it unless he was interested. Right? She drove down the road and a strange feeling overtook her. She was like a fallen leaf floating on a stream, waiting for its destination to unfold, but the stream was headed dead on course.

She knew someday she would go out with Jeff Garrison, and somehow their lives would intertwine. She knew it, and she knew he knew it, too. Fate had brought them together three times as if to give them a chance to look each other over like the two cardinals she'd watched doing their mating dance outside her window that past spring. She laughed to herself. She certainly grasped the opportunity to look him over that afternoon as he lay on the tarp.

A year ago, she'd had no hope of finding out where she came from. Now, without any doing of her own, she was being swept along on a current leading to the answer she'd been searching for all her life. Was it chance, or luck, or something else that brought the cousin she hadn't known existed to her doorstep? Or walking into the post office, and one hour later, landing in the lap of one of the kindest persons she'd ever known at a time when she needed kindness the most? Or Ella taking up her quest like Joan of Arc? Then again, maybe it was none of those things. Maybe it was simply time for her to know.

AFTER SUCH AN eventful day, Holly ached for a quiet dinner with Myrt as she pulled in the driveway. The unmistakable aroma of apple pie fresh from the oven hit her the minute she walked in the door. She strolled into the kitchen and said hello to Myrt who was busy at the stove. Holly put an arm around her shoulder and gave it a squeeze, then went to the open window and inspected the pie on the sill. She noticed a small tart next to it and smiled knowing the delightful morsel would be in the lunch bag Myrt would pack for her in the morning.

"I need to go up and shower and change," said Holly. "When's dinner going to be ready?"

"Not long. I'll call you."

As she was leaving the kitchen, Holly eyed three place settings on the table. "Let me guess," she said. "Ella's coming over tonight."

"Yes. And from the sounds of it, she has some news for you."

Holly was drying her hair when Myrt called up to her. She quickly put it into a ponytail and ran down. Happy to see Ella at the table, she went over and gave her a hug.

"Now, now. Enough of that," said Ella, shooing Holly away. She looked over at Myrt. "When's that dinner gonna be served? It was a stampede at the post office all day, and I couldn't take a moment to grab a bite. I'm so hungry I could eat a horse."

Myrt finished carving the chuck roast and brought it to the table. With everyone seated, Ella picked up her fork and was about to spear a piece of meat when she glanced up to see Myrt and Holly staring at her.

"What's everyone lookin at me for?" she asked, then waved a hand in the air. "Good Lord! The blessing! That hunger of mine was gonna send me straight to hell."

Holly bowed her head and eyed Myrt as Ella raced through a

condensed version of her usual blessing.

As the food was being passed, Holly spotted a folded sheet of paper on the table next to Ella and reached for it. Ella slammed her hand over it, making Holly jump.

"Hold your horses, young lady. I'm gonna get to that soon as I finish eatin."

Holly and Myrt did everything they could to rush the meal along. The minute Ella finished her plate, it was whisked away and a piece of pie put in its place.

"You got any coffee?" Ella asked as she finally put her fork down.

Myrt had anticipated the request and quickly poured her a cup.

"Now, Ella," said Myrt as she sat down and folded her hands in front of her. "You've drawn this out long enough. The suspense is killing us. Tell us."

Ella sat erect and took on the air of authority that came natural to her. "To start with, there's no question Holly's aunt owned that place everyone calls Edelweiss. It's off the Chimney Rock Road on Edelweiss Road. Bessie Freeman's boy works for the county, and I got her to tell him to find out who all owned it. Today, she brought this in." She picked up the paper and handed it to Holly. "Says so right there, and you can trust it cuz her son looked right straight at the deeds in the county courthouse."

Holly read the hand-written list aloud. "J. R. Freeman bought it from the state in July of 1901 and sold it in 1914. Helen Baldwin bought it in October of 1914, and she sold it in August of 1934." Holly put the paper down and thought for a moment. "She adopted me that February right after I was born. So, I could've been there at Edelweiss that summer."

"I have more," announced Ella. "I remembered Gabby Edney has all the old ledgers from the Edney Inn. Her mother carried them out before it burned. She's quite the local historian. Always lookin people up in em. So, I asked her to look for your aunt, and sure enough, she stayed at the Edney Inn for three summers—1912 to 1914. Kinda looks like she came for the season and liked it here enough to go out and buy herself a cabin."

"It's amazing. She actually lived here all those years," said Holly. "Can I keep this paper?"

"It's yours. Now, that doesn't prove you were born in these parts," said Ella.

"No, but it doesn't prove I wasn't." Holly appeared confused. "Why did she want to keep all this a secret from me?"

"Makes you think she was hiding something, doesn't it?" asked Ella.

"She could've stole her," said Myrt.

"Naaah!" said Ella. "Think back. With all the fevers goin round in those days, there were so many orphans they couldn't find homes for em all. Heck, they had to put a lot of em out to work."

"That's true," said Myrt.

"I could go for another cup of coffee and another piece of pie," said Ella. "Gotta make up for missin my lunch."

Myrt poured the coffee, and Holly served them all another slice.

"Our old pastor from the Church of the Transfiguration came in the other day, and we got to talkin," said Ella. She gave Holly a slow, meaningful wink as she said, "Discreet like." She continued. "He's been livin in Winston-Salem for years, but was born and raised in Edneyville. He's gettin along in age and came home to retire. He couldn't remember hearing of Edelweiss or your aunt, but he told me his mother used to talk about a doctor woman who rode all over these mountains on horseback dressed like a man, just like Annie said. She was much loved, and when called upon, would go anywhere to help someone no matter how hard it was to get to, even up to the Lost Colony."

Holly almost sprang out of her chair. "I heard my aunt talking to an old friend about a lost colony. Where is it?"

"Up on Chimney Rock Mountain next to Sugarloaf," said Ella.

"Can you take me there?"

"It's too much of a climb for these old bones," said Ella. "Anyway, they say there's not much to see. Only grown-over stone foundations."

"Why do they call it the Lost Colony?"

"Cuz that's what it is," said Ella. "There were folks who'd been livin up there since just after the Revolutionary War. A remote, self-sufficient community. They had plenty of water, their own grist mill, and a forge. Never saw a need to go anywheres else. But when the wars took their men folk, many of the boys didn't want to go back. Like the song says, 'How ya gonna keep em down on the farm once they've seen Paree.'

"A lot of them got to working for the Chimney Rock Company that was making that big rock sticking out of the mountain a tourist attraction," Myrt added. "They helped build a lot of that 800-step stairway from the village right up to what they call the Skyline Trail. From what I understand, it's a tortuous zigzagged path to the top of the mountain above the chimney and leads to the Hickory Nut Falls. From there, I understand the heart of the colony is a two-mile hike through dense forest."

"My grandpa worked on a crew for that company," said Ella. "It was dangerous work. He said they had to fasten that stairway into the granite face of the mountain with iron hooks and stirrups sunk deep into the solid rock. Most of the time, he was hanging from a rope like a yoyo while he was doin it. They put up railings on both sides made of locust saplings they cut right out of the forest up there. My grandpa always said it was a heroic battle of man against mountain."

"Is that the only way to get up there?" Holly asked.

"No. People say the best way is from the Edneyville side of the mountain. They drive as far as they can up Little River Road to a trailhead, and hike up from there. At any rate, Holly, you'd need a guide to find the place."

Noticing disappointment on Holly's face, Ella patted her hand and said, "That's okay, darlin, I'm gonna help get you the answers. Remember, I'm the Bat Cave postmaster. Every little thing that happens around here flows through that little building, either on paper, on foot, or by word of mouth."

They were quiet, eating their pie and mulling over all that had been said.

"I appreciate all you're doing for me, Ella," said Holly.

"Never you mind, girl. Besides, this is more fun than chasing down the culprit who keeps stealing my 'Wanted' posters."

"She'll have the FBI in on it before she's done," piped up Myrt.

Ella tapped her finger on the table and thought. "We know you were born, we just don't know where and from whom. Are you sure your aunt never told you anything about where you came from?"

"I'm sure."

"Well, you didn't just fall from the sky," said Ella. "We gotta get to the bottom of this. I've just about asked everyone that comes into the post office, and I've talked to all the pastors special." She was quiet for a moment as she thought. "It's strange. Your aunt wouldn't be talkin about the lost colony unless she was connected to it somehow. We know she was here up until '34. Heck, that's but twenty-six years ago. I'm sure there's someone in those mountains who knows somethin."

"Old Granny Garrison used to live up there," said Myrt. "They say she was the last to leave. She wouldn't budge until her son finally went up there and brought her down. But I haven't heard her name mentioned in years. I wonder if she's still alive?"

"She better be," said Ella. "The government's sending her a check every month. She lives in a trailer on her grandson's land up on Garrison Road, and he picks up the mail for her."

"She's got to be in her late eighties, by now." said Mert.

"Can't believe I missed talkin to him about all this," said Ella. "Sometimes they come get the mail from their boxes after I'm closed. I'll put a note in his box to call me."

"Oh, please don't!" Holly piped up. Then she looked at the two, embarrassed. "It's just that I know him. He helped me get my car out of a ditch today. I'll get his number from his cousin who works at the school and give him a call myself."

"I sure hope you plan to be plenty friendly to him," said Ella. "He might be a good feller fer ya. Talk is that he's an up-and-comer. He goes to the Mountain Home Church, and I know for a fact there's quite a few gals who have set their sights on him." She gave Holly a calculating look. "Take it from me, an opportunity like this aint gonna come by every day. It won't hurt you none to sidle up to him. Lord knows you've been around women too much. Men folk aren't half bad once you get used to em."

Holly slowly shook her head as the three of them fell into laughing.

CHAPTER TWENTY

H olly hated to have to put on her uniform on a Saturday to visit Patsy's parents, but this was the only day the girl's father was available for a visit other than Sunday, and Patsy's mother had insisted he be at the meeting. She pulled up to the house and rang the doorbell.

Patsy's mother opened the door and gave her a somewhat stifled greeting before leading her into a simple, but comfortable, living room. The woman introduced her to her husband who sat staring at her. The tension in the room was palpable.

"What's this about Patsy's back?" the father snapped.

Holly sat down and talked directly to him. "Every year we examine all the students between the third and fifth grades for scoliosis of the spine since it most often develops during the growth spurt before puberty. I examined Patsy the other day, and it does appear she has this condition. I would like to set up an appointment for you to take her to the clinic where they can x -ray her and give you a prognosis."

"How serious is it?" asked the mother.

Holly turned to her. "It's hard to say without an x-ray. Mild cases may simply correct themselves, but if she has moderate to severe scoliosis, if gone untreated, it can lead to her having chronic pain and increased deformity, even heart and lung dam- age."

The woman looked to her husband, waiting for him to say

something. Unlike his wife, he seemed more agitated than concerned.

"Adolescent scoliosis usually isn't due to any medical condition," Holly continued. "Current research suggests it's inherited. Does anyone in your family have scoliosis?"

"Not that I know of," he answered with a degree of indignation.

"Can I set up an appointment at the clinic for Patsy?" Holly asked. "It won't cost you anything."

"I guess it won't do any harm," he answered grudgingly.

Holly left, relieved she didn't have to pull out all the grim photos of what could happen if the condition wasn't treated; however, she had an inkling the mother already knew.

Being a Saturday, Holly was enjoying a leisure drive on Route 64 on her way home when she noticed the "Edelweiss Road" sign nailed to a tree. Realizing that was where Annie said her aunt had lived, she swung into the next driveway and turned around. She hadn't dared go looking for the house before, because she didn't want to trespass, but now that she was sure her aunt had owned it, she had a valid reason to be visiting.

She pulled onto the rugged dirt road, flanked on one side by gigantic oaks and black locust, and on the other by a steep drop. She came around a curve and saw a huge log cabin in a clearing up ahead on a hill. It appeared the road ended in a circular driveway in front of it. She started up and noticed an odd little hut.

As she neared the house, she saw a car parked on the side. She lost her nerve and wanted to turn around and go back, but the only way out was around the circle. She approached the house, and a bald, middle-aged man came from behind a huge hemlock. Their eyes met, obliging her to stop.

"Sorry to impose on you," Holly called out to him from her window. "I'm Holly Baldwin, and my aunt used to own this house. I was just driving by to take a look at it."

The man tossed some clippers in a bucket and approached the car. "I'm John Randall, and I own the place. You're welcome to look around if you like."

At first, she was hesitant. Her aunt had always warned her to be cautious with men, especially when in an isolated area. But something about the casual splendor of the house and the man's kindly face made her feel safe, and she got out of the car.

"You say your aunt used to own this place?" he asked.

"Yes, she sold it in '34."

"That's when my parents bought it."

A bulldog that had been asleep in the grass came over and sniffed her. She bent down and petted it.

"He's cute," she said. "What's his name?"

"Hector," he responded. "What was your aunt's name?"

"Helen. Helen Baldwin."

He shook his head. "No. That's not the name I remember. An old man came by one time and told me a woman... what they used to call a doctor woman used to live here. She had an unusual name." He pointed to the hut Holly had noticed when she drove up. "He said she used that building as a drugstore. I guess at the time it was the only one for miles around."

"I don't know what her name was either," said Holly, "but I've been told such a person used to live here with my aunt."

"You can go in the house and look around if you like."

"I would, thank you. Can you show it to me?"

"Sure, right after I turn off the water in back. I've been burning brush."

She meandered up on the porch and was about to peek in a window when he came out the front door. He held the screen door open and said, "Come on in. I'll show you around."

The living room almost took up the whole house with a staircase going up to a balcony she presumed led to the bedrooms.

"Do you live here year-round?" she asked.

"No. Only get up here a couple weeks out of the year if I'm lucky. Mostly to make repairs and beat back the forest. My sisters haven't been here in years and want me to sell it, but I don't have the heart. I keep telling myself I'm going to retire here someday." He looked around wistfully. "It's a shame really. Even when we were kids, my parents could only bring us for one or two weeks a summer." He eyed Holly's uniform. "I see you're a nurse."

185

"I'm in public health."

"I teach at NC State in Raleigh."

He seemed embarrassed to be going on about himself.

"Here, let me show you the kitchen."

They strolled into a typical '40s kitchen with a porcelain sink mounted on the wall, a little gas stove, and small refrigerator.

"As I remember," he said, "none of this was here when your aunt owned it. My father had to have electricity and plumbing brought in before my mother would set foot in the place."

They spilled back into the living room.

"The fireplace is original, as is everything else in this room." He pointed to a door next to the staircase. "That was my parent's bedroom." Seeing her eyes follow the stairs up to the balcony, he said, "Go on up and take a look if you want."

Holly started up the stairs, then stopped at the landing midway up and looked across at the massive room. As rustic as it appeared and as elegant as her aunt was, she could still picture her and all her treasured furniture in it. There was an intrinsic beauty in the sheer naturalness of the place that would've appealed to her. Holly pictured the grand piano in the corner next to the window and could see her aunt occasionally glancing up at the mountains as she played.

She continued up the stairs and looked in the first bedroom. It was small, but nicely lit with windows on two sides. She opened the door to the next room and strolled in. It was definitely large enough for her aunt's cherished Eastlake bedroom set.

She went back on the balcony and started to descend when her host called up.

"Take a look in the hall closet. That's where we stashed anything your aunt left behind. You'll find it a mess. My sisters used to play dress-up with everything in there."

Holly was intrigued as she slowly opened the rustic, handmade door. Articles of clothing hung on nails in the back and lay in a pile on the floor. She fingered a long, silky, sequined dress hanging limply from a nail. It was somewhat torn and soiled, but she could still see her aunt wearing it in its better days to some elegant party. Maybe on one of the ocean voyages to Europe she had always talked about.

She slid to her knees and began rifling through the pile. The reek of aged mildew kept making her pull back to take a breath, but she couldn't stop. Most of the clothes looked like they were her aunt's, but then she pulled out a skirt that had to have belonged to a young girl. She was overcome by a chilling feeling of expectancy as she went through the pile. She found a dress that resembled a sailor suit for a girl of seven or eight, then a dress for a girl of twelve, and then another. She made note of the fact that she didn't come across anything that would've belonged to a boy or an infant.

She fell back on her haunches listening to herself breathe. Who was this girl who wore these clothes? She thrilled at the possibility that it might have been her mother.

She started to put everything back when she noticed a pile of books in the corner. Nothing but a bunch of old novels. She reached for a larger book on the bottom and pulled it out. "The Sapphire, 1933" was embedded on the cover along with a seal with the word "Fassifern." It was a school yearbook.

She flipped through the pages, and seeing all the photos of elegant balls and dances, she could tell Fassifern was a finishing school for upper class girls. She stopped at one titled "Faculty" and skimmed through the staff. She could barely believe her eyes. There was her aunt. She had to have been in her fifties, but she was still beautiful. The caption read, "Miss Helen Baldwin opens the door to France as she leads us through our French lessons."

"That's why they couldn't find her in the county schools!" escaped from Holly's mouth.

"Are you all right?" the man called up.

She scooted to the banister and poked her nose through. "I'm fine. Just found a book with my aunt's picture. Do you think I can have it?"

"Sure. Take anything in that closet you want. I've been meaning to get rid of that stuff for years."

Holly tossed everything back in the closet except the yearbook and the sailor dress and took them downstairs where the man was waiting for her.

He handed her a slip of paper. "Here's my address. If you have any questions about the house, feel free to send me a note. I'll be happy to answer them."

Holly stuffed the paper in the pages of the yearbook, thanked him, and left walking on air.

She couldn't wait to get the book home and almost flew down Route 64. She pulled into Myrt's driveway, hoping she could get the dress and yearbook in the house without her seeing it. She wanted to consume this delectable treasure in the solitude of her room. She went in through the front door and started toward the staircase when she saw Myrt busy in the kitchen packing food in a box.

Myrt barely looked up. "Your supper's in the oven. I'll be working at a church dinner tonight and won't be home til around nine."

Holly dropped her things on a step and went into the kitchen. "I'll help you take everything to your car."

Once Myrt was waved off, Holly came back in and ran up the stairs with her cache. She spent the better part of the evening browsing through the yearbook searching for a girl with the last name of Baldwin, but there were none. She sat cross-legged on her bed eating the stew Myrt had left in the oven and kept glancing at the clock on her nightstand.

She knew it was a cheesy thing to do, but she was going to call Jeff at eight. Whenever her old roommate at school wanted to know if a potential beau was going with someone, she'd call him on a date night to see if he were home. The only difference was that her roommate would always hang up once the call was answered, and she had no intentions of doing so. She needed to talk to his grandma. Maybe the woman could provide her with a clue to why a sophisticated teacher in a deluxe girls' school would be involved with a rustic colony in the back woods.

Seeing it was eight, she went downstairs to the kitchen, picked up the phone, and dialed the number she'd gotten from the secretary. She was ready to give up after six rings, when he answered the phone. The way he said hello, she could tell he was eating. All of a sudden, she felt ridiculous. It was possible he was having dinner with a date he had brought home.

"Hi, Jeff. It's Holly Baldwin."

"Have you been thinking it over?" he asked.

"You mean the date?"

"Yeah. The date."

"I'm sorry, Jeff, but I'm so wrapped up in something right now, I don't want anything to sidetrack me." She took a deep breath and let it out. "But I think you're a nice guy."

"Well, at least we're getting somewhere."

"Actually, I'm calling to ask if you'd take me to visit your grandma."

"Any reason in particular. You know she's pretty old."

"Yes. I want to talk with her about the Lost Colony."

"Why the Lost Colony?"

"My aunt who raised me mentioned it once, and I'm curious about it."

"Well, if you want to know anything about the Lost Colony, she'd be the person to talk with. She was the last to leave."

"So, you'll set that up and get back to me?"

"Sure."

They were silent.

"Are you doing okay," he finally asked.

"Un-huh."

"Good."

Holly sighed. "At least I haven't fallen off a cliff or gone into another ditch."

By the relaxed cadence of his voice, she could tell he was alone, so she fluffed up a pillow and lay back.

"Can I tell you about that ditch?" she asked.

"Go ahead."

"I was driving along... slowly, because of the rain. This vehicle was tailing me before it hit my bumper, then it came up next to me and kept moving closer. Each time, I'd move over to avoid hitting it, and all of a sudden I was in the ditch."

"What kind of vehicle was it?"

"It was big. A pick-up. It was raining too hard for me to see anything except the lights. I couldn't see if it was a man or woman driving."

Jeff didn't say anything, and she knew he was digesting what she had told him.

He finally spoke. "Since you're interested in the Lost Colony, how about letting me take you up there tomorrow."

Vexed that he changed the subject, she said, "Maybe another time. I want to talk to your grandma first."

"I keep striking out with you," he said.

"No. Like I said, Jeff, I like you, but I need to concentrate on something else right now."

They were silent again, as if they didn't have anything to say, yet didn't want to disconnect.

"So, you'll let me know about your grandma?" she finally asked.

"Yeah. I'll let you know."

CHAPTER TWENTY-ONE

H olly had come out of the shower and was slipping into a pair of jeans when Myrt hollered from downstairs that Ella was on the phone. She dashed down to the kitchen and picked up the receiver.

"I got news for ya," said Ella. "Last week, I was talkin to Sarah Clarke, and I got around to tellin her about ya. She'd never heard of your aunt, but remembered hearing about a place called Edelweiss. Well, today, she dropped in and said she'd been thinkin about it and recalled her ma once tellin her she used to play with a girl who lived there."

"Who was this girl? What was her name?"

"You know as much as I do. I'm bringin her over to see you tonight after supper. She has something to show you."

Holly went back upstairs and continued browsing through the yearbook. There were photos of all the seniors and group shots of the rest of the classes. Pictures of their social functions intrigued her—balls, galas, porch parties. There were clubs of all sorts and all kinds of events requiring formal gowns. The curriculum was definitely structured to instruct the South's future debutantes.

She couldn't help wondering why her aunt would leave a post in a school that suited her so well to teach in a rural public school in Pittsboro where her breeding and grace stuck out like a sore thumb. Then she wondered about the girls in the senior class. Her aunt adopted her nine months after they would've graduated. Did one of those girls get pregnant? From what she had culled from all the photos and activities, there was no question their plans for a life of social prominence would've been ruined if anyone found out. Had her aunt taken pity and harbored the girl during her pregnancy and then adopted the baby?

Holly remembered tender moments between mothers and their babies she had witnessed in the hospital. If one of these girls were her mother, it must have torn her apart to let her go, but in the end, she had made her choice. Her baby would ruin her life. She didn't want it.

With tears trickling freely down her cheeks, Holly yearned to lay eyes on someone she could call mother as she studied the senior pictures. After close examination, she decided on three girls who looked enough like her to possibly be her mother. Yet, reading the accolades in the captions, she felt only two of them were anything like herself. One girl volunteered at the hospital and the other was voted the senior class athlete. The one who volunteered had an unusual name, Lula Mae, unlike the typical Anglo-Saxon Protestant ones the book was crammed with.

Holly had always accepted that she'd come into the world unwanted, yet, for as far back as she could remember, she had made up stories in her head of being torn from her loving mother's grasp by some catastrophic event she had no control over. Holly sat stunned, realizing that her being given away at birth was probably nothing more than a cold, calculated decision. "Oh, Helen!" she softly cried, "If it wasn't for your kind heart, I could've ended up in an orphanage, or even worse.

Myrt's call from the bottom of the staircase startled her.

"Sarah's here, darling."

Holly slapped the book closed, slid it under her pillow, and rushed to the bathroom to wash her face. She stared at herself in the mirror thinking there was a good possibility she had the answer to her birth. But niggling at her was the question of who was the little girl who wore all those clothes she found in the closet at Edelweiss, or why had her aunt talked to a friend about a lost colony in such guarded whispers? None of it added up.

She went downstairs and found Ella, Myrt, and Sarah assembled around the circular table in the dimly lit living room, looking like they were ready to hold a séance. After introductions, Sarah took a book with a pink satin cover from her lap and lovingly placed it on the table.

"This is my mother's diary," she announced. "When Ella told me about you looking for your kin, and that your aunt used to own Edelweiss, I knew I'd heard my mother mention that place and something about a little girl she played with there, but I wasn't sure enough to speak up. So I read through her diary to see if she mentioned it. My mother wrote a lot about her summers in Edneyville as a child. Sometimes I sit down and read from it, and it brings her back to me just as if she were sitting right here talking to me."

"Does she mention a Helen Baldwin?" Holly asked.

"No, but..." Sarah opened the diary to a page with a bookmark. "Here it says, 'Today, my sister took me to Edelweiss again. Me and my dear new friend saw convicts blowing up rocks for the new road.'"

Holly fell back in her chair. "I wonder who this new friend was. Does it say how old she was?"

"No. That was the only mention of a playmate I came across. But my mother writes about a doctor woman who lived there." She flipped the pages to another bookmark. "Here she's telling how her sister worked there summers and would get herbs from this doctor woman to take to our ailing grandma. She says there was a little drugstore on the property."

"Oh, my God!" cried Holly. "A man showed it to me on Saturday!"

"Where is your mother's sister now? Can we talk to her?" asked Ella.

"Oh, she's been dead for years. Died in childbirth."

Myrt brought out tea and cake, and the three women sat talking about old times while Holly wondered how she was going to get her hands on the diary. She was convinced there was more buried in it.

As Ella and Sarah were leaving, Holly summoned her courage. "Sarah, can I please keep the diary for a while to see if there's anything in it that might tell me more about my aunt? I promise to take good care of it."

"I don't know. I already went over it pretty good," she answered.

"Heavens to Betsy, give her the diary," said Ella. "That is unless there's something unchristian in it you don't want anyone to read."

"Of course there isn't! My mother was a decent, God-fearing woman." She handed Holly the diary. "You take good care of this now. Call me when you're done, so I can come by and get it."

TWO WEEKS LATER, Holly was at the health department getting ready to go out on calls when she looked up to see Patsy Burrows' mother.

"I came to talk to you in person," said the woman.

Holly motioned to the chair next to her desk. Another nurse, who was getting ready to leave, hurried out to give them privacy.

Mrs. Burrows sat down. "Thanks for seeing me without an appointment. I didn't know who else I could talk to. Last week we took Patsy to the clinic for x-rays, and it was worse than I had feared."

"I know. They sent me a copy of the report," said Holly.

"I was hoping all she'd need was a brace for a couple of years, but they're telling us they need to fuse her vertebra because her spine is already pressing against her lungs. The doctor said it should be done right quick." She wrung her hands. "When you came to the house and asked if anyone in our family had the affliction, I was afraid to talk about it, but I had a sister who had the same problem as Patsy. By the time she was seventeen, she was in a wheelchair and gone to be with the Lord at twenty-seven."

She broke down in tears. "I don't know what's going to happen to my little girl. They said this should've been done years ago." She wiped her tears with a hanky and sniffled. "God knows it's not our fault. We moved here from Alabama, and no one in the schools there ever checked her out."

"If you don't have insurance to cover the operation, I'm sure the clinic can find a way to have it done," said Holly.

"Oh, I wish to God that was all," she said. "Her father won't allow it."

"Can't you sit down and talk to him?"

"You don't understand, Miss Baldwin. There's no talking to him. Not by me, anyway. A week after we got married, he said we were going to dinner at his mother's house, and I told him I didn't want to go, that I was going to stay in and rest. He slammed me against the wall and left. When I finally came to, I crawled to the phone and called my mother. I had a concussion and was in bed for a week. My mother sat down and explained to me that I had married a man who believed a woman's place was to obey her husband, and I had to make up my mind to do just that or leave him." She wiped her tears again. "He's been a good provider, a good father, and he loves me and Pasty, but that's the way it is."

"Didn't the doctor explain the possible outcomes to him if you didn't go ahead with the operation?"

"He did, then Robert stood up and said 'Nobody's gonna cut on my baby,' and walked out." The woman grabbed Holly's arm and pleaded. "Please talk to him. I know if you can make him understand, he'll do the right thing."

"All right," said Holly. "I'll come and talk to him this Saturday."

AFTER DINNER that night, Myrt poured Holly a second cup of coffee and was about to sit down at the table when the phone rang. She picked it up and chatted with the caller. It sounded to Holly as if she were talking to one of her former students.

Myrt turned to her and said, "It's for you, Holly. It's the Garrison boy."

Holly picked up the phone and said hello.

"I set it up for you to visit my grandma this Tuesday after four like you asked. I'm in the middle of bringing in my apple harvest right now, so you'll have to go yourself. I'll try to make it there if I can. Go up the road you had the flat tire on, then turn left on Garrison. Her trailer is a half mile up. You can't miss it."

All day Tuesday, Holly had the visit to Jeff's grandmother on her mind, and now she was finally making her way up Garrison Road. She didn't know what would come of it, but it was a lead, and she had to follow it. She pulled onto the drive and got out. Drifts of black-eyed Susans and cleome on both sides of the walkway swayed in the breeze as she went up to the door and knocked.

"Come ye in," a scratchy voice called out.

Holly went in and was stunned to see a wisp of a woman sitting in a rocker wearing a long dress and granny bonnet. She'd heard there were still mountain women dressing like that, but this was the first time she'd seen it herself. The woman's age and dignity commanded respect, making Holly feel suddenly honored to be in her presence.

"Come set ye next to me, so as I can see ye," she said as she patted a stool next to her.

Holly sat down, and the woman took her hand. "Jeff speaks well of ye, lass. I is right proud a him. Done gone to farming college." Her laugh exposed several gaps where teeth once had been. "We done plenty good fer ourselves up on the mountain without no college, but jist the same, we is proud a him." She patted Holly's hand. "Tell me now what ye aims to be speakin bout."

"I was born an orphan in 1934." Holly's voice cracked to hear the seven sad words summarizing her lineage. "I don't know who my parents were, but I believe my aunt who raised me did. She lived and taught around here, and I once heard her talking to an old friend about a lost colony. I'm hoping you might've known her or maybe heard of her."

"By what name?" she asked.

"Helen Baldwin."

"What was she sayin bout the colony?"

"I was only seven, and all I remember is 'the lost colony.'"

"Is that all ye know?" she asked.

"Yes," Holly answered. "Have you ever heard of her? There

was a doctor woman who used to live with her, too. Do you know who she was?"

"I knowed Granny McDowell from a top a the mountain. She's gone many yars now."

Holly was going to ask her again if she knew her aunt, when they heard a vehicle pull up. The woman stared at the door waiting for someone to knock or come in.

Holly took the opportunity to look around the small trailer. It was old and sparsely furnished, but neat and clean. Seeing a walker next to the woman's chair, she decided the lack of furniture was to make it easier for the old woman to move around. She noted a few framed photographs hanging on the walls, but other than that, they were bare. She looked over at the old woman. She was definitely asking more questions than she was answering. Why? Does she know something she doesn't want to tell me?

The door burst open and Jeff, wearing a sweaty t-shirt, came in carrying a box of groceries.

"Hi, Granny. Hi, Holly." He put the box on the counter. "Granny, these are from Mom." He went to the refrigerator and took out a soda, then leaned against a wall guzzling it down.

Seeing everyone staring at him, he wiped his mouth with the back of his hand. "Don't let me interrupt you."

"We is done, son. I not be havin knowledge fer the lass."

The sudden dismissal surprised Holly. With her cheeks warming from the awkwardness of the moment, she thanked the woman and said goodbye before starting for the door.

Jeff, who obviously hadn't sensed what had happened between the two women, said, "Let me walk you to your car," then tossed out, "Granny, I'll be right back to put your groceries away."

Walking Holly to her car, he said, "Now that you've talked to Granny, I hope you'll let me take you for a hike up to the Lost Colony this Saturday to see it for yourself."

Holly got in her car wanting to tell him about her conversation with the old woman, but didn't feel she should. She liked him too much to even hint that his beloved grandma was coyly maneuvering her, and she decided, instead, to take him up on his offer. This place called the Lost Colony was getting under her skin.

"Okay. I'll go," she said, "but it has to be on Sunday. I have an important meeting on Saturday I can't miss."

"I'll have to skip church," he said, "but Sunday it is. I'll pick you up at seven."

"Seven?!"

"And wear good walking shoes."

"I suppose you want me to pack a lunch, too."

He folded his bronzed arms across his chest. His chiseled jaw was covered with a days-old beard, and damp ringlets of golden brown hair fell across his forehead. "That would be mighty nice of you. I'm working dawn to dusk in the orchard these days."

Holly said she would, then started the car, smiling to herself as she pictured the disappointed faces of the girls at the Sunday service at the Mt. Moriah Church. As she drove away, the perplexing meeting she'd had with Jeff's grandma took over her thoughts. The woman definitely knew more than she was willing to tell. Why all the mystery? What was everyone hiding?

AS MUCH AS he needed to get back and finish spraying his apples, Jeff went back in the trailer to put away his grandma's groceries.

"How'd you like her, Granny?" he asked as he made room in the cupboard for a bag of sugar. He waited for a response, and when he didn't get one, looked at her over his shoulder. "Well?"

"She's a right nice lass, but I'm afearin she be lookin into things better left alone. There be folks round here who aint gonna cotton to it. There be things that took place up in them thar mountains that best be forgottin."

Jeff wondered what his grandmother meant as he finished putting things away, but he knew questioning her would be hopeless. He had to wait until she told him. That was the way with the old ones from up in the colony. He kissed her gently on the cheek and left. On the way back to his orchard, he recalled his grandma's words, and an uncomfortable feeling surfaced.

Holly's incident on the road already troubled him. Maybe he should drop in on Cal Hackett and see if there was anything going on. He'd know if there was.

CHAPTER TWENTY-TWO
1934

Helen came down from the porch at Edelweiss and took the baby from Lula. "The house needs a thorough cleaning, but other than that, the renter left it in good order."

Lula, in a pair of slacks, went to the back of their new sedan and opened the trunk, while Helen gently bounced the baby in her arms.

"Unpack all the food first, Doris," Helen called out to their housekeeper.

Doris, a plain-looking, but spirited widow in her forties, hurried in the house with a load for the kitchen. "We sure brought a lot of stuff for five days," she complained.

Lula lugged two suitcases up the steps and into the house. She stood in the living room slowly taking in all the familiar smells and memories. Helen came up beside her and the two locked eyes.

"I know how you feel," said Helen, "but we had to sell this place. We couldn't stay here with the baby. People would talk, and it could get back to the hospital."

Doris came out of the kitchen. "Well, it sure has character. I can say that much for it. But I don't know about cookin in there." She sighed and went back outside for more groceries.

Helen and Doris prepared lunch while Lula gave the baby a

bottle; then, with the house in utter disarray, they sat down to eat.

"Doris, you straighten up the kitchen," said Helen after the lunch. "And Lula, you see to making the beds. I have to go to the attorney's office and sign the papers for the sale, then I want to stop in at the movers and make sure they're bringing all the crates early tomorrow so we can start packing."

Helen noticed the dreamy look on Lula's face as she stared out at Little Fork Mountain. "Don't worry, darling. In three more days, we'll be visiting with your mother. I'll stop by Gus's tomorrow and make sure he's all set to take the two of us up there, then come get us the next day like I wrote him. I hope he found time to go up and tell your family we'd be coming this week." She smiled. "Or, like you said for me to tell him, when the black snakeroot blooms."

THE NEXT MORNING, Lula held the stuffed billy goat she'd brought down from her room. "Aunt Helen, can we take him back in the car? I don't want him to get hurt. I know Holly will love him."

"Once we're all packed, if there's room, yes; if not, he'll have to go with the movers," said Helen. She raised an eyebrow. "I don't want anything to happen to him either. After all, it's taken us years to find the perfect child to give him to."

They heard the sound of a truck and went out on the porch. The crates had arrived and were swiftly hauled into the living room. Everyone got busy packing the china, and after a quick lunch, Helen announced that she had to go into town.

"It shouldn't take long to close out my accounts at the bank," she said as Lula went upstairs to change baby Holly and put her down for a nap. Once Lula was out of earshot, Helen said, "Now, Doris, I want you to remember what I told you."

"Yes, yes. How could I forget being ordered to commit a sin."

"You mustn't think of it that way, Doris. I'm sure our Creator makes allowances when necessary. Besides, we're only going to be here for a few days, and we don't expect any visitors. However, if on the off chance we do, and they see the baby, you're to tell them Holly's your daughter's child, and we're taking care of it because she and her husband had to travel for a funeral."

"I thought I was supposed to say she was ailing," said Doris.

"Lula and I talked it over while you were asleep in the car, and we like this better."

"Goodness gracious," Doris grumbled. "I hope no one shows up. That way, I won't have to lie." She looked up at Helen, her brows furrowed. "What are we going to tell folks about the baby when we move into the new house?"

"Don't worry about that now, we'll cross that bridge when we come to it."

Doris plopped down on a couch. "I don't know, Miss Helen. I don't think I can keep doing this. It wasn't so bad our being way out in the country."

Helen sat down next to her and took her hand. "You must, Doris. When Father Ryan brought you to live with us, he said you would understand our situation and help us."

"He didn't say anything about all this lying."

"Doris, I never told you how Lula got in this condition, and I think it's about time I did."

Helen told her what happened to Lula on the mountain, and when she was done, they were both crying.

"You know Lula's going to start nursing school in Greensboro in September. Even though none of this was her fault, if they find out about Holly, they'll make her leave, and it'll just about break that child's heart. There could always be someone from around here who'll be at the school. That's why I bought the house in Pittsboro. It's close enough for her to visit the baby on Sundays, yet far enough away to keep her secret. She's been through a lot, and look at her. She's showing all the resiliency of the sturdy mountain folks she came from. Doris, you just have to do this for her."

"How could such a terrible thing happen to such a sweet girl," said Doris. She dried her eyes with her apron. "When we come to that bridge, you tell me what I'm supposed to say, and I'll say it."

AFTER PACKING and sorting most of the day, by evening, Lula lay on the couch with Holly in her arms. She had started the fire after dinner as dusk began to fall, and soft flames now danced over the hot coals. How she would miss the sound of crackling dry oak. The Pittsboro house had a fireplace, but it wouldn't be the same. A fire on a mountain hearth burns in communion with everything around it—the deep, dark outside blanketing every window, the drumbeat of chirping katydids, and the comforting feeling as the dewy air dissipates into a cozy warmth.

Helen broke the silence. "What are you thinking about, Lula?"

"Nothing. I'm just content to have my little girl here in my arms." She turned her head and kissed Holly's cheek.

Helen got up, stoked the fire, and put on another log.

"You told Doris about what happened to me, didn't you?" said Lula.

"She had to know," Helen replied.

"I could tell by the way she looked at me after you left. Once I even caught her crying, and we hugged."

It was a while before anyone spoke. Only Helen sniffled.

"I never want Holly to know how she came into this world," said Lula. "It'll make her sad like it did Doris."

"Once you're out of school," said Helen, "we can move to Charleston or even somewhere in Virginia where you can get a job at a small clinic, or work for a doctor, and we can tell everyone you're a widow."

"I don't know. All this seems so dishonest," said Lula. "But I guess we have no choice. I don't want Holly to grow up with the burden of shame for something she didn't do. It's not fair."

"Don't worry about anything, darling. And as far as you being widowed, we'll come up with something."

"Aunt Helen, thank you for everything."

"Thank you, Lula. You are my everything."

THE NEXT DAY, Helen had to go back to town to see her attorney, hoping to be back by early afternoon. Lula swept up the straw while Doris finished packing the china. They heard a wagon pull up, and Lula, not expecting anyone, peeked out the window. It was someone she didn't know. She went out on the porch.

"Are you Lula?" he asked.

She nodded.

"I've been sent from Gus Gibson's place. They got word this morning that your ma's ill, and thought you should know."

"How ill is she?"

"I don't rightly know. It has to be bad for them to send word down."

Distressed at the news, Lula began to fret. "Are you going back up the mountain now?" she asked.

"After I deliver these oak planks in Edneyville," he said.

"How long will it take?"

"Not long."

"Can you pick me up and give me a ride to Gus's place?"

"I won't be going up quite that far, but I can git you most of the way. It'll help if you can be waitin for me down on the road."

"I'll be there."

Doris watched agape as Lula pawed through the closet searching for her hiking sack. Finding it, she tore through the cabin, throwing in every kind of medicine they had on hand, then she filled a canteen with water.

"What are you doing?" asked Doris.

"You heard what he said. My mother's sick. I must go to her."

"I think you better wait for Miss Helen."

"Tell her I'll get Gus to take me up and bring word down. If I can't find him, I'm going alone."

Lula remembered a small gift she had for her mother and ran up the stairs to her room. She grabbed a small box off her dresser, shoved it in her pocket, and started out. She couldn't resist taking a moment to look at Holly asleep in her cradle on the floor. Despite the harrowing way she came to be, the small darling bundle filled Lula's heart with joy. Tears filled her eyes as she crouched down and touched one of the delicate pink fingers. It broke her heart that she couldn't share this secret treasure with her mother. Lula tenderly adjusted the blanket, then hurried down the stairs, anxious to be on her way.

Once downstairs, she grabbed her sack and ran down the lane to the main road. Shortly, the wagon came from around the mountain and she climbed on. As the horse trotted up the Edney Inn Road, the man went on about how well Gus's new lumber business was doing. "He's even taking on a worker full time," the man said.

Lula barely listened, just nodded from time to time. Her mind was racing through all the illnesses her mother could be afflicted with. She needed to run over to Carrie's house and get Essie to go up the mountain with her and Gus.

The wagon had been climbing the mountain on the dirt road for over an hour, when the man said, "Seein how worried you are, I'm takin you all the way." He clucked for his horse to keep going past the road to his place, and twenty minutes later, turned around in Gus's lot and let Lula off. She thanked him, then checked the sawmill, but seeing no one around, went up to the house.

"Gus's gone over the mountain to the Salola Inn," his wife told her. "He's delivering a load of wood and won't be back for quite a while."

Lula left and rushed up the road to Carrie's house. She knocked at the door, praying Essie would open it.

"My word. If it isn't Lula," said Carrie as she swung the door open. Come on in and tell me what done brought you here."

"I'm looking for Essie. Is she here?"

"Good Lord, no, child. She's staying somewheres else these days." The woman seemed reluctant to continue, but finally said, "I took her in even though I knew her failings. But she worsened a couple months ago, and I had to ask her to leave."

Lula left sick at heart to hear about Essie being turned out of another place. She hurried down the dusty lane to the trailhead, then stopped cold. She stood there fighting off the dark memories until the image of her mother lying sick in her bed loomed. She took a deep breath, slung her sack over her shoulder, and started into the woods.

HELEN BEEPED THE horn three times as she passed the deserted drugstore to signal to everyone at the house that she'd arrived. She was surprised to see Doris waiting on the porch alone. Lula was probably tending to Holly. She pulled up, and Doris rushed down the steps.

"I told Lula not to go, but she wouldn't listen to me."

"Go? Where?"

"Up to see her mother."

"What are you talking about?"

"A man came and told her that her mother was sick. Lula said to tell you that she was going to see if Gus could take her up there. If not, she was going alone."

"Good Lord! How long ago did she leave?"

"An hour, maybe. The man had a horse drawn wagon, so he wouldn't be going that fast."

"I have to go get her," said Helen. "You stay with the baby no matter what." She took off and drove as fast as she could, all the while praying to God this was going to end well. She passed the burned-out hulk of the Edney Inn, and her heart sank thinking how fast tragedy could strike. The road seemed bumpier and the corners sharper as she sped along. She would fly if she could. By the time she reached Gus's, she was already fighting off her old nemeses and struggling to breathe. She got out, and seeing no one in the sawmill, went directly to the house.

"Everyone's lookin for that man today," said his wife. "Even your Lula."

"Did he go with her?"

"No. Like I told her, Gus is off deliverin a load of wood. Don't expect him back til late."

The woman's dog barked and charged out between her legs, almost knocking her over. They both looked to see what the dog was after and saw Gus walking his two horses down the road. Helen ran across the lawn, shouting and waving. He stopped and waited for her.

"Thank God, you're here," said Helen, breathless.

"I don't know what I have to thank him for," said Gus. "My wagon tipped over goin up Sugarloaf. Lost the whole load. It rolled off the wagon and down the mountain. The axle broke, too." He continued leading the horses toward the barn. "I spose you're here to talk about goin up to see Hattie in the next couple of days."

"Didn't you send word that she was ill?" said Helen.

"No. I've been gone since early this morning."

"Someone came to the house and said you sent them to tell us Hattie was sick."

"Oh, that had to be my man. Someone probably came down from the mountain and told him. He must've asked one of my customers going your way to stop by to tell ya."

"Gus, I have to go up after her. She hasn't been well. Please take me."

"Now?"

"Yes! This minute!"

He scratched behind his ears and thought for a moment. "Okay. Let me get Mabel to see to the horses."

He put his fingers in his mouth and let out a shrill whistle. The door to the house opened, and his wife stepped out.

"Come take care of the horses. I'm takin Miss Helen up to see Hattie."

He went over to the well, brought up the bucket, and had a long drink. Then he took off his straw hat and spilled the contents of the bucket over his head. "Let's go. I gotta be back before dark."

With Gus at her side, Helen felt confident she could navigate the climb. Thank God she was wearing a casual pair of slacks and a pair of flat shoes. She'd had too much work to do at Edelweiss to get all gussied up just to close out her bank accounts. They made good time and were going at a steady pace, until the steep section became challenging.

"Let's set a while," Gus said. "You need a rest."

A stream trickled nearby. He went over and drank from his cupped hands, filled his hat with water, and took it to her.

"Put some on your face. It'll cool you off," he told her.

She dipped both hands in the hat and splashed the water over her face. "That felt good," she said. She looked up at him. "I rested at this very spot the first time Lula took me to see her mother." She pulled a hanky from her pocket and wiped her face. "I'm worried about Hattie. Has she been ailing before to-day?"

"I wouldn't know. Haven't been up there going on six months."

"Didn't you go up and tell her we were coming this week?"

"No. I told my hired man to. You know. The feller who used to work for Luke."

"Zeb?"

"I admit, he's not always sober," said Gus, "but sometimes you gotta take what you can get."

"You mean to tell me that man knew Lula would be coming?"

"Sure. I told him so."

She appeared dazed as she spoke almost to herself. "My God. This morning he knew you wouldn't be here if she came, so he sent someone to our house." She jumped up, almost hysterical. "We've got to get going right now!"

Gus grabbed her shoulders. "What's wrong, woman?"

Helen clung to his shirt. "Oh, Gus. He violated that girl something awful the last time she went up there."

It took a moment for him to absorb the weight of what she had said. "Come to think of it, he always showed an interest in her." His jaw tightened. "We have no time to waste. You stay here. I'm goin up alone."

He turned and started off, leaving Helen standing there. She watched him disappear into the woods in disbelief. She covered her face with her hands and cried, but only for a moment. She began climbing the trail with the determination of a mother bear driven to save her cub. Every time she tripped, she got up. Every time she came to a boulder, she dug her fingers into anything she could get a hold of and surmounted it. Her fingers bled and her knees numbed, but she kept climbing.

CHAPTER TWENTY-THREE
1961

Holly pulled into the Burrows' driveway and sat there bracing herself for the challenge ahead. The mother's story of being slammed against a wall worried her, but not as much as what could happen to Patsy if she didn't get the operation. She got out, and as she was about to knock on the door, it swung open. She gasped at the terrifying scowl on Mr. Burrows' flushed face.

"Clear out. We don't need the likes of you around here."

"Please, Mr. Burrows. For Patsy's sake, let me talk to you."

His face twisted into a hideous sneer.

Without taking her eyes from him, she pulled out a picture and held it for him to see.

"Do you want her to look like this?"

She held her breath as he glared at the photo. Suddenly he swiped it from her hand, crunched it into a ball, and threw it at her.

"Get out!"

Mrs. Burrows, cowering in the kitchen, caught Holly's eye. The woman's face was bruised, and one eye was swollen shut. The sight bolstered Holly's resolve. Pulling a handful of pictures from her briefcase, she thrust them in the man's face.

"Look at these, Mr. Burrows! Are you going to let your fear

ruin your child's life! This is what you should be afraid of, not the operation."

Trembling with rage, he slapped the photos out of her hand and sent them flying. He took a menacing step toward her, and she quickly pulled back.

"I said, get out of here!" he roared.

She refused to move, but caught her breath when he neared close enough for her to feel the heat of his body.

"I'm warning you," he said. "Don't you dare show up here again. And God help you if I hear you've been talking to my wife."

He backed into the house and slammed the door.

Holly's shoulders sagged. She hadn't gotten through to him. She bent down to retrieve one of the discarded pictures, but stopped. No! She'd let him pick them up.

THE NEXT MORNING, Holly finished lacing her hiking boots and ran downstairs to find Myrt stuffing something into her backpack.

"What are you doing up so early?" Holly asked.

"Packing your lunch."

"I said I'd do that last night."

"I had to get up early anyway to bake some of my William's favorite cornbread for you two. Has honey in it. After climbing up the mountain, that Garrison fella should really go for it." She tore off a piece of wax paper and wrapped a large chunk of cornbread. "I taught that boy in the fourth grade. He had a tendency to be a little too big for his britches at times, but he was kind and hard working." She winked at Holly. "Like Ella says, it won't hurt you none to sidle up to him." She put the cornbread in the pack and shoved in two moon pies. "I figure, the way he's showing you all this interest, you've got a good chance at reeling him in."

"Really, Myrt! I have no intentions of reeling him in."

"Well, start entertaining those intentions right now, girl. It's about time you got married."

Holly rolled her eyes. "Where are the thermoses?" she asked, in an effort to change the subject.

"Filled them with cold water and packed them already," said Myrt.

Hearing a vehicle pull up, Holly gave Myrt a fleeting hug and ran out the door. She tossed the backpack in the truck's bed and got in.

"I see you know how to dress for a climb," said Jeff.

"After I finished college, I had a boyfriend who used to take me hiking."

A fleeting frown crossed Jeff's face as he started driving. Turning left off Route 64, the truck started climbing, but instead of turning on the road going upward, he continued across the mountain.

"Weren't we supposed to turn back there?" she asked.

"I want to show you my orchard first."

They passed his grandmother's trailer, came around the mountain, and stopped. He got out and went and opened her door. She stepped onto the truck's running board, and he took her by the waist and swung her to the ground before leading her to the side of the road where the land dropped off. Hundreds of apple trees ran row after row in the distance like a bolt of striped cloth spooled across the rolling hills.

"How beautiful," she said.

"When I'm in the orchard, all I see is the work ahead of me, but when I drive around this curve and see them spread out like that, I'm kinda proud."

"You should be," she said.

They got back in the truck, and after a short drive, he pulled onto a driveway and up to a trailer. He sat back and gazed at the house next to it.

"I've been building that place for two years now, and once this harvest is in, I'll have the money to finish it."

Holly couldn't resist giving him a coy, little smile. "You remind me of the bowerbird that builds a fancy nest to attract a mate."

He raised an eyebrow and eyed her. "Is there anything wrong with that?"

She blushed. "No. Actually, there isn't."

They drove on, hardly speaking a word. Holly sensed that his offer to show her the colony was meant to be more than a casual date. They arrived at the trailhead, and Holly jumped out and reached for her backpack.

Jeff grabbed it up and made a face. "What do you have in here?" He took out the two thermos bottles, unscrewed the cups, and threw them in the backpack, then left the thermoses on the front seat.

"There's plenty of springs up there," he said as he adjusted the backpack's straps to fit his broad back. He put it on. "Let's go."

Holly was surprised that the trail was nothing more than an overgrown foot path and soon found that her muscles for steep climbs weren't as limber as she had thought. She'd never faced a hike so relentlessly steep or littered with so many boulders. Much to her consternation, it didn't take long for the two of them to fall into the routine of Jeff breaking ground ahead of her, then automatically reaching for her hand to pull her up every time they came to a steep climb or boulder.

Holly heard the trickling stream in the inviting shade well before she spied it.

"Can we rest here?" she asked.

After taking off the backpack, he brought out the cups and handed her one. Holly eagerly helped herself to a drink from the stream, then took off her shoes and socks so she could wade barefoot in the rock-strewn stream.

"Ooo... it's freezing!"

Jeff leaned against a tree grinning.

"What's so funny?" she asked.

"Nothing. It's just the first time I've seen you in anything other than that territory nurse outfit of yours."

"Don't you be making fun of my uniform," she said as she cautiously stepped from stone to stone. She wobbled on one, and losing her balance, readily accepted his outstretched hand.

By the time they started up again, the sun was high in the sky. Luckily, the path followed the course of the stream, helping to cool the nearby forest. The forbidding woodlands constantly vied for her attention, and Holly found it hard to keep her eyes on the trail as they entered a dark, mysterious section. A giant oak tree canopy hovered a hundred feet overhead, creating a haunting cathedral where moss-covered rocks and decades of leaf litter yearned for sunlight's salvation. Awed, she looked up at the scattered specks of blue, visible through the lacework of leaves.

Next, they came to an area where a huge tree had been struck down by lightning, allowing beams of sunlight to dance on the ground to the tune of the breeze. The path abruptly ended at the stream's bank where it grew much wider and deeper. Holly could see that the path continued on the other side of the racing water. Seeing Jeff sitting on a rock taking off his boots, she began to unlace hers.

"That's okay," he said. "I'll carry you across."

He tied his laces together and hung his boots around his neck. "Here, put the backpack on, and hop on my back."

He started cautiously into the water gripping her legs, while she hung onto him with her arms around his neck. Midway across, the water grew deeper, and he hefted her up to keep her from getting wet. Feeling his strength, Holly fought off the stirring feeling racing through her.

Two hours into the climb, they came through a large drift of rhododendrons on each side of the path. It suddenly opened to a dramatic view of endless blue sky. Holly ran out onto an expansive granite cliff and thrilled to the spectacular view of the valley below.

Jeff came up next to her, and they both stood on the landmark that was visible for miles, enjoying the breeze wafting up from the valley.

"It's beautiful at night." He pointed in the distance. "Over there, you can see Hendersonville all lit up, and lights sparkle throughout these mountains. I'd sometimes camp up here with friends and never felt so small as when we'd lay on this rock at night and gaze up at thousands of stars. And the fireflies in early June. Man! Do they put on a show!"

Almost as if he was embarrassed to be talking about his place in the universe, he took her hands and examined them. "Healing hands," he murmured.

He held them longer than he needed to, and finally said, "We better get moving."

She took two moon pies from the backpack and handed him one, and they casually walked from the cliff, enjoying their treat before starting another strenuous leg of the journey.

Now that she had caught her second wind, Holly was taking the trek in stride. She savored the sheer beauty all around her and was beginning to understand the lure of the mountains. She was touched by Jeff's obvious intentions. She felt honored by them and believed he was prepared to carry her all the way up that treacherous mountain on his back if that's what it took to win her over. Recalling what Ella had said about the girls at Mt. Moriah, she couldn't understand why she was the one he'd chosen to woo. Nevertheless, judging from the tender way he was caring for her, she was convinced that was exactly what he was doing.

How she wished this was the right time to take him up on it. But it wasn't. She needed to find the answers to her questions first. Hopefully, he would wait until then.

The incline started to taper off, and as they broke through a thicket, a massive, thickly forested rolling plateau surrounded by mountains lay in front of them.

"You're looking at what folks in the valley call the Lost Colony," Jeff announced. "If it wasn't for the years of bear hunters beating down this path, I don't know if we'd ever have found it. Makes you wonder how those early settlers discovered it in the first place."

The heat grew intense without the protection of the shade, and the almost deafening chirping of cicadas pierced the resounding silence in waves. They followed the path to a huge open meadow with birds flitting from flower to flower. Jeff stopped and listened.

"Can you hear that?" he asked.

All Holly heard was the sound of chirping birds.

"Listen. Can you hear the bob white?" he asked.

She shook her head.

"Let's see if I can call it in." He whistled "bob white, bob white," then listened for a moment to see if the quail would return his call. Not hearing anything, he tried again. "Bob white, bob white." He pointed to the brush beyond and smiled when the call was returned. "Did you hear him?" he asked Holly. "He's over there."

She nodded. "Do it again," She whispered.

Jeff whistled the call, and Holly grinned when she heard the bird return it.

"How did you learn to do that?" she asked as they continued making their way through the meadow.

"As a kid I sometimes got bored, living in the woods like we did, so I started mimicking all the sounds I heard. My uncle taught me to whistle, and I got good at different bird calls. If you sound enough like one, they'll come in close so they can look you over and see who's come into their territory."

"How many birds can you mimic?"

"Doves, cardinals, blue jays. Pretty much all the birds you'll find around here." He laughed. "And by the time I was ten, I could do mules, horses, and chickens, too."

They came out of the meadow and back into the forest where the path wound around a huge boulder. A vine-covered mound stood in front of them. Holly could barely make out what was left of a stone chimney through all the foliage.

"Let's keep going," he said. "I'll show you the old Garrison homeplace if I can find it."

They continued up the path until Jeff stopped and began pushing aside the thicket before reaching what was left of a log cabin. He tore off layers of vines, finally revealing a door. He rattled it until it swung open on one hinge.

"Let's see if it's anything like I remember. I was four the last time I was actually in it."

He peeked in and went inside. Holly pushed aside the tangle and followed him into what was left of the dark, musty cabin. The only light came from either the doorway or from what was left of the vine-covered roof. A fireplace and hearth took up one whole end. Other than that, there was nothing more to see.

"It's hard to believe my grandma and grandpa raised eight kids in this place," he said.

Holly stepped over to the stone fireplace and spotted something smothered in a thick coat of cobwebs hanging from a nail on the mantle. Curious, she neared and took a closer look. A shiver ran down her spine. It appeared to be a string of seeds like the one in her aunt's jewelry box. An eerie feeling settled on her like a fog.

Jeff neared to see what she was looking at. He peeled away the mass of webs, took it from the nail, and brushed it off before showing it to her. "It's a necklace made out of apple seeds. Granny must've left it behind when we took her down from the mountain." He smiled. "That's the way they lived up here. They learned to take some simple little thing like an apple seed and turn it into something beautiful." He put it in his pocket. "I'll take it to her."

Holly shook off the shock of seeing an exact copy of the necklace in her aunt's jewelry box. It convinced her that she was getting closer to the answers she was searching for. They went outside, and Jeff wrestled the door closed, then found a rock and jammed it up against it. "That should hold it. Now let's go to the falls and see what you've got in that backpack."

They found the path again and started toward a creek that ran and splashed as if it were in a hurry to get somewhere. They hadn't gone far when Holly got a whiff of perfumed air. She followed her nose until she spotted a rose bush climbing up the remains of a chimney. She tugged on Jeff's shirt and pointed to it.

"Can you smell that?"

He started toward it. "I'll pick one for you."

She watched him thrash through the vegetation and held her breath as he climbed on a pile of stones to reach the flower on the highest part of the chimney's remains, returning with a small, but plush pink rose.

"It's funny," she said as she brought it to her nose. "I know this fragrance. It smells just like the roses from my aunt's trellis in Pittsboro. She prized it and told me it wasn't like the ones you buy these days that don't have any scent."

"That's because most of the ones you get from the stores are cultivars propagated for their size and color, not their scent," said Jeff as he looked over at the rose bush. "That one could've come over with the original settlers ages ago."

"I bet it was once part of a garden," said Holly.

"You should see this place in the spring," said Jeff. "All you have to do to find the old cabins is look for the daffodils."

Holly studied the rose. "If I ever have a house of my own, I'd like to have this rose growing in my garden."

He slowly brushed a stray wisp of hair from her forehead with a finger. "I can make that happen."

Her face flushed, and she looked away.

They followed the stream until Holly thought she saw a couple of headstones sticking up from the briars. "Look. I bet that was their cemetery. Let's go take a look."

"Aren't you hungry? We can check it out on the way back."

She nodded, and they continued up the trail running alongside the creek for a couple of miles when they heard the roar of a waterfall up ahead. The trail led them away from the creek and up a steep climb to a bald cliff. Holly stepped out onto it in wonderment. The creek below was rushing over the face of a massive bald and cascading hundreds of feet down before disappearing into the woods and finding its way to a wide rocky river that ran through the gorge.

She looked up and down the cavernous gorge blanketed in forest. Occasional giant balds and bold rock-faced ridges exposed its granite underbelly. Jeff came up next to her and put his arm around her waist in a way that pleased her, for it was as if he wanted to make sure she wouldn't fall off the cliff.

"That's Chimney Rock Village down there," he said. Pointing directly below them, he said, "And that's what they call the Hickory Nut Falls. You can't see it from here, but around that ridge is the Chimney Rock itself." He nodded toward a grassy rise above the bald. "Let's go eat up there."

At the rise, Jeff took off the backpack, and Holly pulled a checkered cloth from it and spread it on the ground. "My aunt loved this old thing and took it on all our picnics. It makes me feel like she's here with us."

He sat hugging his knees, content to watch her unpack the lunch. She handed him a chunk of cornbread.

"Here," she said, "Myrt baked it special for you this morning."

He took a bite. "Oooo, I do love Miss Myrt's cornbread."

Sitting shoulder to shoulder, they ate their sandwiches mesmerized by the hawks soaring in circles on thermal drafts above the gorge.

Holly handed him a cupcake. "I made these for you last night."

"Wow! I'm not used to all this attention," said Jeff.

"Come now," said Holly. "From all the gossip going around, it looks like you're getting plenty from the girls at Mt. Moriah."

He laughed. "Oh, how right you are. I'm almost afraid to go there. They make me feel like a prized bull."

Holly looked at him in amazement. "There you go again. Every time I start to think you're a great guy, you say something so egotistical I want to slap you. Especially as far as women are concerned."

"Me?! Egotistical?! As far as women are concerned?!"

His laugh was laced with cynicism.

"Don't you worry, my dear. That might've been true at one time, but I've been duly humbled. And the picture perfect, always beautifully dressed Tammy Lee Wilcox was just the girl to do it. Yessiree, I've had my comeuppance."

"Something tells me I'm really going to like this Tammy Lee Wilcox," said Holly, laughing.

"We weren't even engaged for a whole year before she threw me over for anyone else she could get her dainty little hands on."

"Tammy Lee threw *you* over?" she asked teasingly. "Do tell."

"Well..."

"Come on, you can tell me," said Holly, nudging him. "After the way you lifted, carried, and dragged me all over these mountains, we've got nothing to hide from each other."

"Okay. You asked for it." He reached for a chocolate chip cookie, took a bite, and thoughtfully examined it. "Things were going pretty good, or at least I thought they were. That is up until last summer when I was getting ready to start picking apples. A hailstorm hit us, and my apples weren't good for anything but sauce. I knew if I didn't get them to the processing plant that day, I'd pretty much lose my shirt. I didn't have pickers lined up yet, so I had to call in everybody I could—my mother, my sister and her husband, all my cousins, every friend—and start picking.

"I was on a ladder reaching for an apple when this big, fluffy pink mass at the far end of the row caught my eye. It suddenly hit me. It was Tammy Lee. I'd forgotten I was supposed to go with her to her best friend's wedding that afternoon."

Holly threw her head back and laughed. She slowly shook her head. "This doesn't look like it's going to end well."

"I'd seen her all riled up once before," he continued, "and by the determined way she marched down that row I knew I was in for it. I kept picking while I waited for her to reach me. She didn't even give me a chance to say anything before she screamed, 'Jeffery! Get down this minute! You're going to Annie's wedding with me!' Naturally everyone heard her, and boy, did they come running," he said with a rueful smirk.

"Naturally," offered Holly.

"I tried to reason with her. When I told her if I didn't get everything picked and delivered that day I could lose everything, she hollered, 'Good! Then you can get a decent job like everyone else. The last thing I ever wanted was to be married to a farmer.'"

He shook his head. "The way she said that word... like it was something nasty..." He grew quiet, staring into the distance, remembering the scene. "Boy, for a minute, I thought my mother was gonna go for her." He tossed his head and chuckled. "The only thing that saved Tammy Lee from my mother's wrath was her ultimatum. 'Jeffery, you either get down from that ladder and go with me right now, or we're through!'

"When I didn't get down, she let loose." He blew a long, slow whistle. "Oh, boy, did she let me have it. She kicked any ounce of pride I had left right out of me. Right there, in front of almost everyone I knew and loved, she spit out a humiliating list of my many flaws, right down to my stinky socks."

"You poor thing," said Holly, feigning sympathy.

"My buddies still ride me about it."

They both laughed.

"Let me tell you, it was painful," he kept on. "Over her shoulders I could see my two best buddies laughing their guts out. She finally took off her engagement ring, and flung it at me."

Suppressing a smile, and with a twinkle in his eye, he shook his head and tsked. "It was sad the way it finally ended."

"Sad?" said Holly, leaning forward so she could look him in the eye.

"It happened so fast I couldn't do anything. She flung the ring with such force, it made her step back in a puddle of mud. Her shoe got stuck, and there she was, pulling and tugging, trying to wiggle it loose when she lost her balance and..."

"Don't tell me," said Holly. "She didn't."

"Yep, she did. It was one sad sight watching her limp away wearing one shoe and that flouncy pink dress covered in mud."

After having a good laugh, Holly said, "Did you ever find the ring?"

"It took me and my mom a good hour the next day, but we found it. I brought it back to the jeweler, and we worked something out. I guess these things happen often enough. I hope those other guys didn't get as humiliated as I did."

They sat with their thoughts and watched the hawks for a while. Holly smiled to herself, pleased to be getting to know Jeff. His invitation to take her to the Lost Colony was part of the age-old mating ritual, and this strenuous trek was a chance for him to show her his ability and fitness to take care of her. True, there was a pridefulness about him. But it was more honest than arrogant. She respected the way he was forthrightly offering himself as a candidate for her hand, and she knew that someday she would consider it.

She looked down the gorge contorting its way to the back and beyond and wondered what the future held for her.

A serious expression appeared on his face as he ran the back of a finger slowly down her cheek. "Now that I've bared my soul, it's your turn to tell me about the guy who took you hiking."

"It's not as colorful as your story. They're so strict in nursing school, I hardly ever dated until I graduated and met George. He was interning at the hospital where I worked. When he was offered a position as a resident at Mass General in Boston, he wanted to get married. But, my aunt had just died, and I'd just found something out that I had to track down."

She took a deep breath and slowly let it out. This was going to be a lot harder than telling her story to Myrt and Ella.

"Jeff, you need to know something about me. I was an orphan, and Helen Baldwin adopted me. I always called her Aunt Helen, but I believe she was no relation to me. All my life I wanted to know who I was and where I came from, but mostly why my mother gave me away. I used to daydream about finding her so she could see who I was and like me. I never really had a clue until my aunt's funeral. A distant cousin of her's told me she used to live near Bat Cave. That's why I'm here."

"What made you want to talk to Granny about the Lost Colony?"

"When I was little, I overheard my aunt talking to an old friend who mentioned it. I remember how upset she was when she found out I heard him." Holly wrung her hands. "I'm convinced she was somehow connected to this place. That necklace we found today was exactly like one that was in her jewelry box." She bit her lip and thought. "And when I smelled the rose you picked for me that was exactly like the one my aunt had, I got the willies."

"Did my grandma tell you anything?"

"No. She answered every one of my questions with another question."

"That's the way of the old ones."

"Jeff, I know my aunt used to own a house in Edneyville called Edelweiss and was teaching French at the Fassifern School for Girls in Hendersonville as late as 1933. She sold Edelweiss in 1934, the year I was born and she adopted me. That same year she bought a house in Pittsboro, and sometime after that, started teaching in the local public school. Everything points to my being born out of wedlock to one of her students at Fassifern. In those days, a girl like that would've been a pariah. My aunt was really kind and would've helped her, even going as far as adopting the baby.

"All that makes sense," Holly continued, "except, when I visited Edelweiss, I came across clothes that would've been worn by a young girl. I'm sure there was a young girl living there, because I read it in someone's diary. I keep asking myself, who was she? And now that I saw a rustic old seed necklace hanging in your grandmother's cabin that is exactly like the one I found among all my aunt's valuable jewelry, I'm sure there's more to this story.

"Jeff, I won't find peace until I get these answers. I keep thinking my mother is out there somewhere, and I want her to know me. To know how I turned out. Maybe to love me. I know I want to love her."

Holly hesitated as if she couldn't make up her mind. Finally, she turned to him and said, "I didn't tell you why I broke up with George." She wiped one eye and then the other. "When I told him why I wanted to come here, he said it was better that I never find out where I came from, so I'd never have to lie about it. The way he said it, I could tell it would make a difference to him if what I found out was scandalous, which it may very well be. He's from an old Boston family and proud of his heritage. It gave me that same old feeling of being rejected."

Jeff put an arm around her and gently squeezed. "If he loved you, none of that would matter. You are the person you've become. All that matters to me, Holly, is you." He kissed her gently on the cheek.

She leaned into him for a moment, comforted by his kind words. There were other feelings in there, too; feelings she couldn't give in to until she had answers. She straightened abruptly and snatched up the wax paper wrappings. "We better start packing."

As he helped her gather the remnants of the lunch, he said, "I want one last word about that ex-boyfriend of yours. He's missing out on someone who's probably as dedicated to helping folks as anyone could be. Anyway, that's what I thought the minute I saw you trying to change your tire that first day. I took one look at you and said to myself, 'Any pretty girl who can go around in those godawful black shoes and turn her uniform inside out in broad daylight so she won't get it dirty, is either so totally committed to a cause that she's willing to wear any kind of getup, or she's just plain crazy.'"

Holly's mouth fell open as she uttered, "Awww."

Laughing, he caught the backpack she threw at him.

With the trail blazed, the trek down the mountain proved to be much easier than the climb. Holly kept a keen eye out for the remains of the cemetery as they approached the cabin ruins.

"There it is!" she cried, spying the top of a tombstone.

Jeff cleared a path to what looked like a cluster of grave markers. The stones were pockmarked with age and the words etched in them barely legible.

"Wow," sighed Holly. "This one says 1798."

"A bunch of Garrisons are buried somewhere in here," said Jeff, "and according to Granny, they go back at least that far."

Holly stumbled on a small stone no bigger than a shoebox, and noticed five more in a row. "Gee. How sad. I bet these were for babies."

They looked at a few more and were ready to start back down when Holly noticed something glistening through the thicket on a rise overhead.

"I wonder what that is up there?" she said.

"I suppose you want to go and take a look," said Jeff in an accommodating tone. Without waiting for an answer, he grabbed hold of a small tree and lifted himself to the rise. Out of sight for a moment, he reached down for her and yelled, "You gotta come and see this!"

Holly took hold of his outstretched hand, and he pulled her up onto the ledge. He pointed to a headstone he'd partially cleared from vines. "This marker isn't at all like the rest of them. It's made of white marble, and the etching's been done by machine."

"Can you get more of those vines off?" she asked.

He proceeded to rip them away.

Holly studied part of the inscription, now black with mold. *Lula Mae McWade* jumped out at her, making her gasp.

"Is something wrong?" asked Jeff.

"That was the name of one of the Fassifern girls! The one who volunteered at the hospital."

She started tearing off the rest of the vines until she read, *1916 -1934.* "Oh my God. She died the year I was born. Look! She was only eighteen. Could this be... I mean... she could've been..." She fell to her knees and feverishly yanked up weeds.

He lifted her up and said, "Don't. You'll tear up those healing hands. I'll come up here another day with a sickle and clear everything away."

She rose and started pushing aside the foliage.

"What are you doing?" he asked.

"Looking to see if someone's buried next to her."

Not finding another headstone, Holly murmured, "I wonder if he's still alive."

CHAPTER TWENTY-FOUR

Jeff hated to take the time away from the orchard, but he was worried about Holly. That strong will of hers wasn't going to let her stop riling up half the county until she got all the answers she was searching for. He decided it was time to pay a call on his old buddy, Cal Hackett. He still hung out with the old gang up on the mountain. One of Jeff's tractors had to be fixed before the pickers arrived in the morning, so he had to make the visit short. No kicking back over a couple of beers and a few laughs. Hopefully, Cal would be in his shop and not hiding out in the woods working on his still.

He pulled into Cal's compound and was surprised to see a new steel building and his old friend inside working on a motorcycle. Cal looked up, giving him a welcoming nod as he walked in.

Jeff found it hard to believe that this guy with long hair, beard, and doo rag was the same clean-cut kid who went every Sunday scrubbed and polished to the Mountain Home Baptist Church. Had to be the years he spent in the navy. Cal was skinny, but his sleeveless shirt revealed a set of biceps that testified to hard work, only they were marred with bizarre symbols.

"What are you gonna do when you run out of skin?" asked Jeff, gesturing at the tattoos.

Cal laughed. "Man, you gotta be on some kind of mission to tear yourself away from your apples this time of year. Don't tell me you're finally in the market for some of my hooch."

Jeff crossed his arms and leaned against a wall.

"Well, let's have it," said Cal.

Jeff nudged a ball lying on the floor with his foot. "Seeing that a lot of the old gang hangs out here, I wondered if you've heard any talk going around about a nurse?"

Cal looked up from the motorcycle he was working on and studied Jeff for a moment. "Some. Heard she got Joey the fixins for a chicken coop." He laughed and went back to the bike. "They say she's a whole sight better looking than the last one."

Jeff looked around at the boxes of parts neatly stacked on shelves next to a display of expensive leather jackets. "Looks like business is booming."

"You could say that."

"Heard anything else about her?"

"Some of the boys talked about giving her a fright."

"What for?"

"From what I can tell, she's got that nosey bitch at the post office poking around in things the old folks up on Stony Mountain want kept buried."

"What sort of things?" Jeff asked.

He shrugged. "It's got to be shit you and I obviously don't know anything about." He finished unscrewing a sparkplug and looked over at Jeff. "You sweet on her?"

Jeff gave him a hard stare.

"Don't worry. Nobody's gonna hurt her. The boys were told to give her a scare is all. And if anyone can do it, those dudes from Stony Mountain can." He chuckled. "Just looking at them is scary enough. And when they get her on edge, they're supposed to tell her to lay off asking about her family." He went back to working on the bike and called out, "Hand me that wrench on the counter."

When he didn't get an answer, he looked up to find Jeff gone.

Jeff's truck raced up Garrison Road, his tires spitting out rocks and dust. He pulled into his grandma's drive, slammed on the brakes, and jumped out. He ran up the walk and unto the porch. He was about to open the door to the trailer when he noticed his grandma on the porch rocking.

The very sight of her calmed him. Swelled with love, he strolled over and sank onto the railing.

"Ye look muchly aboil," she said.

"You're right about that, Granny. You remember Holly, the girl who came to visit you? Well, I took her up to the colony, and we found a gravestone with a name carved on it. Lula Mae McWade. She's pretty sure it's her mother's grave."

The old woman rocked and looked off in the distance.

He sat down on the rocker next to her and took her hand. "Granny, some of the boys are trying to scare her off the mountain. Cal Hackett told me the old folks on Stony Mountain don't want her looking for her family. I'm worried. They're a rough bunch."

"Aww, aint nothin, son. They be warnin her is all."

"I don't understand."

"Don't give mind to it none. No one be harmin her."

Jeff scratched behind his ear. "Granny, when I was up at that gravesite with Holly, I kinda remembered something. It's hazy. I had to be four... five at the most since it was the summer I spent with you before Pa took you off the mountain. I remember I was asleep in your cabin, and an awful wailing woke me. You were gone, so I went outside to look for you. There was a light coming from a cabin below, so I went down. When I got there, the door was open, and I pushed my way through the mountain folk gathered around. A girl was lying on the table, and two women were crying in each other's arms." He looked into her eyes. "That gravestone up there said she died in June of '34. That would be about the time I saw that girl lying on the table. Tell me, Granny, was that Lula Mae McWade?"

"Hush! I don't wanna hear none a that talk, son. Ye got no part in it, an ye be best not talkin bout it. Jist get yer girl to tell the woman at the letter office to stop the tongues waggin. Lula was one a our own, an we done seen to it ourselves. It best be forgotten. It would jist dirty up God-fearin folk's memories."

"What's best forgotten, Granny?"

She stared ahead and rocked.

Jeff knew it was hopeless to try to get more out of her than she wanted to give, so he took off for the orchard. Tonight, he had to go see Holly and warn her, even though it meant he'd probably be up all night with the tractor.

HOLLY WRAPPED UP her final visit to the woman who'd had the problem with the chickens with a hopeful feeling of accomplishment. The baby girl was thriving, and a schedule of regular visits to the clinic had been set up. But once back in her car, the cloak of sadness at finding what she suspected was her mother's grave settled on her again.

She pulled out from the dirt road and onto Sugarloaf, expecting to see the black pickup that had been tailing her all day parked on the side waiting. Relieved that it wasn't, she started down the mountain. After the emotional revelations of the day before, she was looking forward to a quiet evening at home and the possibility of Jeff giving her a call, when up ahead, she saw the pickup tucked in a wooded lane.

She slowed down as she passed and tried to get a look at the driver. His cap hid his face, but she could see he was big and burly. She drove with one eye on the road and the other on her rearview mirror. Then, just as she had feared, the pickup came from out of the woods and followed her down the mountain.

Worried the man might try to force her off the road again, it wasn't until she came to the straightaway with open country at the bottom of the mountain, that she was finally able to loosen her iron grip on the steering wheel. She passed a church and several houses and couldn't image him trying anything out in the open. The last thing she wanted was for him to follow her home, so she slowed, hoping he would pass her. But no such luck. Up ahead, the road ran into Route 64 at Freeman's grocery store. She could swing into the parking lot, go in, and hang out until the truck was gone.

As she neared the store, anger at the thought of having to run in and hide got the best of her. She slammed on the brakes, jumped out onto the pavement, and stood in the middle of the road with her fists on her hips, staring at the pickup. It swerved and skidded to a stop. Holly's heart pounded in her throat.

The man jumped out of the truck shouting, "What the hell's wrong with you, woman!"

"I'll tell you what's wrong! I'm sick and tired of you following me! I could've been killed that time you forced me off the road!"

Her fury shocked the man, and he clutched the back of his neck and shook his head in confusion. Holly was surprised to see he was somewhere in his early twenties.

"You should be ashamed of yourself!" she shouted. "How would you like someone doing this to your sister... or your mother?"

"Calm down, ma'am. I aint meanin you no harm."

Even though he was of an intimidating stature, his contrite demeanor told Holly he wasn't going to hurt her. "Tell me, why are you doing this?"

"Ma'am, why don't you tell me why you're trying to hurt our family."

"Hurt your family? How dare you say something like that! I get up every morning and drive all over these treacherous mountains to bring comfort and aid to folks. I'm not from around here, and I'm scared half out of my wits most of the time, but I do it! You know why? Because I want to make a difference! Me! Myself! Every day when I go home I want to know that I made someone's day better. Especially the babies."

Her voice cracked. Holly stopped and took a deep breath.

The man rubbed his forehead as if it ached. "I'm sorry, ma'am, but my grandpa says you're aiming on causin a heap of trouble on us. Anyway, I was just supposed to scare you is all and tell you to stop askin about your kin. That's all he be wantin."

"Well, you can tell your grandpa you succeeded in scaring me, but you can also tell him nothing's going to stop me from finding out who I am and where I came from. I have a right to know."

Seeing he was feeling guilty, she kept pressing. "What does your grandpa have to do with me or my kin?"

"Heck, ma'am. I don't know. Those old ones never tell you nothin. I do know he doesn't cotton to that nosey old woman at the post office gettin everybody to talkin."

A car came from behind, and the driver stared at the two before passing them.

"I better be gettin along," the young man said. He gave Holly a sheepish look. "I only did what I was told. Don't worry. I'm aimin to tell my grandpa I aint doin this no more."

Holly, stunned at what had just happened, stood on the road and watched him get back in his truck and drive away.

MYRT, ELLA, AND Holly sat at the table discussing the gravestone with all the zeal of conspirators. The diary Holly borrowed from Sarah lay open in front of them.

Holly pointed to a page. "Here she's saying, 'The woman Katie works for took Lula Mae and me to town today and bought us peppermint sticks. I sure wished I lived with her. She is most generous and kindly, and I could be Lula's friend and companion.'"

Holly sat back and folded her arms. "That proves it. That girl who lived with my aunt was named Lula... Lula Mae McWade."

"Okay, we now know the girl who is buried up there is Lula McWade," said Ella, "and she lived with your aunt, and according to the yearbook, went to that fancy school your aunt taught at."

"We also know she came from the colony or they wouldn't have buried her there," Myrt added.

"You say she died the year you were born?" asked Ella.

Holly nodded, appearing dazed. "It all adds up to Lula being my mother. But why all the secrecy? It would've been easy for my aunt to tell me I was born out of wedlock, and my mother died bringing me into this world. After all, I'm a nurse and know what can happen to women. No, there's more to this than that. Something unspeakable. I'm sure of it. Especially after what happened to me today."

Holly told them about confronting the man who had been

harassing her, bringing looks of concern.

"I knew all along this had something to do with your searching for your kin," said Myrt.

"Come to think of it," said Ella, "many of the folks who came down from the colony years ago settled at the foot of Stony Mountain below the plateau. Some of them are pretty high and mighty these days. In fact, they've got some of the biggest orchards in the state up there." She reached over and squeezed Holly's hand. "This is getting dangerous. We got no choice. We gotta go see Granny Garrison. She has all the answers and can put a stop to this."

"Okay," said Holly. "We'll go tomorrow, after work."

A tap on the kitchen door startled them. Holly looked over and saw Jeff through the door's glass window. The sight of him made her feel suddenly whole. He entered, and his tall, muscular frame seemed to fill the small kitchen—a palatable masculine presence she wasn't accustomed to, but knew she needed if she ever wanted to be complete.

"The exact person I want to see," said Jeff as he pulled out a chair and sat down next to Ella.

At that remark, Ella sat up straight and assumed her managerial persona. "If it's about what Holly discovered up on the plateau, we're gonna see about that tomorrow. We're all goin up to pay a visit to your granny."

"Oh no, you're not," he said.

Ella jerked her head back in indignation. "Well, I..."

"You don't really think you three going up there will get anything out of her, do you?" he asked with a good-natured grin.

Ella waved her hand in the air. "Well, dag gum it, someone's got to do somethin. We can't just sit around. They're gonna kill that girl the way they're runnin her off the road and chasin her down the mountain."

"Think about it, Ella," said Jeff. "If they wanted to do her any harm, they'd have done it by now. Can't you see they're just trying to frighten her?"

"We know that," said Ella. "One of them said as much to her today."

Holly proceeded to tell him about her encounter on the road.

Jeff put an arm around Ella. "Can you do me a favor?"

"Shoo!" She said, fluttering him away. "You cut out all that huggin stuff, and maybe I will!"

The way Jeff chuckled as he sat back and folded his arms, Holly could see he was starting to warm up to the woman.

"For Holly's safety," he said, "I want you to pass the word around that she's given up on looking for her kin."

"Of course! You think I didn't have no raising? I was already planning on doing just that!"

He looked at Holly. "This has gotta stop. And I know it's not gonna until you're satisfied. My granny knows what happened to Lula, and the old ones will listen to her if she tells them to leave you alone." He looked over at Ella. "My granny's not gonna tell you a thing since you've got no connection to the colony. But, if Lula is who we think she is, they'll consider Holly one of their own."

He took Holly's hand. "You're the only one she's gonna tell."

"Jeff's right," said Holly. "Ella, Myrt, I'm truly grateful for your offer to go with me, but I have to do this myself. I need to talk to her woman to woman. With eight children, she understands the bond between mother and child. Once she knows how much it means to me to find out about my mother, she's gonna tell me."

Ella's response surprised Holly. It was the first time the woman allowed herself to reveal her maternal nature.

Ella patted her hand. "You're right, darlin. It's your place to go see her."

Jeff eyed Holly. "Are you sure you want to do this yourself?"

"I'm sure."

Jeff stood up. "Okay. I better be going. There's a tractor waiting on me."

Seeing Jeff start for the door, Ella quickly motioned for Holly to get up. "Aren't ya gonna see him off?" she whispered loud enough for everyone to hear.

Myrt ushered Holly to the door like a mother hen with her chick. "Why don't you go sit with him on the porch a spell."

Holly rolled her eyes and followed Jeff out.

It had gotten cool, and a dew had settled. Jeff stopped at the steps and looked out into the night. Holly went up next to him, and he put his arm around her shoulder.

She looked up at him as he pulled her close. "You can kiss me if you want."

His eyes met hers. "No. If I do, it'll kill me to stop."

She reached for his hand. The heat in it took her breath away.

He pulled away and started for his truck, then stopped and turned. "Are you sure you don't want me to go with you to see Granny? What she tells you might break your heart."

"I'll be all right. I think what she's going to tell me will put it back together again."

CHAPTER TWENTY-FIVE

Holly picked up the lacy gold frame and felt a lump in her throat as her eyes fixed on the woman who had cared for her as if she were her own, yet had always kept a whisper of space between them. It was as if her aunt were reserving that niche for the woman who gave her birth. The lovely clothes in the closet at Edelweiss, the exclusive school, and the marble monument proved to Holly that her aunt had loved Lula Mae.

It suddenly dawned on Holly that Helen felt she'd be trespassing on Lula's grave if she didn't leave room for her in her daughter's heart, and a calm slowly fell over her like a soft blanket gently laid upon a sleeping child.

"Aunt Helen, I know you couldn't stand to see me hurt," said Holly, "but I need to know what happened to my mother, or I'll never put her to rest. As painful as it might be, I'm ready." She kissed the picture and placed it back on her bedside table. Helen was no longer here, but would always be near as long as she lingered in Holly's thoughts.

She went over to the big oval mirror on her dressing table and searched for the semblance of the girl in the yearbook. If only she could remember the face gazing down on her as she was cuddled in her mother's arms. What happened to her when the heartbeat she recognized as mother was no longer pulsating next to her. Was that the moment when the unabated yearning was imprinted on her brain?

All her life she had wanted her mother to know her. With every accomplishment and award, there'd be a hollow feeling knowing she wasn't there to share it with her. Yet, a renewed hope quickly would follow, reminding Holly that someday she might find her. Sadly, she now accepted that was never going to happen. A wistful desire to at least get to know what her mother was like was all she had left. Dozens of scenarios of what could've happened to her streamed through her thoughts, most of them frightful. Why else would her aunt have so stubbornly kept the secret for so many years.

She awoken that morning with Jeff on her mind, and it had filled her with hope and promise for the future. A future where there wouldn't be room in her heart for the cobwebs of regret. She ran a brush slowly through her hair, strangely confident she would end her quest that day. She would grasp this moment for the truth and put it behind her. Granny Garrison wasn't going to live forever, and once she was gone, buried along with her would be the story of Lula Mae McWade.

HOLLY DROVE AROUND the curve where she had gotten the flat tire and wondered if the embarrassment for offering to pay Jeff for changing her tire was ever going to wear off. She arrived at the trailer and went up to the door. Again, after her knock, came the high-pitched, "Come ye in."

Granny Garrison sat smoking a corncob pipe. "I be spectin ye. Come be settin down."

Holly went and sat next to her. She had planned to pour her heart out and beg Granny to tell her about her mother straight off, but sensing the woman was already on the verge of revealing her secret, she kept silent.

Granny barely rocked in her chair, staring ahead at the mysteries of the past. She took a bit of a puff. "I knowed ye were Lula's chile the day ye stepped in that door. Yer her spittin image."

Holly was spellbound.

"The kinfolk of the man who sired ye been sayin thar were a chile, but us folks up in the colony didn't rightly cotton to it. Tis

235

they who don't want ye be askin bout yer ma. They be too big fer thar boots nowadays, an looks to me like they don't want the pitiful sad mess brought up again." She shook her head. "Caint blame em a whole heap."

Granny rocked back and forth puffing. "Spose you want to know what happened to yer ma."

Holly nodded.

"We all be in the fields when word came Lula Mae went plumb off a cliff."

Holly gasped.

"I went ta give Lula's momma, Hattie, comfortin while men folk went bout fetchin the poor lass. I twernt thar with Hattie but fer a short spell when the lady Lula'd been stayin with in the valley fell in the door. She was doin poorly, all scratched an bleedin an rantin bout how Zeb done made an ugly mess a Lulu once afore. We done tended to her an Hattie, an set by the fire prayin til jist bout dark when they carried Lula in an laid her out on the table."

Granny slowly shook her head. "The lady sure did a heap a carryin on. Mr. Gibson, the man who done brought her on the mountain to be lookin fer Lula, made her accept a good deal a whiskey to git her settled. Then he told Hattie bout him an the lady chasin up the mountain after Lula so as Zeb McGee wouldnt be catchin her unawares agin. Mr. Gibson came rushin through the thicket to see Lula fightin Zeb off, an then her steppin clear off the rock. It bout broke that man's heart, fer he be but a moment late in comin to Lula's aid.

"We jist bout got the lady calmed when we seen Hattie twernt amongst us. We heard the shotgun jist once an reckoned Hattie done gone an shot Zeb. The men folk dragged him off to a cave an put him down a hollow where the mountain opened up." She looked straight at Holly. "We be takin care of our own up in the colony." She bit on her pipe and rocked. "Zeb's kinfolk ner forgave it, an sayed it was Lula's doin. Her roamin the mountains in breeches. But, we knowed that twernt the truth." Granny put her hand on Holly's. "Ye go now, chile. There be no more tellin."

Holly stumbled from the trailer and sat in her car numb. It all made sense now. No wonder Helen kept the truth from her all these years. She felt her anger rise. *That man sentenced me to a lifetime without my mother!* She broke down and sobbed, letting all the bitter sorrow and anguish she'd felt as a motherless child rage.

HOLLY DIDN'T KNOW how long she had sat there, but she finally came back to her senses. She turned on the car and eased out of Granny Garrison's driveway. Her old boyfriend, George, had been right. It would've been better if she didn't know. Shame reared its ugly head as she imagined how he would look at her if she had married him and this horrid story had come out.

She headed home, her cheeks burning and ears ringing. How could her mother ever have loved her? She would've been a constant reminder of what had happened to her. Her grandma's vengeance on the man who sullied her daughter and the clan throwing him down a fissure in the mountain like a butchered snake were too grim to imagine. *Did he push Lula off the cliff? Had she slipped? Oh my God, had she jumped? As she fell through the air, what had raced through her mind?*

Then she thought of Helen. What had she seen to put her in such a state? Holly recalled the years of nightmares that had haunted her aunt. In her later years, she'd rarely had them, but Holly remembered, as a child, the frequent nights she'd awakened to Helen's screams. She would run into her aunt's bedroom and find the housekeeper, Doris, rocking her aunt in her arms. *Had Helen seen Lula go off the cliff?*

A WEEK HAD PASSED since Holly's visit with Granny Garrison, and she couldn't shake the sadness that dragged her down. Myrt and Ella had been comforting angels after she told them what Granny had said, and Jeff had called her every night after dragging himself in from the orchard. Twice, he'd fallen asleep on the phone. Yet, the minute she was alone, the weight of her sad discovery bore down on her.

School was back in full swing, and as she walked in the building, she hoped a day with gleeful children would raise her spirits. She spent most of her time planning her schedule and reviewing the list of students. Concerned Patsy wasn't on the rolls, she mentioned it to the sixth grade teacher when she ran into her in the hall that afternoon.

"Oh," she said, "she's being home schooled."

Holly's spirits sank even deeper. Patsy's father must've pulled the poor child from school after her visit.

"She's had an operation," the teacher continued, "and won't be back til after Christmas."

Holly rushed back to her room, closed the door, and fell back against it, crying. "If coming to the mountains and hearing the ugly truth of my birth is the price I had to pay to help Patsy, I'm okay with it," she told herself. She went to her sink and rinsed her face. She had to stop all this crying before people started noticing. The school bell rang, and the clamor of kids rushing out of the building echoed through the halls. Thank God. Now she could go home and have a good cry in the sanctity of her room.

After leaving the school, she feared she was intruding, but couldn't resist driving up Garrison Road and parking in Jeff's driveway. She got out and walked to the edge of the road. The scene below churned with activity—forklifts loading huge apple boxes onto trucks, tractors coming and going, men on ladders and on the ground picking. The neatly mowed ribbons of green grass were now trampled and cluttered with rejects as far as the eye could see. She found comfort in seeing so many people so earnestly dedicated to reaping the earth's bounty.

Two days earlier, she had taken a pie Myrt made for Jeff to the orchard at dinner time only to find it abuzz with people bringing food for the pickers. A woman swiftly took the pie from her and whisked it away to a picnic area. The way people were waving and greeting each other, made her feel like an outsider, so she hurried to her car and left before Jeff could notice her.

As she stood there gazing at the activity below, Jeff appeared from between two rows. Warmth shot through her with such force her knees almost buckled. She closed her eyes and dreamt of returning in the middle of the night and slipping into his bed.

She shook the thought away. He had made his intentions clear, and she must wait for him to woo her in the manner he'd been raised. The thought of it, however, was all that was holding her together.

She checked her watch. Past five. She'd better be going. As she neared Myrt's house, she could see two cars parked in front. One belonged to Ella, but the other she hadn't seen before. It had to belong to one of Myrt's friends. Good. The three of them would sit and chat the evening away, and she could go up to her room and be alone for the night.

She ran up the steps to the back porch and was about to open the door when she saw the woman who connected her to everything she had ever known and loved. It was Helen's best friend and housekeeper.

"Doris!" Holly exclaimed as she rushed in and gave her a big hug. "How did you get here? Why didn't you let me know?"

Ella pushed a chair under Holly and pressed her shoulder to sit down, while Myrt put a glass of iced tea in front of her.

"I needed to see you, but all I had was the Bat Cave post office address on the letter you sent me. So that's where I went. Miss Ella was kind enough to bring me here."

The instant Holly noticed the guilty look on Ella's face, she knew she had told Doris everything. She fell into her old friend's arms and burst out sobbing.

"It's about time you knew about your momma," said Doris. "It was an argument me and your aunt had for the whole time I knew her."

Holly pulled away and looked at her with a face twisted in incredulity. "You knew my mother?"

"Your aunt swore me to her charade before you were born. I can't count all the lies I had to confess to Father Ryan."

"I can't believe you knew her! All those years you never told me!"

"I wanted to tell you about your momma so much my heart ached. Land sakes, child, all those stories you made up about where you came from were just your way of healing a wound. As much as it pained me not to tell you, I knew Helen would never forgive me if I did."

Doris suddenly dropped her head in her hand and let out a tearful sigh. "You look just like your momma." She took a tissue Myrt handed her and wiped her eyes.

"Doris, did she love me? Did she even want me?"

Doris threw her head back. "Good Lord, child! She adored you. If it hadn't been for you, I don't think she'd of fought so hard to get into that nursing school. Those two vixens plotted and planned and made me tell all sorts of lies so you could grow up without that man's mark on you."

Myrt pulled out a tissue for herself, then one for Ella.

"I'm getting old, Holly, and I didn't want to leave this earth without you knowing your momma. No matter what I promised, it wouldn't be right. So, here I am."

Doris reached for a bag she had brought. "My sister's moving us to Sarasota. When I was packing, I ran across some things I've saved for you all these years." She wiped her tears again and pulled out a small white sweater and cap from the bag. "Your mother made these for you before you were born. Your aunt gave all your clothes to charity as you were growing up, but I couldn't part with these." She lovingly pointed to a spot on the sweater. "This is where she picked up an extra stitch. But other than that, it's perfect."

Lula examined the small articles with reverence. "My mother made these for me?"

"Yes, darling, she did."

Holly clutched the sweater to her breast and closed her eyes. "You'll never know how much this means to me."

"Your aunt, God bless her, insisted your yearning to know was a lesser burden than growing up ashamed of the circumstances surrounding your birth and your mother's death. She felt it would put a permanent stamp of sadness on your heart if you knew." She slapped her hands on her legs. "Your aunt was right. Look at the way you turned out, girl. You're as right as rain."

Holly took the woman's hands in hers. "Doris, I want you to tell me all you know about what happened to my mother the day she died."

Doris looked at Holly, then searched the faces of the two women and found approval in their eyes. She took a deep breath and slowly let it out as she gazed in the distance. "I'll never forget that day as long as I live. Helen had gone into town, so Lula and I were in a dither over getting packed and moved to the new house in Pittsboro. Oh, your momma was so excited about going to nursing school. It was something she had wanted all her life, and she was determined to get there. Imagine the grit it took the year before, after all that had happened to her and the condition she was in, to march into that school and get her admission deferred by telling them she had to take care of her ailing aunt. Whatever it took, that child was going to get in that school."

Doris sniffled in her tissue and blotted her eyes. "In the middle of getting the dishes packed, word came down that Lula's momma was sick. After what happened to that poor girl on that mountain, she would never have gone up there alone, except to care for her momma.

"But your grandma wasn't sick. That awful man who did that wretched thing to her knew she was back at Edelweiss and that she would come to her momma's aid, so he sent someone with the lie and waited for her on the mountain. I'll never forgive myself as long as I live for not stopping her from going. If only I had, none of this would've happened."

Doris broke down in tears, and Holly reached over and squeezed her hand.

"Go on, Doris. I want to hear it."

Ella quickly handed Doris another tissue.

Doris blew her nose and continued. "Your aunt came back from running errands and went chasing after her with a man who had a sawmill near the bottom of the mountain. It wasn't til they were a good deal the way up the mountain that your aunt found out your grandma wasn't sick, and that the man who sent the messenger to the house was the same one who had attacked Lula. He worked at the sawmill and knew the owner would be gone for the day and Lula would have to go up alone.

"Once your aunt and the man figured that out, he ran ahead to catch up with Lula. He had no choice, but to leave Helen. She would only slow him down. Helen was never one for the out-doors, but somehow she made her way up to a place where she could see this big cliff way off in the distance." Doris stopped and stared as if she were replaying the scene in her head.

Holly squeezed her hand. "Go on."

"That poor woman described that tragic moment dozens of times, dozens of ways—after waking up screaming in the night or crying uncontrollably in the middle of the day while clutching Lula's picture. She relived that horrible moment Lula went off the cliff a thousand times. Helen was clawing her way up the mountain and heard Lula screaming. She looked up at the cliff and saw her struggling with a hulk of a man. He grabbed Lula's blouse, and she pulled away with such force, it ripped away, and she sailed right off. In that one irreversible instant the lives of you and your aunt were permanently changed. It just about broke your poor aunt's heart. I swear, if it wasn't for you, she would've laid down and died."

Holly buried her face in Doris' shoulder and the two of them quietly wept.

Myrt and Ella pulled out tissues and blew their noses.

Doris regained her composure and took a notebook from the bag. She picked up a photograph lying between the pages and handed it to Holly. "It's you and your momma."

Holly was thunderstruck. A young woman was holding a newborn and looking at the tiny face with so much love Holly burst into renewed tears.

"Your aunt kept that picture hidden, but when you were away at college, I'd sometimes catch her looking at it. When she realized she was dying, she gave it to me. Holly, I believe she knew I would give it to you when it was time."

She gave the notebook to Holly. "There's no need for me to be telling you about your momma. It's all in here. These are stories she wrote waiting for you to be born. We spent most of that time in a house Helen rented way out in the country. She was afraid if someone saw Lula in that condition, it might get back to the nursing school. Lula would write down her memories of growing up in the mountains, and at night, we'd sit around eating popcorn and listening to her read what she wrote that day. Oh my, how we would laugh at the stories of that feisty little thing riding all over the mountains on the back of a horse, clinging to a doctor woman named Essie."

Doris wiped her eyes with a tissue. "You can see now why I broke my promise to your aunt. How could I go running off to Sarasota without giving you these things? They belong to you. I know Lula would want me to do this. She would want you to know your momma." She pulled an envelope from her purse and handed it to Holly. "Here's a receipt. I put your aunt's bedroom set with the same storage company you put the rest of her things. It's only right that I give it back since it's too big for our small place in Florida. And now that you're getting married, it'll come in handy."

"Married?!" Holly flashed a glare at Myrt and then Ella, then shook her head.

"I hope you can have supper and stay the night with us," Myrt said, hurriedly trying to change the subject.

"No. In fact, I must be going. My sister and I came up together, me to see Holly, and her to give some of her husband's things to his family in Morganton. She'll be expecting me."

Holly walked Doris to her car with Ella and Myrt, and the three waved as she drove away.

"I'll be getting along, too," said Ella.

After Ella's car disappeared down the road, Holly and Myrt walked arm-in-arm back to the house.

"You go upstairs. I know you want to be with your mother's things," said Myrt. "I'll bring you up a tray."

Later that night, Holly sat cross-legged on her bed reading one of her mother's stories. Except for eating the dinner Myrt brought up, she had spent the whole evening getting to know Lula Mae McWade, and she was liking her. Slowly, as she devoured the pages, she started to feel whole and at peace knowing what a wonderful life her mother had lived, one that spanned two different worlds. Holly could clearly see that her mother, from the age of seven, spent her whole life taking care of people. For as far back as Holly could remember, she wanted to be a nurse, and she finally knew where it came from.

She was glad Jeff had taken her up to the colony. All the people and places her mother wrote about came alive as she read. Tears streamed freely down her cheeks as she read about the touching encounter between her grandma and Helen when she gave her the gift of a seed necklace. Holly slid off the bed and dug her aunt's jewelry box from her trunk. She pulled out the precious necklace and clasped it to her heart. For that instant, they were all together—her mother, Helen, Hattie, and her.

Holly started to read a story that told of a whippoorwill her mother always listened for from her bedroom window at Edelweiss. Holly stopped for a moment and wondered what the bird might sound like, when she heard a truck pull up. She ran to the window and seeing it was Jeff, raced down the stairs and out the back door to the porch. The moon reflected off his face as he came toward her. She ran down the steps and into his arms. His hair was wet, and he smelled of shampoo and clean clothes.

She thrilled to the promise in the heat of his lips as she kissed him.

"Whoa!" he said as he let go of her and stepped back. "Let's not get ahead of ourselves here."

She reached for him.

"You stay right there, young lady." He pulled a small box from his pocket and took out a ring. He dropped to one knee and reached for her hand.

She looked down at the handsome face and into the heart of the man she knew she would always love.

"Holly Baldwin, will you marry me?"

"Yes! Yes!"

He put the ring on her finger and stood up. "I'll have the house finished in a month. We can get married then."

"Jeff, I can't wait that long."

He picked her up laughing, then twirled her around shouting, "I love you, Holly Baldwin!" He put her down and tenderly brushed her hair back from her forehead. "I can't either. Can you get off work early tomorrow so we can make it to the county courthouse? Then we'll have the whole weekend together."

"I'll do all my urgent calls in the morning. Pick me up here at one."

"Woowee!" he shouted loud enough to wake the neighbors. He raced to his truck and jumped in.

Holly ran after him and stepped onto the running board. "I'm not gonna get off til you give me a kiss."

He gave her a quick peck on the lips.

"Is that all?!" she pouted.

He winked at her. "Don't you worry none, darlin. I plan to make it up to you tomorrow." He started the engine, and she jumped off.

"Jeff, can you make the call of a whippoorwill?" she shouted out to him.

He stuck his head out the window, and the haunting whistle "Whip-poor-will, whip-poor-will, whip-poor-will" faded into the night as he drove off.

EPILOG
1979

B en, put your backpack on. I want you to see if it's too
heavy," said Holly to her youngest son.

Patrick, who was seventeen and four years older than Ben,
came in the kitchen and playfully shoved his brother. "The last
time we went up there, Dad had to carry you down the mountain on his back."

"Really, Patrick, he was only six," said Holly as she helped
Ben take the pack off.

Jeff came in, put an arm around her, and gave her a peck on
the cheek. "You ready, babe?"

The phone on the kitchen counter rang, making Jeff groan.

"Can't they let you take one single day off?"

Holly answered the phone and listened.

"Get her enrolled in WIC, that way they'll have food, and set
her up for an examination at the clinic," she said. "No, it's okay.
We were just leaving."

Holly put the phone down and gave Jeff an apologetic smile.
"She's new, honey, and wants to make sure she's doing everything right."

"Okay, you guys. Let's go!" said Jeff.

Everyone grabbed their backpacks and piled into the Jeep.

It had been over seven years since Holly last visited her

mother's grave, and the prospect was putting her in a sentimental mood as they drove to the trail.

"It's funny," said Holly, "That new nurse is going to be able to help that family this very day. When I started in these mountains almost twenty years ago, I'd pretty much have to go to the churches and charitable organizations to come up with food and medicine for women and children in need, and now we have WIC and Medicaid. These were the kind of programs we knew we needed back then, but hadn't gotten yet." She nodded to herself. "What a godsend."

Patrick patted her on the shoulder. "Mom, I know you're running that place, but let's just have fun today."

Holly laughed and rubbed his hand. "Of course, darling."

As the jeep got farther along, the road went from asphalt, to gravel, to dirt, and the terrain grew rougher and steeper until Jeff could go no farther.

He grabbed his backpack. "This is it. We walk from here."

Everyone was strapping on their packs when Ben said, "It's not fair. Mom doesn't have to carry anything."

Patrick gave him a shove. "Where's your chivalry, man?"

Ben's face reddened at the reprimand.

Holly mussed the boy's blond hair. "That's all right, son."

The boys ran ahead, only stopping when they lost the trail. Jeff wasn't far behind. Holly enjoyed the serenity at the tail end of the convoy where she could be alone with her mother's stories. They came alive and wrapped her tenderly in the past.

"Wait up, boys!" echoed in the woods up ahead.

Holly came around a huge rock and saw Jeff standing above on the gnarled roots of an ancient chestnut. He reached down, grabbed her hand, and pulled her up.

"You, doing all right, honey?"

She looked into the kind eyes. "I'm doing just fine. Go on with the boys and wait up where we have to cross the stream. We'll have lunch there."

Holly continued on the trail with a haunting feeling seeping into every pore. She saw a small flower and pictured a barefooted little girl in a homespun dress gently picking it and putting it in her herb basket. When she came to a small clearing in the woods and spotted remnants of a chimney, she saw her mother with the granny doctor in her long dress and sunbonnet trading herbs with a settler.

Almost two hours into the trek, she heard the small waterfalls ahead, then the boys laughing and calling out to each other. She reached the cool, shaded spot to see both boys in the stream in their bare feet. Her eyes met Jeff's and she knew he was remembering, like herself, the first time he had taken her up the mountain and she had done the same thing.

She laughed and took the lunch from their backpacks and spread it on her aunt's checkered cloth. "My mother used to wade in this same stream whenever she climbed the mountain with the granny doctor," she told the boys as they all sat eating. "Only, she didn't own any shoes to take off."

They finished their meal, then drank from the stream before continuing the trek. This time, Jeff stayed close to Holly and kept calling for the boys to wait up. Holly knew it was because they were nearing the cliff her mother had fallen from. The trail barely fit between two enormous rhododendrons and opened to an endless view. Jeff took her hand. The boys stood on the cliff gaping at the view, just like she had the first time she was up there. Holly squeezed Jeff's hand.

"Boys, come off that cliff. It's making your mother nervous."

"Gee, Mom," said Ben. "Don't worry about us. We're never going to go so far out that we'll slip off like your mother did."

Patrick nudged Ben with his elbow. "What did I tell you?!"

"Let's keep going, boys," said Jeff.

As Holly trudged the rest of the way to the plateau, she wondered when she would tell the boys the whole truth about Lula. Granny Garrison and the old ones on Stony Mountain were now long gone as were her three beloved friends, Doris, Myrt, and Ella. Holly believed they all took what they knew of Lula Mae with them to their graves.

Holly, hearing the boys shout, "We're here, Mom!" hurried along. The three of them were looking out over the rolling hills of the plateau waiting for her. She found a reservoir of strength and charged ahead. Brushing aside the tall weeds and saplings, she made her way to the cemetery with Jeff and the boys close behind. She saw the rise with her mother's grave and realized it was now in a clearing. She looked at Jeff, surprised.

"I tend to it every time I come hunting up here," he said.

Holly put her arms around him, pulled him close, and kissed him tenderly, then spying the two boys over Jeff's shoulder with sheepish grins, she drew away.

"Help me up there, honey," she said.

They climbed to the rise, and Jeff started ripping out errant saplings near the grave. It was sheathed in a thick layer of needles from several nearby tall hemlocks. The boys took off their backpacks and joined in clearing the brush that had taken hold.

"Gee whiz, Mom, this is a pretty nice gravestone," said Ben.

"My aunt Helen had it brought up here special."

"Man, she must've been rich!"

"She was rich, but not in the way you're thinking."

"Can I take a picture of it? It's neato."

"Sure, darling. I'd like that."

He pawed through his pack for his camera, then took several shots, including one with Holly standing behind the stone.

"I guess we're done here," said Jeff, looking around.

"Can we go to the falls now, Dad?" asked Patrick.

"Yes," said Holly. "You three go. I'm staying here."

"We'll be gone for at least an hour," said Jeff.

"Take your time. If I get bored, I'll look around and see if I can make out some of the other gravestones."

The boys whooped and hollered as they slid from the rise and found the path.

"You gonna be okay, babe?" asked Jeff.

"Sure. Go on."

He started to leave, then turned back, took her in his arms, and kissed her.

She caught her breath. "Wow. Now that was a kiss!"

He winked and jerked his head in the direction their sons had disappeared. "Gotta be careful in front of those two."

She touched him lovingly. "Hurry along, honey. They're

waiting on you."

Holly stood on the rise and watched the tall, broad-shouldered figure move agilely through the thicket. It had been quite a few years since she had studied his physique as he lay on the ground hooking a chain to her car. He was now even stronger and leaner than he had been then. She couldn't take her eyes away until he disappeared from sight, then she pulled her aunt's checkered cloth from one of the backpacks, spread it out, and sat down. She ran a finger along the stone's inscription and spoke to her mother.

"Thanks for writing all those stories, Momma. Sometimes I wonder if you had a premonition that something was going to happen to you, and you wrote them for me so I would know you.

"What a fascinating life you had, born in one world and thrust into another. When I read your stories, it's as if I'm sitting with you, Helen, and Doris, listening to you read them with all of us laughing together. I know someday I'll have to tell my boys how I longed and searched for you. They have a right to know their mother's whole story, but I can only tell it with the telling of your whole story, too. Just like Doris, I'll know when it's time."

Holly was comforted by the memories of the things her mother had written. She thought it sad that so many stories through the ages were taken to the grave without ever being told. Stories no one wrote down or retold, stories kept secret, hidden, or lost. Do they disappear into thin air and float away like the scent of a rose, she wondered. Or do they find a place to hide until they're rediscovered—in the depths of fading photographs, in the weave of old, frayed quilts, in the rust of abandoned toys, or on the pages of forgotten diaries.

She jumped when she heard the shouts coming from the woods. The boys were back! She quickly got up, folded the cloth, and stuffed it in the pack. As she waited for her family to appear, she turned to the grave. "You can rest now, Momma. I'm all right."

ACKNOWLEDGEMENTS

Falling Off a Cliff evolved from thoughts that have been drifting in and out of my mind ever since 2007 when I met a group of retired public health nurses, some of whom have since become close friends. Over the years, I'd also thought about the Lost Colony that thrived in the 1800s on the plateau between Chimney Rock and Sugarloaf Mountain in the northeast sector of North Carolina's Henderson County, and I was pleased to finally be able to fold its history into a novel.

In the 24 years I have lived in the Carolinas, I have enjoyed collecting and reading the homespun stories written by folks who wanted their histories and those of their forebears to survive. These treasures exist in the form of everything from photocopied typewritten pages put together with staples, to polished booklets. One such effort was *Without the Master's Knowledge No Sparrow Falls* by Ellen B. Heydock. The stories of her life in the 1920s in Bat Cave, NC, where the area's Lost Colony had existed, were the inspiration for the character, Helen Baldwin.

I do hope you enjoy meeting Lula Mae McWade and Holly Baldwin who personify the dedication and passion to help their fellow man that public health nurses possess.

I want to thank my editors, Sandy Horton, Jamie Stanton, and Annie Pott who made this book better. Special thanks go to nurses Jackie Price, Harriet Harvey, and Barbara Stanley. The character of Holly Baldwin embodies their dedication to this honorable profession. I also want to thank all the nurses in their group whose careers in public health inspired me to write this novel: Sheila Devine, Kathy Baluha, Pat McCall, Linda Weldon, Louise Brazillac, and Robbie Goolsby. Also, my thanks to my reader, Gail Trump and my diligent researcher, LuVerne Haydock. But most of all, I want to thank my loyal readers who I think of every time I sit down at my computer to write. You folks are my inspiration.

BLUE RIDGE SERIES of Stand-Alone Books

Winner of the 2019 Historical Fiction Award from the N.C. Society of Historians, Inc.

Catching Fire. *The thrilling story of the Party Rock Fire.* Pushed to the breaking point with over twenty fires raging in the NC mountains, how does the state's emergency response network combat this fire of biblical proportions threatening to devour four mountain communities. Woven throughout this tale of two firefighters in love, yet torn apart by swirling suspicions and mistrust, is the story of a family's struggle with its past.

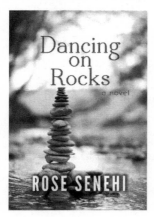

Winner of the 2014 Indie Reader Discovery Award

Dancing on Rocks. Nursing her mother back to health wasn't all that drew Georgie Haydock back to the little mountain tourist town. Hiding around every corner, are a family's painful memories of a child who disappeared in the middle of the night 25 years ago. The summer roils as her mother thrashes in her bed, insisting that the woman stalking her store downstairs is her missing daughter. Meanwhile, Georgie aches to reunite with the hometown boy she's never forgotten.

Carolina Belle. Belle McKenzie is obsessed with finding the best apple anyone ever bit into and determined to rekindle the love this obsession destroyed. She risks her life rescuing four hundred antique apple trees her neighbor has collected from all over the South. Pap thinks of Matt as a son, but Belle thinks of him as the man she loved and who betrayed her. Rich in emotion and driven by suspense, woven throughout this story is the fascinating history of the American apple that started when settlers planted seeds all over the country and kicked off one of the biggest evolutionary experiments this nation has ever seen.

AWARD WINNING HISTORICAL FICTION

Winner of the 2012 IPPY Gold Medal Fiction-Southeast

Render Unto the Valley. *Karen Godwell isn't as much ashamed of her mountain heritage as of what she once had to do to preserve it.* She reinvents herself at college and doesn't look back till her clan's historic farm is threatened. She returns only to come face to face with who she was and what she did. Cousin Bruce sees life through the family's colorful two-hundred-year past; Tom Gibbons, a local conservationist, keeps one eye on the mountains and the other on Karen. Her nine-year-old daughter is on the mission her dying father sent her on.

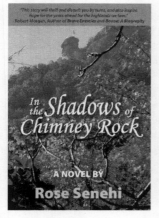

Nominated for the 2009 SIBA Book Award

In the Shadows of Chimney Rock. *A touching tale of Family and Place.* A Southern heiress reaches out to her mountain roots for solace after suffering a life-shattering blow, only to be drawn into a fight to save the beauty of the mountain her father loved. Hayden Taylor starts to heal in the womb of the gorge as she struggles to redeem her father's legacy, never suspecting the man who killed him is stalking her.

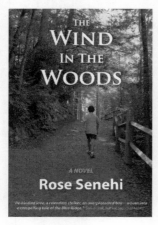

Nominated for the Thomas Wolfe Memorial Award

The Wind in the Woods. A romantic thriller that reveals a man's devotion to North Carolina's Green River Valley and the camp he built to share its wonders; his daughter's determination to hike the Blue Ridge—unaware that a serial killer is stalking her; and nine-year-old Alvin Magee's heart-warming discovery of freedom and responsibility in a place apart from the adult world.

OTHER NOVELS BY ROSE SENEHI

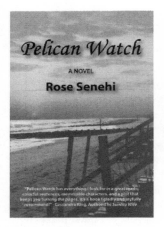

Pelican Watch. *Laced with the flavor of South Carolina's low country, this love story is told against a backdrop of murder and suspense.* Nicky Sullivan always nurses injured animals, but this time she's going to heal herself. She flees to a SC barrier island and discovers a kindred spirit in Mac Moultrie, a salty retired fisherman. From the moment she meets Trippett Alston, she's smitten, but the dark forces swirling around the island threaten to keep them apart.

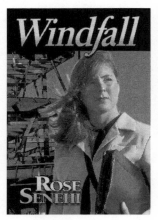

Windfall. *Meet Lisa Barron, a savvy marketing executive with a kid and a crazy career in the mall business.*
Everyone knows she's driven, but not the dark secret she's hiding. She's keeping one step ahead of the FBI and a gang of twisted peace activists who screwed up her life in the sixties, while trying not to fall in love with one of the driven men who make these massive projects rise from the ground. What will she do if her past catches up with her? Grab her daughter and run, or face disgrace and a possible murder charge?

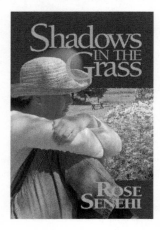

Shadows in the Grass. Striving desperately to hold onto the farm for her son, a widow comes into conflict with the handsome composer who builds a mansion on the hill overlooking her nursery. All the while, she never suspects that the man who moves into the rundown farm behind her has anything to do with the missing children.

Visit Rose Senehi

www.rosesenehi.com

or email at:

rsenehi@earthlink.net